SHE KNOWS

AJ WILLS

Cherry Tree
Publishing

ALSO BY AJ WILLS

HIS WIFE'S SISTER
BETWEEN THE LIES

PROLOGUE

The phone ringing.

Her heart pounding.

She peels open her eyes. Where the hell is she? Certainly not in her own room. Or her own bed.

She groans as she tries to recall how the evening ended. But her mind is blank. She remembers dinner. A smashed glass. Her head swimming. Knees buckling. A plate flying. Hitting the ground.

And after that, nothing at all.

'It's me,' whispers the voice on the phone she sweeps off the floor.

She can't understand why the woman is calling. Not when they're under the same roof. It makes no sense.

'Where are you?'

'You don't remember anything, do you?' the woman says.

'No.'

She kicks off the thick duvet. Still dressed in her jeans and t-shirt, the material sticking to her skin.

She looks down and gasps. Her clothes are soaked in blood. It's all over the sheets too, like the scene from a horror movie.

'Take deep breaths,' the woman whispers in her ear.

'What the hell's going on?' Her stomach churns. She fights the urge to be sick.

'You need to go downstairs,' the woman says.

'I don't want to.'

'You have to.'

Fingers of fear creep up her spine. She wants to get out, to get some air. She spills out of bed and rushes for the door but jumps back at the sight of the knife. Lying on the carpet. As if it's been dropped casually. Its thin, curved blade and ebony handle smeared with scarlet streaks.

With legs like water, she steps around it and steals down the stairs, into the kitchen, following the woman's instructions. What other choice does she have?

A strange metallic smell is partially masked by the stale cooking aromas from last night's meal. The long table where they'd eaten has been wiped down and cleared of dishes.

Everything exactly as it should be.

But then she sees the feet. A pair of brown brogues. Poking out from under a sheet over a body lying in a sticky pool of congealing blood.

She drops the phone. It bounces across the tiles.
She gasps for breath, panic rising.
Oh my God.
What has she done?

CHAPTER ONE

The sound that made me look up from my feet as I kicked through the sand was like an animal in pain. A low keening, pitiful and hollow. The sort of noise that lifts the hairs on your arms and plants fear in your mind. It stopped me dead in my tracks as the last light of day was slowly slipping away and a chill breeze whipping off the sea grazed my skin.

That's when I saw her.

A woman rocking gently back and forth on a boulder near the base of the cliffs where a patch of scrubby vegetation skirted the top of the beach. She was virtually lost in the gloom of the failing light, staring out to sea. So glamorous, so fragile, and so completely out of place beneath the angry black clouds that had amassed as the evening drew in.

As I watched, her shoulders shook and she sobbed pitifully. Then she dropped her face in her hands and wailed as if her entire world had collapsed.

My instinct was to walk on, to put my head down and to leave her alone. Whatever had upset her was none of my business. And besides, what could I do? I had enough problems of my own and I was hardly qualified to offer emotional support to anyone else.

But how could I leave her? The woman was in obvious distress. And now I'd seen her, I couldn't pretend I hadn't.

'Hello?' I said, taking half a cautious step closer. 'Is everything okay?'

Her head jolted up. She blinked into the gathering darkness, eventually picking me out, staring at me with wide, wet eyes.

I could see she'd once been an attractive woman, but her beauty had waned, stolen by too much sun and the cruel advance of the years. Her hair was cut short in a smart bob, coloured like a burnt sunset, and around her throat she wore a stunning necklace set with emeralds and diamonds that looked totally inappropriate for the beach.

As I approached, slowly, like she was liable to bolt at any moment, she stopped crying and watched me curiously, dabbing the tears from her eyes with a screwed-up tissue in her fist.

She slipped off the rock, her movements slow and precise, as if she were wary I might pounce.

'I didn't mean to startle you,' I said. 'I thought I heard you crying. Is there anything I can do?'

'No, it's nothing. I'm fine, thank you,' she muttered, stooping to pick up her handbag but knocking it over in her haste, spilling its contents across the sand.

She clawed frantically for her things, scratching around with blood-red painted fingernails, while never once taking her frightened eyes off me. Then after straightening her dress, she scurried away, heading in the direction I'd come, towards the two wartime pill-boxes that had collapsed onto the beach from the top of the receding cliffs. She marched with purpose, stumbling in her hurry; not exactly running, but not hanging around either. She never once looked back.

I shrugged. Some people could be so rude. Was I really that scary? Maybe I ought to go easier on the eyeliner and do something with my hair.

It was only when the woman had become a speck in the distance that I spotted she'd left something by the rock where she'd been sitting. Something small, flat and black. I brushed the sand off it and discovered it was a notebook, no bigger than a tobacco tin with a faux leather cover, its pages secured with a thin strap of elastic.

'Hey,' I yelled. 'You left this behind!'

But the woman had already vanished into the dark shadows. I waited for a response, hoping the wind might have carried my voice further than I could see, but there was no reply beyond the hissing surf and the lonely screech of a bird.

I turned my attention back to the book, wondering what I'd found. An address book, maybe? I knew that some people who distrusted smartphones still liked to write down names, numbers and addresses. Or was it something else? There was only one way to find out.

I peeled it open and flicked through lined pages filled with dense rows of scrawled handwriting, the thin, cream paper indented where the author had pressed too hard.

At the top of one page was a date in capital letters. Underlined. My heart raced faster. A diary! A little black book chronicling someone's deepest, darkest thoughts and feelings. My fingers tingled with excitement at what scandalous secrets and lurid gossip it might contain. But in the low light, all I could pick out was the odd meaningless phrase here and there. Nothing juicy, especially as the tiny handwriting was difficult to decipher.

With my pulse galloping, I snapped the diary shut. I shouldn't be looking. A diary was private. Personal. I had no right to read it. It was voyeuristic and perverse. How would I like it if someone had read my diary? Not that I kept one these days. My cheeks burned with shame. I shoved it into the bottom of my bag, appalled by my lack of self-control.

As I rushed home, my mind was in turmoil. I knew it was wrong to have looked, but it didn't quell the temptation to read more. But then, would it really be that bad to take another quick glimpse?

Of course it would. I had to be strong. I had to fight the urge.

Back at the caravan, I threw my bag into my room, out of sight. I didn't even mention the diary to my flatmate, Amber. I knew what she was like. She would have been wild with excitement and wouldn't have stopped going on about it until my resolve had weakened and we'd ended up dissecting it word by word over a bottle of wine or two. And no matter how rude the woman on the beach had been to me, she didn't deserve Amber and me poring over her secrets.

As I climbed into bed that night, I still couldn't stop thinking about why that woman had been so upset or whether she'd noticed her diary was missing yet. Maybe she was back on the beach, looking for it.

I made up my mind. I'd found it, so it was my duty to return it. In the morning, I would set out to track her down and deliver it back safely. And in the meantime, I wouldn't give in to the burning temptation to sneak another peek.

CHAPTER TWO

As I lay in bed that night, chasing sleep, the diary was all I could think about. It was also the first thing on my mind when I woke the next morning. I'd been dreaming I was on the beach, struggling to reach the woman on the rock. Except the woman wasn't the woman at all. She was my mother, crying and begging for my help, but every time I took a step closer, my feet sank deeper into the sand until I was up to my neck and it threatened to fill my nose and mouth.

'Hey, you awake yet?' Amber hammered on the door. 'Don't forget you're supposed to be at work by ten.'

'What time is it?' I moaned, rubbing my eyes as I rolled back under the duvet.

'Nearly quarter to.'

I groaned. I couldn't be late again. I fell out of bed, picking up my underwear and jeans from the floor. No time for a shower. A spray of deodorant would have to do.

When I arrived at work twenty-five minutes later, Michelle, my boss, was waiting with her hands on her hips and a sour expression on her face.

'You were supposed to be here to open up,' she sneered.

I pulled out my earpods and resisted the urge to roll my eyes. 'I overslept,' I explained, refusing to apologise.

'This place doesn't run itself, Sky. I need someone I can rely on.'

I glanced around the deserted amusement arcade. Hardly anyone came in before midday, especially in April, before the start of the summer season. I had no idea why she insisted on opening so early.

'You want to take a long hard look at yourself. What are you now? Nineteen? Twenty?'

'Twenty-one,' I said.

'Right, and you can't even get to work on time. You're already on a warning for your time-keeping.' She had the most unpleasant manner. 'If you don't want this job, there's plenty who'd bite my hand off for a chance to work here.'

I could have laughed. Who in their right mind would choose to work at the Golden Sands Amusement Arcade? The job was boring as hell, they paid a pittance, and the boss was a total bitch. Even the name was a joke. There was no golden sand. Coarse, muddy sand was more like it.

I'd never warmed to Michelle and her constant nagging. And what exactly did she do all day anyway, other than hiding out in the back office reading novels on her e-reader and writing scathing one-star reviews? As if she could have done any better. She liked to boast about how she was going to be a famous author one day, but she'd never finished a manuscript in her life. She preferred criticising other writers than putting her own work on the line.

Eventually, she left me to get on with my job. I wiped down and polished all the machines until they were gleaming, grabbed a mug of tea from the staffroom and collected my cash float. In my booth, I arranged the coins on plastic trays in rows of different denominations. But my mind was already drifting. All I could think about was the woman on the beach and the diary she'd dropped. It was like an old scab that needed itching. It consumed me.

When I was sure no one was looking, I retrieved the little notebook from my bag and laid it on the counter. With the lightest of touches, like I was examining an ancient relic, I ran my fingers over its scuffed and pock-marked cover. Just a quick look. Surely it couldn't do any harm, and besides, if I was going to return it, I needed to see if it contained any clues to the woman's identity.

With trembling hands, I unhooked the elastic strap and opened it at a random page. At first, I was disappointed to find nothing of interest beyond some long-winded and meandering musings, like a tumbling stream of self-consciousness that meant nothing to me. But then I stumbled on a brief paragraph that jumped off the page, shocking me like a bee sting on my neck.

I snapped the diary shut, my pulse galloping.

I wish now I hadn't looked but I couldn't unsee the words. They'd imprinted themselves on my mind.

I'd crossed a line. But at least now I understood why the woman on the beach who'd run off like a terrified rabbit had been so upset. She was in serious trouble. No, worse than that. Her life was in danger. The words she'd written bringing back terrible memories I'd tried so hard to bury and forget.

'What are you doing?'

I jumped like a naughty child caught passing notes in class. I dropped the diary in my lap and tried to hide it under my thigh as a prickle of heat spread across my neck and cheeks. 'Jesus, you scared the life out of me,' I said.

Amber, my flatmate, peered into the booth holding two cardboard cups of takeaway coffee.

'Aren't you supposed to be at work?' I said.

'I'm on a break. Thought you could use a latte,' she replied.

I eyed her suspiciously. She rarely came to see me during the day, and she never brought coffee. 'What's going on? Are you in trouble?'

'No!' she said. 'Of course not. I just thought it would be nice to hang out.'

'Right,' I said, waiting for the bombshell. There was something on her mind. It was written all over her face.

'What've you got there?' She angled her head to see what I was hiding under my leg.

'Nothing.'

13

'Come on, what were you reading?'

'I told you, it's nothing. Is one of those for me?' I nodded at the coffee cups she seemed to have forgotten she was holding.

'Can you take ten minutes?' Amber asked, handing me a cup.

'No, I'm not supposed to be on a break for another couple of hours yet.' I couldn't just take a break whenever I fancied it.

Amber frowned. 'What's eating you?'

'Nothing.'

'Well, there's obviously something wrong. Is it Michelle? Has she said something?'

'No,' I snapped. 'I'm fine.'

'No need to bite my head off.'

I sighed. 'I've got a few things on my mind, that's all.'

'Want to talk about it?' Amber asked.

'Not really.'

'Come on, a problem shared and all that. I am supposed to be your best friend.'

Although Amber was the only genuine friend I had on the island, I wasn't sure about telling her about the woman I'd met on the beach and the diary she'd left behind. But then, I had to tell someone before I burst.

'I found a diary on the beach last night,' I said. 'And I think the woman who lost it is being abused by her husband.'

'Jeez,' Amber hissed. 'What makes you think that?'

'I read some of it,' I said. 'Just a little.'

The words that had jumped out at me swirled around and around my mind.

What he did was unforgivable. He tells me he loves me – but I'm not sure anymore. He says he feels bad, but how can we go on like this? I realise I should have left him months ago. Is it so awful that sometimes I want to kill him?

'What are you going to do?'

It was a good question. What could I do? I didn't know who she was or how to find her. And I'd not read anything that explicitly said that her husband *had* physically harmed her, so I could hardly go to the police. But I knew I had to do something. 'I don't know,' I said.

'Is her name in it?'

'I was just about to look when you came in,' I said.

'Come on, then. Do it now. Let's see if we can find her.'

Reluctantly, I hooked out the diary from under my leg and opened it on the counter. Amber squeezed into the booth and watched over my shoulder as I opened it from the front, peeling back the pages reverentially.

The first was blank, but the next two were covered in a repeated scrawl that looked like someone was practising their signature. I'm not sure how I'd missed it before.

'Mum said she did that when she first married Dad and had to try out her new name before signing the mortgage papers,' Amber said.

The woman seemed too old to have been a newly-wed, but I suppose she could have been a divorcee or a widow on her second, or even third husband. I lifted the book closer to my face. 'I can't quite make out the name.'

'Esme someone,' Amber said, leaning over my shoulder. 'Wilder? Wilton? I'm not sure.'

'It's Winters,' I said. 'Esme Winters.'

'Great. You've got a name. What now?' Amber asked.

'I need to work out how to find her. Anyway, what was it you wanted to talk about?' I asked, remembering Amber had come to see me clearly with something on her mind.

'It doesn't matter,' she said. 'I've got to get back to work.'

'Are you sure?' I slipped the diary safely back in my bag. I couldn't risk losing it before I'd tracked down Esme Winters.

'I'll tell you tonight,' she said, finishing her coffee and tossing the empty cup into a bin. 'It can wait.'

CHAPTER THREE

Garrett Hanlon focused on the road ahead, aware of the danger of losing control through the damp and twisting back lanes, especially with all the weight over the back wheels. He didn't want to end up wrapping the car around a tree. That would be a disaster.

Like him, the vehicle was showing signs of its age. Its suspension rocked through every corner, the gears were stiff and the engine asthmatic. At least it had been easy to steal. No central locking. No immobiliser. No tracking. In fact, its owner would probably be glad to see the back of it. He doubted they'd even bother to report it missing. At best, it was an insurance claim. Nobody was going to investigate its theft. The only risk was if the police stopped him, but if they did, he had far bigger worries in the boot than being concerned about driving a stolen vehicle.

It had been one of those quick and dirty jobs that paid well but didn't test his skills as an investigator. A dealer muscling in on a patch, distributing through a network of kids on their BMXs, too young to appreciate the consequences of what they were doing. It didn't take Hanlon long to find the guy. He ran the operation from his flat on the seventeenth floor of a decrepit tower block overlooking the estate where he peddled his misery. The kids had given him up easily, blindly leading Hanlon right to his front door. He was only young himself. A guy in his early twenties chancing his luck on making some easy cash. Not that Hanlon felt a spark of regret or guilt. The guy must have known what he was getting himself into, setting up a rival operation under the noses of a bigger, more organised gang. Surely he'd known the risks?

On the passenger seat, Hanlon's phone trilled with an incoming call. He didn't recognise the number.

'Hanlon,' he answered, jamming it against his ear with his shoulder so he could keep both hands on the wheel.

A woman's voice. A foreign accent. Exotic sounding. She repeated his name, confirming she had the right number. The line hissed. Hanlon checked the call hadn't dropped, amazed he had any reception at all so far out in the middle of nowhere.

'Hang on,' he said. 'Let me turn the music down.'

He'd had the radio up loud to drown out the howl of the wheezing engine and the insistent banging coming from the boot. The only station he'd found with a decent signal was playing cheesy classics from the eighties, music that reminded him of his childhood and a different era. The lyrics flooding back to him from a deep recess in his brain, even though he couldn't remember the names of the bands.

As he reached for the volume, the phone tumbled from his shoulder, falling between his legs into the footwell.

'Shit,' he hissed, ducking his head below the dashboard, momentarily taking his eyes off the road as he clawed for it by his feet.

When he looked up, he was drifting across the road, heading towards an oncoming white van which flashed its lights and blasted its horn.

'Wanker!' he yelled, swerving out of the way at the last moment. He watched the van disappear in his rearview mirror and dialled the music down to barely a whisper before pressing the phone back to his ear. 'Who is this?'

'You don't need to know my name.' Her voice was husky. Her accent sultry. She sounded Eastern European, like the Bulgarian cleaner with the unsightly hairy mole on her chin who came to his flat twice a month.

'Okay,' Hanlon said. 'What can I do for you?'

'I need you to find someone.' Blunt and to the point. No small talk. Professional and efficient. He liked that.

'Sure, I can help. Let me just pull over and take the details.'

Hanlon turned off onto a rutted track at the

entrance to an apple orchard surrounded by a tall hawthorn hedge shielding it from the road. It was as good a place as any for what he had in mind. He pulled up out of sight of passing traffic and killed the engine. He hauled himself out of the vehicle, grimacing at the stab of pain in his knee from the old injury that had forced his early retirement from the force.

'Where did you get my number?' he asked, perching on the bonnet and swatting away a fly buzzing in his face. The banging from the boot started up again.

'It doesn't matter,' the woman said. 'Can you do it?'

'Find someone? It depends.'

'On what?'

'A lot of things,' Hanlon said. 'I don't come cheap.'

'Money's not a problem. I'm told you're good at what you do.'

'I'm the best at what I do. Do have any details?'

She gave him a name. It meant nothing to him. Nor did the home address or the name of the shop the guy owned. She offered nothing more.

'What's he done?'

'That's not important. Can you find him?' the woman asked.

'Of course, but it helps to know what I'm dealing with.'

'Call me on this number when you find him. You have five days.'

Hanlon opened his mouth to protest. Five days was pushing it, especially with a standing start. The guy could be anywhere. He might even have gone abroad.

'I'll pay double your usual fee,' the woman added, nipping Hanlon's protestations in the bud. 'On the understanding you find him.'

'Double?'

'Plus reasonable expenses, of course. When you've located him, I'll give you further instructions.' There was something intoxicating about the way she said it that brought a smile to Hanlon's face. 'I was told you could handle anything.'

'You have excellent sources of information,' Hanlon said, noticing a spray of blood on the sleeve of his jacket. Little spots of the red stuff. How careless. It was one of his best jackets, too. Now he'd have to get it dry cleaned. He was normally so fastidious about his work. He took pride in doing things right. Silly mistakes like that were what tripped you up. It was a rare slip.

'Good. I know you won't let me down.'

The underlying threat wasn't lost on him. It came with the territory. The people who hired his services weren't the sort of people you messed around. They certainly didn't accept failure easily. It's why they always paid so well. Hanlon guaranteed success. If he'd had business cards, that would be his motto. *Garrett Hanlon, private investigator. Success guaranteed at all costs.*

'Alright, I'll phone as soon as I've located him,' Hanlon said.

The woman hung up. No goodbye. No pleasantries. Hanlon saved the number in his mobile with his hackles rising. The noise coming from the back of the car was getting under his skin.

He pushed himself off the bonnet, limped around the back to the boot, and flipped it open.

'Will you stop banging!' he screamed at the guy, who stared back at him, wide-eyed with fear. 'I was trying to take a phone call.'

The guy went quiet and stopped struggling. His face was bloodied, and one eye had almost entirely closed. He tried to speak, but his words were indistinguishable through the thick tape across his mouth. The same tape Hanlon had used to bind his legs and wrists, trussing him up like the animal he was. Hanlon grimaced at the wet patch around his crotch. Disgust was the only emotion he felt. No sympathy. No regret. It was nothing more than a guy like him deserved.

Hanlon grabbed a fuel can and an old t-shirt by the guy's feet and slammed the boot shut. He doused the petrol liberally inside the vehicle, watching it seep into the fabric of the seats, the strong vapours filling his nostrils, making his head spin. He poured the last of it over the t-shirt, unscrewed the filler cap, and shoved one end of the material into the fuel tank. Then he stood back. Took a lighter. Put a flame to the material. It caught with a satisfying whoosh, which flushed his face with heat.

He hurried away and didn't give another thought to the guy in the boot. Nor did he flinch when the car exploded with a deafening boom and a plume of oily smoke. He just put his head down and kept walking. Back to the road with his thumb out to hitch a ride, his mind already thinking ahead to the next job and the five days they'd given him to locate a man he knew nothing about.

CHAPTER FOUR

T he rest of the day dragged with my mind restless as I mulled over how to find Esme Winters. All I had was her name and a vague memory of what she looked like. At a guess, I would have put her in her sixties. She obviously had money from the look of that necklace she was wearing. And she probably lived somewhere near the beach. But that was all I had. It wasn't much to go on.

That evening, when Amber insisted we go to a party on the beach so she could hook up with some lad, I didn't put up much resistance. Even though I wasn't much in the mood, she persuaded me a change of scene would do me good. Anything to take my mind off Esme Winters for a few hours.

The problem she'd come to speak to me about at the arcade that morning turned out to be not much of a problem at all. Her ex, Aaron, had been pestering her to get back together. I told her she was lucky to have two guys chasing her and to be grateful. I'm not sure that's what she wanted to hear, but it was how I felt. She would never struggle for male attention.

I wasn't sure what to make of Amber when we first met. She was already living in the caravan, a perk of the job working for the holiday park, and although I'm not sure she really needed help with the rent, she'd advertised for a sharer around the time I found myself searching for new digs. A caravan wasn't exactly what I'd been looking for, but when my old flatmate walked out, drawn back to the bright lights of London, I wasn't left with much time to make alternative plans. I had little money and the rent on the caravan, by the time we split it two ways, was cheap.

Amber was like nobody I'd ever met before. She could have been a model with her stunning blue eyes and high cheekbones, but it was her verve for life that I found most attractive. She revelled in every day. Nothing ever seemed to get her down, and she never stressed or worried about anything. She just enjoyed having fun. And when I told her about my previous life, of growing up in a tower block in London, being put into foster care when I was fourteen, running away and living on the streets, she never passed judgement or thought she was better than me.

I wish I could have been similarly non-judgemental. Amber didn't talk much about home, but I gathered her father was something important in the City. They lived in a big house in the country with horses and tennis courts. It was a world apart from anything I'd ever known, and as much as I didn't like to admit it, part of me resented her for it. She would always have her family. I had nobody.

She'd run away from home because of the pressure from her parents to succeed. They'd not only expected her to achieve top grades in her exams, but had her entire career mapped out. She told me she needed space to find herself, so threw some things in a bag and walked out.

Even though I resented that she'd squandered those opportunities I'd never had, I recognised how good she was for me, always encouraging me to be sociable, dragging me out to parties and drinks with her friends when I could have easily spent the night curled up in front of the TV. She was my best friend. Probably my only real friend.

The party was one of those typical mid-week affairs with a relaxed vibe, where everyone was chilled and the music ambient rather than thumping. We sat by a roaring driftwood fire, already buzzing from the wine and vodka shots we'd consumed at the caravan.

I'd brought the remains of the vodka with me and set the bottle in the sand between my knees. As the heat from the fire warmed our faces, I took another sip, not wanting the glowing fuzz to pass but conscious that for me there was a fine line between the alcoholic euphoria that made a party go with a bang and a much, much darker place. I passed the bottle to Amber, who was already getting into the swing of things, swaying her head in time to the music as I watched the smoke from the fire swirling into the darkening night sky.

Amber was wearing a short skirt and crop top which not only showed off her long legs and toned mid-riff, but made me feel frumpy and fat in my t-shirt and scruffy jeans.

'Are you cold?' I asked. 'Do you want to borrow my hoodie?'

Amber threw her head back and laughed, her long blonde hair cascading over her tiny shoulders. 'Lighten up. We're supposed to be having fun.'

'I am having fun.'

Out of the gloom, a waif-like figure bounded up to us, squealing with delight. She collapsed in the sand next to Amber, showering her with pretentious air kisses.

'Karma! Babe!' Amber screamed. 'You know my flat-mate, Sky, right?'

I raised a hand in greeting. I couldn't be doing with all that gushing haven't-seen-you-in-ages nonsense. We'd only been with Karma at the weekend. Or had it been the weekend before that? It was all a bit of a blur. Instead, I offered her the bottle of vodka, but from the look of her voluminous, black eyes, she was already lit.

She waved the drink away and produced a joint from a pouch strapped around her waist under her t-shirt. She lit it curling her hand around the flame from a lighter, and took a deep drag, squinting as the smoke drifted into her eyes. When she exhaled, her body melted. She collapsed on her back with a sigh of contentment.

'Anyone else?' Karma held the joint up between bony fingers.

I knew I shouldn't, especially on a stomach-full of wine and spirits, but after the day I'd had, I needed something to help me forget, to park my worries about Esme Winters for a little while. I took the joint and drew the smoke down deep into my lungs, waiting for the smooth caress of the drug to flood my veins. It arrived slowly as I exhaled, liquefying my muscles, jellying my limbs.

'Tell Karma about the diary,' Amber said as my gaze drifted to the stars blazing in the beautiful night sky, pulsing like they were dancing to the beat of the music.

Karma sat up, her interest piqued.

'It's nothing.' I shot Amber a barbed look that seemed to pass her by completely as she continued to explain how I'd found the diary on the beach.

'Did you bring it with you?' Amber asked, breathlessly.

'What?'

'Is it still in your bag?' Amber pulled her skirt down over her skinny thighs, that stupid grin that always gave away when she was drunk, stretching from ear to ear. 'Read some of it to us.'

'No!' I stared at Amber, trying to read her expression, but I couldn't focus on her face. Her features and everything around her were losing their shape, shifting and morphing like molten lava. I wasn't sure if I was imagining it, but Amber and Karma seemed to be edging closer to me, crowding me. Amber's hand reached for my bag. I half-heartedly slapped it away. 'Stop it. No.'

'It's only for a laugh,' Amber said.

Karma raised an eyebrow, and I felt my resistance evaporate. What harm could it do if I read them a few pages, especially some of the more innocuous passages? Not the stuff about her husband. That would be wrong.

Before I could stop myself, my hand was snaking into my bag, rummaging through my things. I giggled as I pulled out the little black book, not sure what was so funny. What Esme Winters was going through was no laughing matter.

Amber wrung her hands in anticipation. 'Go on then,' she said. 'Find a good bit.'

I cleared my throat and opened the book on my lap, planning to read a few lines, that's all. Just something to keep them happy. I scoured the pages, pretending to search for something salacious, but the truth was I could hardly make out the words in the flickering light of the fire.

I used the torch on my phone to light up the pages, smirking as the handwritten words swam in front of my eyes. 'Are you ready?' I delighted in their anticipation. 'You know I really shouldn't be doing this.'

'Sky!' Amber screamed. 'I'm dying here!'

'Okay, here we go,' I mumbled. 'Just a few lines, alright?' But the more I tried to focus on the words, the less willing they were to remain still. Like the smoke from the fire, they swirled and danced as if they had a life of their own, and the harder I stared at them, the more difficult it became to make sense of them.

I flattened a page and cleared my throat, focusing hard on a couple of sentences.

How can I tell anyone? He'd kill me if I breathed a word of it. None of this my fault, so why do I feel like I'm to blame?

No, I couldn't read that to them. It was too raw. Too personal. I shook my head and squeezed my eyes shut, trying to get a grip on my sobriety, fighting the surge of sickness rolling in my stomach. When I opened my eyes again and tried to speak, my voice stuck in my throat like tar. The words in the diary lifted off the page and contorted into an awful image, a memory as ugly as cancer, one that I'd struggled to keep buried. And now it was back. A ghost from the past.

'Are you okay?' Amber touched my arm lightly, making me jump.

'What? Yes, I'm fine.' I sniffed and wiped my cheek, surprised to find tears rolling towards my chin.

I snapped the diary shut and threw it back in my bag, burying it under the detritus of my life, just like I'd been burying the bad memories for so long.

'You're upset.' Amber was on her knees, her face crumpled with concern.

'It's nothing.' I took another long, hard swig of vodka, willing the alcohol to numb the pain and help me forget. But too quickly it was all gone, the bottle empty. I tossed it into the fire where it smashed with a splintering crack and I stood unsteadily. 'I need another drink,' I slurred.

'Why don't you have some water.' Amber tried to press a plastic bottle into my hand.

'I don't want water,' I yelled, throwing the bottle towards the sea. 'I need a proper fucking drink.'

CHAPTER FIVE

The shop Garrett Hanlon was looking for was sandwiched between a beauty parlour and a charity store in the busy high street. A sign above the shuttered windows was written in gold leaf on a dark blue background above a canvas awning. *Whittakers of Chelmsford*. Classy. Professional. Alongside it, a letting agent's board had been hastily screwed to the wall. Hanlon rattled the shutters more in hope than expectation, but they didn't budge.

He'd already run a series of checks online for the man he'd been hired to find but there was little information available. Usually there was something, a name in the local squash league or a forgotten LinkedIn profile. A lead of some kind. But there was nothing. It was like the guy didn't exist, which was no surprise. Why else would they have hired him if he'd been easy to find?

'You're out of luck. The shop's been shut for a few

weeks,' said a woman with heavily pencilled eyebrows and plump lips as she emerged from the beauty salon next door.

'Any idea when they're opening again?' Hanlon asked.

'They've closed down. I mean, for good. It's a shame for the town.'

'I was looking for the owner. Duncan Whittaker? Do you know him?'

The woman shook her head. She had fingernails like talons and her dark tan, the colour of mahogany, looked fake, especially in the middle of April. 'Not really. I saw him from time to time to say hello, but I wouldn't say I knew him well.'

'Any idea where I might find him?'

'Sorry, no. We didn't even know he was shutting up. One day he was here, the next he was gone. Good luck though.' She smiled, showing off a gap between her front teeth, then walked off.

Hanlon watched her totter down the street on high wedges that made her calf muscles bulge.

The shop was a dead end then. Hanlon took a step back and stared up at the sign above the folded awning as he pondered his next steps. If Duncan had departed in such a hurry, it was possible he'd left a clue behind. Hanlon pulled out his phone and dialled the number on the letting agent's sign.

A dour-sounding receptionist answered and put him through to someone dealing with enquiries on the tenancy.

'Yeah, that property's currently available. Do you want to make an appointment to view it?' the guy asked.

'I'm in town at the moment, but I'm not here for long. I don't suppose it would be possible to look this morning?' Hanlon asked. When the agent hesitated, he added, 'I have other properties to see later, and this is my only window today.'

'Sure, we can make that work.' The guy must have been desperate for the business.

'Can you meet me in the next twenty minutes?'

The guy hesitated for a beat. 'Okay, I'll get over there as soon as I can.'

To his credit, he made it in fifteen. Hanlon spotted him a mile off in a tight-fitting blue suit and brown brogues which he wore with a confident swagger and an oily charm. He had one of those annoying designer stubbles, not quite a full beard but more like he'd not bothered to shave for a few days. Hanlon hid his disdain as he shook the guy's hand, shooting him a friendly smile despite catching a nostril full of strong cologne.

The agent fingered through a bunch of keys and unlocked the padlocks on the shutters. They opened noisily, shedding light on the empty shop full of vacant glass display cases. There were more locks on the door.

'What kind of business are you in?' the agent asked, as he let Hanlon in.

'Arts and crafts,' Hanlon said.

'Do you have any other premises?'

'No.'

'Your first shop then? That's exciting for you. Don't worry about all these fittings. We'll clear out anything you don't need.'

White velvet display trays and mannequin busts had been left abandoned in the glass cabinets, along with a litter of discarded price tags.

'The last tenants were jewellers,' the agent explained.

'Looks like they left in a rush.'

The agent smiled. 'I think they'd outgrown the space and were looking for bigger premises. As you can see, it's a decent sized retail space. And there's a big office out the back too.'

Hanlon followed him into a back room with a desk, a couple of deep filing cabinets and two heavy-duty safes, their doors hanging open. On one wall, hung a picture of a sun-kissed island with white sandy beaches and coral blue translucent seas. Someone's idea of a perfect getaway? The Maldives? The Caribbean? Hanlon made a mental note.

The agent walked over to the desk and picked up a chair that had been knocked over. 'Like I said, we'll clear this space for you, unless there's anything you want to keep?'

Hanlon ran a hand over one of the filing cabinets and casually pulled open the top drawer. He was surprised to find it full of paperwork.

'We'll make sure it's thoroughly cleaned before you

move in,' the agent said, stepping in front of Hanlon and pushing the drawer closed.

Above the filing cabinet, business cards, a hand-written directory of telephone numbers and a sandwich menu from a local cafe covered a corkboard on the wall. Plus a newspaper cutting. A picture of a grey-haired man next to a woman wearing mayoral chains. Under it, a single line caption: "Business owner Duncan Whittaker receives his award from Mayor Jane Whitford after being named Chelmsford Entrepreneur of the Year."

Duncan was staring at the camera with a grin spreading across his face. Nothing unusual looking about him at all. Charcoal suit. Smart shirt. Bland tie. Not the usual type Hanlon was hired to find. 'Is this the last tenant?' he asked.

The agent glanced at the clipping. 'Yeah, that's him. Duncan Whittaker.'

'Did he leave a forwarding address? I could send the paperwork he left onto him.'

The agent frowned. 'I can't give out any personal details, I'm afraid. But don't worry, we'll take care of it.'

Hanlon pulled open the heavy door of one of the safes and peered inside. Empty. Same with the other one.

'The property comes with one allocated space at the rear of the property as well, which is a nice bonus. I can show you.' The agent sifted through his bunch of keys to open a rear door.

Hanlon scoured the floor while he was distracted. The carpet was threadbare and blackened.

'It's a good-sized parking space for the centre of town,' the agent said. 'I know the previous tenant used to park his Range Rover there with no problem. Would you like to see?'

'Yeah, sure.'

Hanlon was about to follow the guy out when he spotted something wedged between the carpet and the skirting board. He knelt and picked up an inch-long painted wooden spike. A golf tee with white writing on red paint. As the agent grappled with a sticky lock, Hanlon slipped it into his trouser pocket.

'As you can see, the parking's very convenient for the shop. Useful for deliveries too,' the agent said.

As he stepped outside, Hanlon ripped the newspaper cutting from the corkboard and stuffed it in his jacket.

Outside, a wide strip of asphalt had been divided into four parking spaces with white paint, each with a car registration plate screwed to the wall.

'This one would be yours.' The agent indicated to the space nearest the rear door of the shop.

Hanlon smiled at the registration number.

DW1 JWL.

So Duncan Whittaker was one of those guys who needed to flaunt his status with a personalised number plate. Interesting.

'What do you think?'

Hanlon sighed. 'I don't know,' he said. 'The woman

next door said the previous tenant left suddenly. Do you know what happened?'

The agent scratched his chin. 'I can't really tell you too much–'

'I need to know if this is going to be a viable location for my business,' Hanlon said, cutting him off. 'If the previous tenant had any issues, I'd like to know about them.'

'Look, between you and me, and I probably shouldn't be telling you this, but it was all very sudden. He literally shut up shop overnight, cleared his stock and never came back. I don't know why. As far as we were concerned, business was good. I never got the impression he was struggling. Seriously, this is an excellent location for footfall, but maybe the guy didn't move with the times. I don't know. I'm not sure he even had a website. How can anyone expect to survive these days without a digital presence?'

Hanlon smiled and nodded in agreement. No wonder he'd not been able to find anything about Duncan Whittaker online. He sounded like a dinosaur. But it didn't explain why he'd gone missing or why there were people looking for him. His best guess was that he owed money. Not that it was important right now. His job was to find him. That's all.

'And you've not heard from him since?' Hanlon asked.

'Nothing. So, are you interested?'

'What?'

'In taking the shop?'

'No, sorry. It's not what I was looking for.' Hanlon shoved his hands in his pockets and turned to walk away.

'Seriously? We've not even talked rent. Can I at least grab your name and number?' the agent called after him, a note of desperation in his voice.

But Hanlon kept walking. Time was ticking. His fingers curled around the little wooden spike in his pocket. A golf tee embossed with the name of a local club. Duncan's club? He seemed like the kind of guy who might play golf. Maybe somewhere there might know where he was hiding.

CHAPTER SIX

My head was thick and my mouth desert dry. I winced at the brightness of the sun streaming through the thin curtains and rolled over, burying my face in the pillow as daggers shot through my throbbing skull. But at least I was alone, thank God. I couldn't have faced that early morning awkwardness with an intimate stranger.

The room was already warming up, the chill of the night chased away by the early morning rays on the caravan's thin skin. I kicked off the duvet and found I was still in my underwear. At least I'd had the sense to get undressed before climbing into bed, even if I'd not pulled on my pyjamas.

A wave of nausea bloomed in my stomach and it took all my willpower to swallow it back down, my brow flushing hot. A tap at my door. Amber poked her head into my room. 'Are you awake?' she whispered.

'No,' I croaked, my voice harsh and gravelly like I'd

smoked way too much. 'Go away.' I pulled the duvet over my body, embarrassed to let her see me half-naked with all my lumps and bumps in the wrong places.

'Just checking you haven't overslept.' I couldn't believe how fresh she looked. Her skin was glowing, and her eyes sparkled like she'd had a decent ten hours' sleep.

'I can't face going into work today,' I whined. 'Can you call in sick for me?'

'Not a chance.'

'Some friend you are.'

'Seriously?' She put her hands on her hips and shot me a look she reserved for when she was really pissed off with me. 'And who do you think got you home last night? Undressed you and put you to bed when you could barely walk? I even brought you the bucket. Do you want tea?'

'What happened last night?' I asked, not sure I wanted to know.

'You got wasted, as usual. Don't you remember?'

I shook my head and immediately regretted it. I clamped a hand over my mouth.

'Not even going off with Gavin?'

'Gavin? No. What did I do?'

'What didn't you do? Seriously, Sky, you need to be careful, you know. Have a shower. I'll bring you a cuppa.' Amber slammed the door shut, sending a thunderbolt of pain through my temples. I'm sure she'd done it on purpose.

I relaxed back into the warmth of my bed and stared

at the mould-pocked ceiling. I'd only intended to go out for a quiet drink, to keep Amber company while she waited for her date, who I don't think ever did turn up. I could remember bits of the party. The vodka. Karma sparking up a joint that sent my head spinning and tanking beer from cans with a group of lads I didn't know. Everything else was a blank. Hours lost that I'd never recover.

I had a snatched memory of Amber and Karma goading me about Esme Winters and her diary, how I'd been too weak to resist and reading a few brief words that chilled my heart.

How can I tell anyone? He'd kill me if I breathed a word of it.

My anger simmered. It's how abusers controlled women like Esme, wasn't it? The threat of fear and violence. What a total piece of shit. Guys like her husband, hiding behind a pretence of normality while behaving like monsters behind closed doors, deserved to be strung up.

A shower, clean clothes, and a cup of tea weren't exactly a miracle cure, but they made me feel half-human again. And as I dragged myself into work with the sun on my face, my spirits lifted a little, even though I was going to be late again. The third time in two weeks, which meant yet another dressing down from Michelle. I might tell her where she could stick her job if she started on me.

Although I was already ten minutes late, I decided

on a quick detour to grab something to help me through the morning.

The general store on the high street at the top of town was a mecca for tourists in the summer, one of those places that stocked everything from bread and milk to sun hats and beach inflatables which they hung from an awning outside. I headed straight for the chilled cabinet at the back and grabbed two cans of energy drink.

On my way out, I almost bumped into the owners' son, Cam, fussing over a display in the window. He was one of those guys I saw occasionally at parties. He virtually ran the shop since his mother had become ill and his father had taken on full-time caring duties.

He shot me a friendly smile. 'Hey, Sky. How are things?'

'Fine,' I lied. I noticed he was slotting handwritten postcards into a transparent plastic display sheet. Adverts for all sorts of things; a Pilates class in the town hall on Wednesday nights, second-hand lawnmower for sale, a bundle of baby clothes, and an unused footbath. Hadn't these people heard of e-Bay? 'How much does that cost?' I asked, a thought popping into my head.

'Nothing,' Cam said. 'It's free. A community service. Why? Do you have something to advertise?'

'Can I put up a lost and found notice?'

'You can advertise whatever you want. Well, within reason,' he laughed. 'If you've got two minutes, you can do it now. I'll grab a card.'

Before I could stop him, he'd rushed off. He returned clutching a pen and a blank card. 'I'll write it for you, if you like. What do you want to say?'

He was so keen, I didn't have the heart to tell him I didn't have the time right now. 'I'm not sure. I found a lost diary on the beach the other night.'

Cam rested the card against the wall and began scribbling in large capital letters. He wrote 'FOUND' along the top and underlined it. His writing was much neater than mine.

'What did it look like?' he asked.

'Small. Black,' I said.

Cam continued to scribble, the tip of his tongue poking out between his front teeth. 'SMALL, BLACK DIARY,' he wrote.

'And where exactly did you find it?'

'By a rock, close to the pillboxes at Warden Point,' I said. 'I think it belongs to a woman called Esme Winters, but I don't have her address.'

Cam lowered his pen and frowned. 'Esme?' He stepped outside and studied the display of small ads from the other side of the glass. Then with a triumphant grin pointed to a card in the top left corner. He strode back into the shop, pulled it out and handed it to me. 'Here,' he said. 'I thought the name sounded familiar.'

The advert was written in black ballpoint pen.

NEED TO TALK?
FACE-TO-FACE COUNSELLING

UNDERSTANDING AND CONFIDENTIAL
- STRESS
- RELATIONSHIP PROBLEMS
- ADDICTIONS
- PANIC ATTACKS
- PHOBIAS

APPOINTMENTS: MON - SAT 9am - 6pm

And at the bottom was a name with a telephone number. I read them twice, my hand shaking.

CALL ESME ON 07700 900896

'Do you think that might be her?' Cam asked.

Leysdown was only a small place, but despite what Cam said, the name wasn't that unusual. 'I doubt it,' I said.

'It's got to be worth a try though, right?'

I couldn't just ring up a random stranger and ask if they were missing a diary. That would be weird. 'Can you remember what she looked like?'

Cam shrugged. 'Sorry. We get so many people in here and I'm dreadful with faces. Why don't you take a note of her number and call?'

'What if it's not her?' I asked.

'We can still put your advert up.'

'I'll think about it,' I said, snapping a picture of the

advert on my phone. I needed time to work out what I was going to say, how I was going to let her know I'd read the diary and that I wanted to help, without freaking her out.

'Let me know how you get on,' he called after me as I walked away, hurrying for work.

'Yeah, sure,' I shouted over my shoulder. But it was the last thing I intended to do. This was personal business between me and Esme. My shot at redemption.

CHAPTER SEVEN

The clubhouse was like a shrine to golfing achievement. Ancient wooden-shafted clubs, engraved silverware in display cabinets and framed black and white photographs of golfers in plus-fours and Argyle sweaters adorned the walls. Cheap props to capture a wistful nostalgia, as if the place was a grand hall of sporting homage rather than the local golf club.

A low murmur of conversation hummed off the ceiling from a few small groups dressed colourfully and enjoying coffee and cake. Hanlon approached the bar and flashed a fake police warrant card at the barman.

'DC Barraclough, Met Police,' he said. 'I'm investigating the disappearance of one of your members.'

The barman, a tall, slim guy with a distasteful sneer, glanced only fleetingly at Hanlon's identification and showed no emotion. Not even a raised eyebrow.

'Do you know this man? Duncan Whittaker?'

Hanlon asked, unfolding the newspaper clipping he'd stolen from the shop.

'If it's a query about a member, you'll need to speak with the club secretary, Sir,' the barman said, without looking at the clipping. 'Or our general manager.'

'And are they around?'

'I'm afraid they're currently in a meeting. Perhaps you could come back later? I can let them know you were here.'

'A man's missing,' Hanlon hissed, thumping the bar with his fist and narrowing his eyes. He wasn't used to being pissed around. The warrant card usually commanded some respect. 'I don't have time to come back later. Now do you know Duncan Whittaker or not?'

The barman flinched but quickly regained his composure. 'I only work the bar, Sir,' he said. 'I'm not really at liberty to answer your questions.'

'Is there anyone else around who might know him?' Hanlon growled, his patience stretched.

The barman glanced towards a wide expanse of glass with impressive panoramic views of a verdant golf course that stretched as far as the eye could see. The fairways, fringed by a magnificent woodland, were lush. 'You might try Mr Bashara,' the barman said, pointing to a pair of golfers approaching the eighteenth green. 'I believe he's a friend of Mr Whittaker's.'

'Right, thank you,' Hanlon said, folding the newspaper clipping and slipping it back into his jacket pocket. 'That wasn't so difficult, was it?'

The barman gave him a withering look. Jumped up arsehole with a misplaced sense of his own self-importance.

Hanlon stepped out onto a terrace overlooking the last hole and watched the two golfers finish their match. He guessed Bashara was the brash-looking guy with the pink polo shirt and garish red trousers. Even at a distance, his braying voice carried. When he sunk a long putt, he whooped like a kid and punched the air. The grin on his face was a smug badge of victory. He was clearly a man who enjoyed winning. Hanlon took an instant dislike to him.

While his partner disappeared with his clubs over his shoulder, heading towards the car park, Bashara bounded up the steps towards the clubhouse, carrying a single white leather glove.

'Mr Bashara? DC Barraclough, Met Police.' Hanlon held up his warrant card briefly before snapping the wallet shut in the man's face. 'I'd like to talk to you about Duncan Whittaker. I'm leading an investigation into his disappearance.'

Up close, the man showed the signs of taking full advantage of the good life. Expensive clothes. A paunch that stretched the fabric of his shirt. A chunky gold chain around his neck and several fatty folds under his chin.

Bashara looked Hanlon up and down. 'I don't know anything about that,' he mumbled. A thin bead of sweat glistened on his forehead at the line of his thinning black hair.

'But you know Mr Whittaker? When did you last see him?'

Bashara slipped his glove into the back pocket of his trousers and glanced over Hanlon's shoulder into the clubhouse, a cloud of worry darkening his face.

'Mr Bashara?'

'I can't help you. Sorry.'

When he turned and ran, it was the last thing Hanlon had expected. He sprinted the length of the terrace with the spikes on his shoes clattering over the flagstones.

'Shit,' Hanlon muttered under his breath as Bashara vaulted a low privet hedge, heading for a thicket of trees fringing the eighteenth hole.

Hanlon hadn't run anywhere since he'd injured his knee. Walking was painful enough. But he couldn't let Bashara get away. He half jogged, half hobbled along the terrace and stumbled over the hedge, trying to ignore the stab of pain radiating up his leg. He'd never been an active sportsman. Why run when you could walk or even better, take the car? But running had never felt like this. As he entered the edge of the wood, his breathing became heavy and laboured. God, he was unfit.

Bashara was already twenty metres ahead, crashing through the trees and a thick covering of ferns, his arms swinging wildly at his sides as he snatched glances over his shoulder. But his feet were dragging. He was struggling. Neither of them exactly in their prime. A foot race in slow motion.

Hanlon pushed on as the man ahead slowed, gritting his teeth as his calf muscles stiffened and cramped, a stitch needling under his ribcage.

'Mr Bashara! Stop!' he yelled.

The guy made it only another fifty metres before he slowed to a stop, clutching his shoulder. He threw his head back as he gasped for breath.

Hanlon eased into a quick walk to give his leg some respite, sweat patches damp under his arms.

'You want to tell me why you ran?' Hanlon asked as he finally caught up with Bashara. 'Do you have something you need to tell me?'

Bashara wasn't looking so great. His skin was pallid and tinged the colour of an overcast morning. 'I don't know anything. I promise,' he wheezed.

'Try again. Duncan Whittaker's a friend of yours, right?'

'We play a round together sometimes. That's all.'

Hanlon brushed his fringe from his brow with his fingers, his heart racing. In the distance, the thwack of a golf ball carried across the rolling, wide-open landscape. 'He cleared out his shop a few weeks ago and hasn't been seen since. Have you heard from him?'

'No.' Bashara shook his head and winced, bending at the hips, leaning forwards with his hands on his thighs. 'I swear.' Sweat was pouring off the guy.

'Did he owe money? Is that it?'

Bashara dropped to his knees, rubbing his chest.

Hanlon repeated the question. 'Was he in debt?'

'Yeah, I guess.'

51

'What do you mean, you guess?' Hanlon stepped on the man's hand. 'The truth, please.'

Bashara yelped in pain. 'Alright, alright, ' he yelled. 'He had a cash flow problem. The banks had turned their backs on him.' Every word seemed to be an effort.

'And?'

'I gave him a contact. Someone who might help. That's all.'

'What contact?'

'Someone recommended to me. I swear I've never used them. They were offering loans. No questions.'

'Loan sharks?'

'Romanians,' he hissed.

Hanlon let his foot off Bashara's hand. Romanians. That made sense. The woman with the Eastern European accent who contacted him could have been Romanian. Had Whittaker stupidly borrowed money from them and not repaid his debts? Idiot.

'I don't feel so good,' Bashara said. That was an understatement. He looked like death. His face creased in silent agony. 'Help me,' he gasped as he collapsed face down, arms and legs spread wide.

Fuck. Hanlon should have spotted the signs. Classic heart attack. Typical. Just as he was getting somewhere.

'Do you know where I can find Duncan Whittaker?' he asked, raising his voice.

Bashara groaned.

Hanlon grabbed him by the collar and lifted his head off the ground. 'Mr Bashara, where is Duncan

Whittaker? I need to find him urgently. Do you understand?'

But Bashara's eyes were closed, his breathing shallow and laboured. He wouldn't get anything more out of this waste of space. He released his grip, letting Bashara's body drop.

A trio of golfers approached over the brow of a rise. But they were deep in conversation, more interested in their game than what might be going on amongst the trees.

Hanlon shrunk away from Bashara's dying body. Maybe someone would find him before it was too late. Maybe they wouldn't. It wasn't his concern. Finding Duncan Whittaker was all that mattered, and although he now had a clearer idea of why he'd vanished, he was still no closer to finding him. He certainly didn't have the time to waste waiting for an ambulance.

He picked his way carefully back to the car park, giving the clubhouse a wide berth as he brushed dead leaves off his suit and straightened his tie. He climbed back into his van and punched an address into the sat nav. Time to see if Duncan had left any clues at his home.

CHAPTER EIGHT

The house was a thatched cottage with white picket fences, uneven stone walls and a mature garden bursting with the first green shoots of spring. Surrounded by fields and only accessible along narrow country lanes, it was a bit remote. The nearest village was a good twenty minutes' drive away and God only knew how far it was to the nearest supermarket.

Hanlon parked up in a layby a short distance away and walked the last quarter of a mile. His knee was still painful after his exertions at the golf club, but he couldn't risk parking his van outside the house. A little discomfort was the price he had to pay to make a discreet approach.

The cottage had an air of desolation about it. He peered through a window at the front, expecting to find it cleared out, like the shop, but was surprised to discover all the furniture had been left untouched, although covered up with big, white dust sheets. Definitely nobody home.

A lock on a patio door around the back of the house put up little resistance to the crowbar Hanlon had brought from the van. He jimmied it open, splintering the wood around the frame with a sharp crack, and let himself in.

Inside, the air was musty like an old library, but the house was remarkably clean. No cobwebs or layers of dust as he'd been expecting, which was odd as the property must have been shut up for the best part of a couple of months. Why hadn't Duncan sold the place or put it up for rent? Maybe he hadn't had the time, or perhaps he was planning to return when he thought the trouble he was in had blown over.

Hanlon wandered into a spacious kitchen and threw open a cupboard. No food, only plates and bowls, cutlery and pans. The fridge and freezer had also been cleared out and switched off.

In the lounge, a pile of ash remained in the fireplace and a stack of logs piled up alongside the hearth. A television sat forlornly in the corner, and behind a large sofa, floor-to-ceiling shelving was filled with books. Factual stuff, mostly. Not much fiction. Publications on travel, jewellery, history and gardening. The travel books were grouped together in a mess of different sizes and shapes. Hanlon pulled out one about the Maldives, remembering the image he'd seen on the wall in Duncan's office at the shop. The book had been well-thumbed and was packed with pictures of sparkling blue seas, pristine white sandy beaches and palapa-roofed villas perched on stilts in the water. Inside the front cover was an inscription wishing Duncan a happy Christmas, dated December 2003 and signed 'Mum xxx'. That was almost twenty years ago. Was she still alive? Did she know what had happened to her son? He slipped the book back in its place and continued exploring the rest of the house.

He thought he'd struck lucky when he discovered a study at the back of the cottage. More books on shelves. A leather-topped desk in the window. Hanlon tried all three drawers built into it. They were full of pens and staplers, drawing pins and paper clips, scissors, a hole punch and a stack of blank white postcards but no personal papers. Even a small filing cabinet in the corner had been cleaned out. Duncan had clearly gone to some trouble to sanitise the place, ensuring there were no hints to suggest where he might have gone.

Next, Hanlon tried upstairs. The staircase creaked under his weight as he crept up the steps one at a time. Into a master bedroom. A king-sized bed hidden under another dust sheet. Two bedside tables. Two bedside lamps. It hadn't occurred to him before that Duncan might be married. That should make the job of finding him easier. Much more difficult to hide as a couple than alone. Hanlon allowed himself a wry smile.

No surprise that a set of built-in wardrobes were empty, home now only to a bank of empty hangers. He imagined the couple shovelling clothes into suitcases and bags in their frantic effort to get away. Or had they planned their departure in advance, their cases packed and ready ahead of time?

What was that?

A noise from downstairs?

The sound of a door slamming?

Hanlon froze, a surge of adrenaline shotgunning through his veins. There it was again. Movement. Someone below.

Duncan? Surely not. Why would he have returned to the cottage? Who then?

Cupboard doors opening and closing. Footsteps in the hall. Hanlon stalked onto the landing and cocked an ear. An estate agent, maybe? Someone humming. A woman. So not Duncan. His wife possibly, back to collect a few more of their things? But why take the risk?

He crept to the top of the stairs, cringing at every creak of the old floorboards. The flash of a figure walking past, oblivious to his presence. Hanlon snatched his breath and held it. Counted to five and started down the stairs. If she saw him, he'd have no choice. He'd have to deal with her and worry about the consequences later. Deal with her? What the hell was he going to do?

He reached the bottom of the stairs and peered around the corner. The woman was in the kitchen at the sink, her back to him, running water in a bucket. A cleaner? Of course. It made perfect sense that Duncan would have left someone to keep an eye on the place, which meant he *was* intending on coming back at some point.

The front door was straight ahead, where the woman had left her bag and a coat on the floor. Unless she turned around suddenly, he could easily slip out without her noticing. But what if she knew something? She obviously had a key, so what was to say she didn't know where Duncan was hiding? But how could he explain why he was prowling around the house? Even using the pretence of being a police officer was going to raise her suspicions. And if she knew anything about Duncan's whereabouts, what was to stop her tipping him off Hanlon was onto him?

His hand tightened around the crowbar. It was a lethal weapon. But what would he do with her body? He didn't have the time to clean up after him. It was one thing abandoning a guy who'd run away and suffered a heart attack. It was an entirely different matter bludgeoning an innocent woman to death merely to cover his tracks. And he'd not thought to wear gloves, so the chances were his prints were all over the house. No, the risk was too great.

He took a step towards the door, but as he reached for the handle, noticed a bundle of letters under the woman's handbag. Post for Duncan? She must have picked it up on her way in. The sound of water filling the bucket stopped. The woman's hacking cough echoed through the cottage.

Hanlon slipped the post out from under her bag and thumbed through it, hoping to find a bank or credit card statement, something that might inadvertently give Duncan away. But mostly it was just junk mail. Charity appeals. Fliers for double glazing. An invitation to take out a new credit card. The only thing of interest was a plain white envelope with Duncan's name and address printed on a sticker stuck to the front.

Hanlon opened it, wincing at the sound of the paper tearing. Inside was a single printed sheet folded in half. He pulled it out and opened it up. A newsletter. Fuzzy pictures of old people with nursing staff in blue uniforms. Slabs of text. It appeared to be from a home on the south coast. An update of everything that had happened in the last couple of months.

Bingo. Hanlon smiled to himself as he recalled the inscription inside the cover of the book on the Maldives. He shoved the newsletter in his pocket and put the rest of the post back under the woman's bag, before pulling open the door and slipping outside. He crept down the drive back to the road, hardly even noticing the pain in his knee.

CHAPTER NINE

As I left work that evening, the first thing I did was check my phone for messages in case Esme had seen my postcard in the shop window and tried to call.

Nothing.

It had been a stupid idea. Even if she shopped at the store, what were the chances she'd seen the display of small ads? It was a waste of time. I'd probably have more chance of success printing out a load of posters and sticking them to lampposts around town. But the thought of advertising my number to all the wackos and perverts out there quickly put a dampener on that idea.

I'd been putting off calling the number for the woman offering counselling sessions, convinced it couldn't possibly be the same Esme. But Cam was right. What did I have to lose? I pulled up the photo of the advert and scribbled the number on the back of my hand before heading to the beach to make the call in private.

I sat on the sand with my back against the sea wall, punched in the number on my phone and listened to the silence in my ear as the call connected.

Eventually it started ringing.

I held my breath, counting each ring in my head.

One. Two. Three. Four.

'Hello?'

I cleared my throat. 'I don't know if I have the right number,' I said, a tremor in my voice, 'but I was trying to get hold of Esme Winters.'

'Yes?' The abruptness of the woman's reply threw me.

'You're Esme Winters?'

'Yes. Can I help you?'

Oh my God, I'd found her and now I didn't know what to say. 'I… umm… ' I stammered.

'Who is this?'

'You don't know me. My name's Sky. We bumped into each other on the beach the other night. You were upset,' I said.

A taut silence crackled in my ear. Was she still there? I checked the screen of my phone in case the call had dropped. When I heard her breathing, I carried on talking. 'After you left, I found your diary,' I said. 'But I didn't read it or anything,' I blurted out as an afterthought. What did I say that for? Now she was going to know for sure that I had. 'Obviously, I looked to see if you'd written your contact details in it but that was it, I promise. That's how I found your name.' I was rambling now but couldn't stop myself, my nerves getting the better of me. 'And then I saw your advert in the shop window and Esme's such an unusual name around here I thought it might be you. Well, actually I thought it would be too much of a coincidence.' I laughed nervously.

'Where are you?' she asked.

'I live in Leysdown, in one of the holiday parks,' I replied. Why did I feel the need to give out that much information?

'We're in Warden Bay. Would you be able to drop it around to the house?'

The house? Oh my God, she wanted me to deliver it to her. Was that a good idea? 'Sure,' I said, without thinking. 'I can do that.'

'Great. Can you pop around this evening?'

'No problem.'

I wrote her address down on my hand under her number and then she was gone.

Oh my God. Against the odds, I'd not only found Esme Winters, but I was going to see her, face-to-face again.

My skin prickled. All I had to do now was work out how to help her escape from her violent husband.

CHAPTER TEN

I t wasn't the quickest route to Esme Winters' house, but I figured the walk along the beach would give me time to work out what to say. I turned the words over and over in my head, but no matter how I tried phrasing it, I couldn't find an easy way to explain that I'd read her diary, I knew she was in danger from her husband and she needed help.

Would she be angry? Relieved? Or maybe she'd deny everything. The more I thought about it, the tighter my stomach knotted and by the time I'd made it to Warden Bay, I wasn't sure if I was doing the right thing at all. Would it be better to say nothing, just hand the diary back and let her get on with her life?

No, I couldn't. She needed my help.

I pictured Esme lived in a pretty cottage with a Kent peg-tiled roof and wisteria blossoming around the door, a house where she could maintain the pretence of a perfect life. What I didn't expect to find was a drab modern build with a scruffy garden set off a potholed track, with paint flaking off the window frames and a front door that looked leakier than a colander.

At the top of the drive, I stopped and took a deep breath, my heart rampaging, drumming against my ribs. I'd spent the last few days convinced fate had thrown us together, and that it was my destiny to save Esme from the monster who shared her home, but now I was here, my nerve was turning tail and seemed determined to abandon me. I had to fight the urge to turn and run away.

I forced one foot in front of the other, the words I'd been planning to say scrambling in my head with every step, my mouth dry and my breathing ragged.

A little silver Mercedes was parked at the front of the house, but as I drew closer, I had the distinct impression no one was home. A solitary light burned in a downstairs window, but there was no other sign of life. I was running a little late, so typical of me, but surely Esme hadn't forgotten I was coming? I'd only spoken to her a few hours ago.

I psyched myself up and knocked on the door. When no one answered, I knocked again, louder. No footsteps in the hall. No barking dog. Not even a flicker behind the curtains. Irritation stole the place of my anxiety. How could she have forgotten about me, especially as I'd made a special journey? It wasn't like I'd tramped over here for the benefit of my health.

'Hello? Is anyone home?' I shouted through the letterbox. I detected the faint aroma of onion and garlic. Cooking smells. Unlikely then that they'd gone out for dinner.

What a waste of a journey. I'd worked myself up into a frenzy for nothing. I pressed my nose against a window and shaded my eyes to peer inside. A deserted lounge was dominated by a pair of large sofas facing a flat-screen TV on the wall. A gilt-framed mirror hung over a faux fireplace and in the corner, by the door, was the source of the only light I could see in the house, a standard lamp with a voluminous beige shade.

Any sensible person would have posted the diary through the letterbox or left it on the doorstep with a note, regretting we'd missed each other. But returning the diary was only half the reason I'd come. This was supposed to have been an opportunity to talk to Esme and let her know she wasn't alone. That I knew her secret and wanted to help her escape from her husband. I'd imagined the relief on her face, the realisation that her long ordeal was ending, and I'd been positively bubbling with the excitement at doing something so selfless. I could almost imagine Mum looking down at me with a smile of pride, which is why I couldn't walk away. Not now. I'd give it ten minutes. Maybe half an hour. Esme couldn't have gone far.

After five long minutes sitting on the doorstep, curiosity won me over. I'd been inside Esme's head when I read those snatched extracts from her diary, and now I was intrigued to see for myself how she lived. With a quick glance up the drive to make sure no one was watching, I sneaked around the side of the house into a large rear garden that was flanked by a thick hedge on three sides.

An imposing conservatory ran along almost the entire length of the back of the house and inside it was a long dining table and six high-backed chairs. Beyond it, an enormous kitchen with a long wooden worktop, rows of cupboards and a shiny double oven, all lit with hidden downlighters which cast a ghostly glow around the room.

I drank it all in, imagining Esme cooking over the stove, pans on the boil, soft music playing and the looming presence of her evil husband lurking some-where in the background. I shuddered at the thought, wondering what kind of terrible things had played out in this room. I could almost picture him raising his hand to her, screaming in her face, raining down blows on her head. I squeezed my eyes tightly shut, trying to force the image out of my mind.

What was that?

A noise at the front of the house. I froze, my eyes springing open, all my senses alive.

The growl of a car engine. The crunch of gravel. Someone was coming.

I raced back to the front and was blinded by powerful headlights so dazzling I had to hold my arm up to protect my eyes.

A large 4x4 lurched to a halt. A door flew open, and a man jumped out.

'What are you doing here?' he screamed, waving his arms aggressively. 'Who are you?'

I couldn't speak, my gaze fixed on his snarling, angry face. I thought he was going to attack me. I staggered backwards with a pathetic whimper.

'I said, who are you?' He was right up in my face now. It was all I could do not to burst into tears.

'Sky,' I mumbled.

'Who?'

I'd never wondered what Esme's husband might be like. I suppose I'd sub-consciously imagined he was a large man with a threatening physical presence, but he was quite ordinary looking. Not exactly the sort of guy you'd cross the street to avoid. Average height, a little overweight maybe. With his plain, unremarkable face and grey, thinning hair, he could have been an accountant or an insurance salesman. A bit dull. No wonder he had to get his kicks terrorising his wife.

'I-I came to see Esme. I called earlier,' I said.

Behind him, a smaller figure slipped out of the car and stepped towards us. 'Frank? Who is it?'

I recognised Esme's voice immediately.

'Just some girl snooping around. Nothing to worry about. I'll deal with this,' he called over his shoulder.

'Esme? It's Sky,' I said, side-stepping out of the shadow of her husband. 'You asked me to come to the house.' She stared at me blankly. 'I found your diary.' I dived into my bag, frantically pawing through dried up pens, tissues and old sweet wrappers. Where was it? Finally, my fingers curled around its soft leather cover and I yanked it out, holding it aloft like a trophy for them both to see.

'Oh God, I'm so sorry. I totally forgot,' Esme said.

My hand trembled.

'You know her?' Her husband, Frank stood his ground, blocking my way.

'It's a long story.' Esme waved a dismissive hand. 'My diary must have fallen out of my bag when I was on the beach the other night.'

'Right,' said Frank, his expression revealing his obvious scepticism. 'Still doesn't explain what you were doing snooping around the back of the house.'

'I-umm,' I stammered, snatching a glance at Esme. Her wrist was bandaged, a pristine white dressing wrapped around her palm and lower arm. Had she had that when I saw her on the beach the other night? I don't think so. I'm sure I would have remembered. A recent injury, then.

'Well?' Frank demanded.

'When nobody answered the door, I thought I'd check around the back in case you hadn't heard me knocking,' I said.

'Leave the poor girl alone, Frank.' Esme slammed her car door shut. 'She wasn't doing any harm.'

'I didn't know you kept a diary,' Frank said, turning away from me.

Was that surprise or irritation in his voice?

Esme shrugged. 'Maybe you don't know me as well as you think.'

I could have kicked myself. I'd just revealed to him that his wife kept a secret diary that catalogued his abuse. No doubt she'd pay for that later.

Esme stepped in front of Frank and held out her bandaged hand. I gave her the diary, staring into her eyes. If only I could communicate with a look. I'm a friend, I wanted to say. I know the pain you're going through. I'm going to help you get away from him. Don't worry.

But of course, I couldn't say any of that in front of Frank.

'Your hand. You've hurt yourself,' I said, raising an eyebrow, challenging her to account honestly for the injury.

'It's nothing,' she said.

'It's only a cut, although you'd have thought she'd severed a finger from the fuss she was making a couple of hours ago.' Frank said.

As he returned to the car to kill the lights, I watched Esme carefully, looking for a flicker of fear. A tremble of her lip. The darkening of her eyes. But she showed no emotion at all.

'Actually, the doctor said I was lucky I didn't cut a tendon,' she said. 'It still needed three stitches.' She wiggled the fingers poking out from the bandage as if to make the point.

'What happened?' I asked.

'A silly accident. I broke a wine glass,' she said, as if trying to dismiss it as something trivial. An irrelevance. But I had a feeling she was hiding something. Had Frank done this to her? 'But look, thank you for returning my diary. Frank, have you got the door keys? I'm dying for a glass of wine.'

Frank blipped the car locked. 'Was there something else?'

'No,' I said, flustered.

'Can I give you a lift home?' he asked.

'No!' I said, horrified, recoiling at the thought of being trapped in a car with him. 'I can walk. It's not far.'

'Suit yourself,' he said.

He opened the front door and let Esme in first. I pivoted on my heel and marched up the drive with my head down and a hit of adrenaline racing through my veins.

I couldn't get away from that house fast enough, and yet my heart was tearing apart. I'd failed Esme. On the walk over, I'd worked myself up to say something, to let her know she wasn't on her own and together we'd come up with a plan. Instead, I'd said nothing. I'd been a coward and a failure. Again. I'd let Esme down and now I was going to have to find another way to help her.

CHAPTER ELEVEN

H anlon pressed the buzzer on the wall and stepped back, adjusting his jacket. A click and a crackle of static pre-announced the voice that answered.

'Hello?'

He detected a slight Scottish lilt. 'I'm here to see Mrs Whittaker. I called earlier.' He leaned in close to the speaker and smiled for the benefit of the camera, anticipating the uneasy hesitation. He pictured the woman who answered leafing through paperwork on a desk and consulting with colleagues who wouldn't have a clue about his visit.

'I'm sorry, what did you say your name was?'

'DC Barraclough, Met Police.' Hanlon held up his warrant card.

'And what's this concerning?'

'I'm afraid I'm not at liberty to discuss that,' he said.

Another long pause. There would be no record of

any DC Barraclough phoning the nursing home, but Hanlon had banked on her sense of civic duty to let him in. Who in their right mind turned away a police officer, appointment or not?

'There's nothing here to say you called.'

'Really?' said Hanlon. 'I rang at about seven this morning.'

'That would explain it. The early shift,' she said, as if it was a regular issue.

'If it's a problem, I can come back later. I don't want to cause any trouble. It's only that we think Mrs Whittaker might have some information concerning a serious historic crime we've had cause to re-open and time is quite pressing.' Hanlon waited a second or two and then turned as if he was going to walk away.

'No, it's okay, I'll buzz you in.'

He concealed a smug grin as he heard the door click open. 'Thank you,' he said, letting himself in.

The nurse who waddled out of an office into the entrance hall was short and overweight, but she had a wide smile and a kind face.

'Sorry to put you out,' Hanlon said. He did his best to hide his disgust at the stomach-churning smell of incontinence and boiled cabbage.

'It's no bother,' the nurse said. 'After all, it's not every day we have the police turn up.'

'I'm glad to hear it, but I'd appreciate it if you could be discreet. It would be better if my visit wasn't widely broadcast.'

'Absolutely,' the nurse said, tapping her nose.

'Mum's the word. Are you on your own? I thought you detectives always worked in pairs.'

'Budget cuts,' Hanlon said, rolling his eyes.

She tutted. 'We know all about those. Come on, follow me. I'll take you to Maisy's room.'

He followed the nurse along a corridor and into a room with a window overlooking a car park. Maisy Whittaker was sitting up in bed, staring mindlessly into space. Her skin was grey and creased, her floral night-dress buttoned up to her scrawny throat and her hands clawing at the blanket over her legs. Hanlon's heart sank. He'd not considered she might be in a home because she had dementia. What if she didn't remember she had a son, let alone where he could find him?

'Is she okay?' Hanlon asked.

'Yeah, sure, she's fine, aren't you, Maisy?' The nurse swept around the bed and yanked the curtains fully open, allowing more natural light to flood in.

The room was just about big enough for a hospi-tal-style bed, a chest of drawers, a narrow wardrobe, a vinyl-covered armchair and a sink in the corner. Hanlon wrinkled his nose at the trace of stale urine.

'Maisy, my love, there's a police officer here who wants to ask you some questions,' the nurse said. The old woman turned her head slowly. 'He wants to talk to you about an investigation.' She plumped up the pillows behind the old woman's back and smoothed out the blanket.

'Thank you, I'll take it from here,' Hanlon said as the nurse continued to fuss.

'Okay, right, well I'll leave you two to it then.'

Hanlon shot her a thin smile as he ushered her out and shut the door. He drew up the armchair alongside the bed and sat with one foot crossed over his knee, studying the old woman. She stared back at him with wet, rheumy eyes thick with suspicion. Her hair was colourless and so thin her flaky scalp was visible under the wispy strands. Her nightdress hung off her saggy shoulders and her face was gaunt, like someone had sucked all the fat and muscle out, but behind her eyes he saw a spark of life that gave him hope he'd not made a wasted journey.

'What do you want?' she hissed, the venom in her tone taking Hanlon by surprise.

'I'm investigating your son, Duncan,' Hanlon said, studying her reaction, watching for any tell.

She held his gaze defiantly for a second or two before looking away, focusing on the blank wall opposite.

'He's missing and I need to find him. Do you know where he is?' No response. Not even a flicker behind her eyes. 'Mrs Whittaker?'

'No.'

Hanlon breathed in sharply through his nose. 'The truth please. I'm not here to play games.'

'Is he in trouble?'

'Not if you help me find him.'

'I told you, I don't know,' she said.

'When did you last see him?'

The old woman glanced down at her hands. She was twisting the woollen blanket around her bony fingers. 'A few months ago.'

'Did he say anything about going away?'

A slight pause. A definite dip of her head. Not quite a nod, but Hanlon had an eye for these things, the subtle signs people gave off even when they were trying to hide the truth. 'Did he say where he was going?'

She sighed. 'He didn't tell me anything.'

Hanlon read the disappointment written all over her face. Did she feel betrayed? He could use that to his advantage.

'Have you spoken to him since?'

'No,' she said, a little too quickly to be convincing.

'Don't lie to me, Mrs Whittaker.'

'Why are you asking all these questions? What do you want with Duncan?' A flash of anger. Frustration that her son had abandoned her?

'I told you, I'm a police officer. I'm investigating a serious historic crime. Fresh evidence has come to light and we believe your son may have information that would help our enquiries,' Hanlon said.

'Duncan doesn't know anything.' She looked straight at him now as if she was challenging him to contradict her.

'How can you be so sure?'

'He's done something, hasn't he? What is it?'

'I can't discuss the case, I'm afraid,' Hanlon said,

leaning forwards in the chair. 'Are you still in contact with him? I can't believe he'd abandon his own mother.'

'No,' she snapped.

'I don't believe you.'

'Believe what you want.'

'In which case, you won't mind if I look around.' Hanlon stood and glanced around the room. His gaze settled on a cluttered cabinet beside the bed. He reached for a narrow drawer and pulled it open.

'That's private. You can't go in there,' the old woman said, raising her voice. Her panic was a good sign he was onto something. Her fingers searched for the alarm button draped over the headboard, but Hanlon was quicker. He snatched it away and dropped it on the floor, out of her reach.

'I wouldn't do that,' he said.

'Who are you?'

'A detective, which means you need to be truthful with me,' Hanlon said.

'I don't believe you.'

'What's in the drawer, Mrs Whittaker? Something you don't want me to find?'

The old woman folded her arms across her chest and pressed her mouth tightly closed, creating a concertina of thin lines above her top lip.

Hanlon hunted through packets of pills and painkillers, drugs and potions of all shapes and sizes, and there, right at the back of the drawer, was a phone. An old Nokia. A vintage model, as heavy as a brick. No touchscreen, only a grid of plastic buttons. He held it up to show her and raised a quizzical eyebrow. 'Is this how you keep in touch?'

Maisy stared at the wall, refusing to look at Hanlon or the phone.

Hanlon powered the phone on and waited for it to boot up. It eventually demanded a passcode.

'PIN?' he said.

Maisy continued to give him the silent treatment. As if she was in any position to hold out on him. Why did these people always make it difficult for themselves?

'I need the PIN for the phone, Mrs Whittaker,' he repeated. 'To see whether you've been telling the truth.'

Her head twitched, almost as if she was fighting the urge to shake it.

Hanlon lost patience. He was going to get the code out of her come what may. 'I don't have all day, so why don't you cut the crap and just give it to me.'

But the silly old bat persisted in her stupid dumb act. Why didn't she spare herself the trouble?

He reached under the bed, grasping for the lever to release a catch. The mattress under her head dropped, and she fell backwards, Hanlon's hand flying to her mouth before she could scream. He clamped it tightly over her thin lips, creating a seal. Nothing like the panic of suffocation to loosen a tongue.

She stared up at him, eyes wide and bulging, craggy fingers scratching at his arm, desperate for breath, trying to release his hand. In her terror, she reminded Hanlon of his own grandmother. But it was a fleeting memory. It didn't cause any stir of emotion. No connection. No pity. He was there to do a job. Emotions and feelings didn't come into it. Years of being a cop helped.

He shifted his grip as her panic increased, covering her nose and mouth. She thrashed. Death was only a few heartbeats away if she couldn't breathe, especially for someone so frail.

'How long do you think you can hold out on me? You're an old lady, Mrs Whittaker. Your body is weak. Do you think that heart can take it much longer?'

Her eyes darted towards the door and for a second Hanlon feared someone had come in. But there was no one there.

'You'll be dead long before anyone realises anything's wrong. Nobody's going to save you.' Hanlon laughed. He was enjoying how easy it was.

Her grip on his wrist weakened and loosened, the fight in her ebbing away. He relaxed the pressure on her face and let her take a gasp of air.

'Last time I'm going to ask,' he said. 'Give me the PIN.' He held the Nokia to her face, but despite her lungs rasping as she battled for air, she remained resolutely silent. 'Seriously? You want to do it like this?' He couldn't believe the woman's stubborn stupidity. He was going to get it out of her, whether she liked it or not.

He put his hand to her nose and mouth again, shutting off her airways. As the old woman's body convulsed under the sheets, he counted out loud to ten. Slowly. Drawing out time. Presenting her with a sense of hopelessness. But she was losing strength. He had to be careful. Too easy with old people to go too far too quickly.

He reached ten, but this time, when he released his hand, she blurted out a four-digit code without being prompted.

'One, seven, zero, nine.'

Probably a significant date. September the seventeenth. A birthday? An anniversary? People were so predictable. He punched the numbers into the phone and grinned. Bingo!

'Very good, Mrs Whittaker. Now that wasn't so hard, was it?'

He scrolled through a menu to locate the call log as Maisy lay wheezing and pale. Curious. No calls received, but a handful of calls made. All to the same number. What were the chances?

'Is this Duncan's number?' Hanlon asked, holding the phone to the woman's face.

She looked defeated but nodded, unable to look him in the eye.

'That's all I need for now. You've been most helpful. I'll let you know if there are any developments in the case,' he said, keeping up the charade for no other reason than it amused him.

He pocketed the phone and was heading for the door when he noticed a photo frame on the chest of drawers. Why hadn't he seen it earlier? It contained a portrait of a familiar-looking man, his thick, grey hair neatly combed and with bright friendly eyes. It was a better picture of Duncan than in the newspaper clipping he'd taken from the shop.

'Mind if I take this?' Hanlon said, showing the woman the frame as he removed the photo.

'What are you going to do to him?' she asked.

'Good question.' Hanlon slipped the photo into his jacket pocket. The job was only to locate Duncan Whittaker. But there'd been a hint it might go beyond that. 'I guess it depends on how cooperative he is.'

Hanlon limped back to his van. He'd parked a few streets away as a precaution. Who would believe he was a detective if they saw him turn up in his VW Camper? It wasn't anything fancy, not even one of those 1970s classics that hipsters and surfers favoured. It had started life as a builder's van but he'd had it converted with a fold-down bed, fridge, cooker, stowaway tables and plenty of storage. A home and an office which allowed him to travel without the expense of booking into hotels or the worry of leaving a trail when he needed to be anonymous.

He slid open the side door and disappeared inside, pulling off his jacket and tie. He unbuttoned his shirt and changed into a comfortable pair of jeans and a t-shirt.

Maisy Whittaker had put up more resistance than he'd expected, a tough nut to crack for an old lady. He gave her some grudging admiration for that, and although he'd wasted time, he now had another significant lead. A mobile number. Almost certainly Duncan Whittaker was using a burner phone, but that didn't matter. You could still trace a burner's location. That's all Hanlon cared about.

He put the old Nokia on the side and made a call from his own mobile. Time to cash in a favour from an old contact. Neil Beckers owed him. While Hanlon had been passed up for promotion three times and was eventually forced out of the job he loved after a suspect in a stolen car had deliberately mowed him down, Neil had clung onto his job and even made detective sergeant somehow. It had taken Hanlon a year to get back on his feet, by which point the force decided it no longer had a job for him. Pensioned off and thrown out at thirty-six. He'd never forgiven them for that. They'd used his injury as an excuse. He was good at banging heads together, getting scumbags off the streets, but apparently they didn't like his methods, even though they achieved results. You had to follow the rules these days. Neil had been his partner for four years and was no angel, but Hanlon guessed his face was a better fit. At least he was free now to do things his own way.

'Neil, it's Garrett Hanlon.' He heard the hubbub of a busy office in the background. His old office. The rustle of papers. Neil's sharp intake of breath.

'What do you want?' Neil growled. No polite small talk. Not even a "Nice to hear from you. How's life treating you?" It was like he didn't care.

The background noise died away, as if Neil had

walked out of the office for some privacy. At least he'd not immediately hung up.

'How are things, Neil?' Hanlon asked.

'A lot better before you called.'

'Don't be like that. I need a favour,' Hanlon said.

'No. No more favours, Hanlon. I'm done.'

'I need to trace a mobile phone.'

'Which bit of "no" don't you understand? You know I could lose my job if they found out I was talking to you. Your name's still toxic around here.'

'Don't be such a drama queen. Do you have a pen?'

'It's not as easy as it used to be. They've tightened up procedures. You don't understand. A lot's changed since you left,' Neil said.

'I didn't leave. They kicked me out with the garbage, remember?' The memory still left a bitter taste in his mouth. He'd always believed the force would look out for him, especially after he'd been injured in the line of duty. It was supposed to be one big family.

'That's not my fault,' Neil said.

It was partly true. Neil had been with him on the day of the accident, the first to his side when he'd been rolling around in agony on the ground, his knee shattered. Neil called the ambulance, travelled with him to hospital. Visited him in the first dark months of his recovery, keeping his spirits up. But it was what happened afterwards that stung, when someone in a senior uniform had decided it was an opportunity to get rid of him quietly, and Neil had done nothing to stop them. He could have put in a good word, made them see sense. Instead, he'd concentrated on saving his own skin.

'No,' said Hanlon. 'It's not. But here I am scratching out a meagre living while you're still on a decent copper's wage with a cushy retirement looming if you keep your nose clean.'

'Please, don't ask me to do this.'

'It's one phone, Neil. It's not a big deal. You wouldn't want me talking to professional standards, would you?' Hanlon had stories that could bring Neil Beckers down in a heartbeat. Brutality. Corruption. Inappropriate relationships with witnesses. The list went on.

'Stop.'

'Do you have a pen?' Hanlon asked.

Neil sighed. 'I can't just run a trace on a phone without questions being asked. It's not like it used to be.'

'We both know you're a resourceful guy. Bury it in whatever case you're working on.'

'For God's sake. Alright. But this is the last time. Give me the number.'

'That's the spirit,' Hanlon said.

He'd no sooner reeled off Duncan's number than Neil hung up. Now he just needed to wait. Nothing he could do until he had Duncan Whittaker's location.

Hanlon tossed the phone to one side and stretched out his leg. His knee was still aching, but he was buzzing. He was getting closer to Duncan. The net was closing, and now it was only a matter of time before he found him. Hopefully, he'd not done the sensible thing and fled abroad. Most people didn't feel the need. They were arrogant enough to think they had the skills to vanish. But totally disappearing off the grid required money, planning and above all else, the commitment and willingness to cut all ties with friends and family. It was the undoing of most people. Duncan Whittaker was no exception. His need to stay in contact with his mother was going to be his downfall.

Hanlon closed his eyes and relaxed. Nothing to do but wait. But he had barely nodded off when his phone buzzed. He snatched it up and clamped it to his ear, recognising Neil's number.

'That was quick,' he said.

'The Isle of Sheppey in Kent. Specifically Leysdown,' Neil whispered. 'Now piss off and leave me alone.'

CHAPTER TWELVE

A fter failing to communicate my concerns to Esme when I'd returned her diary, I'd had to come up with another plan. It struck me, walking home along the beach, that my best opportunity to speak to her alone might be to book a counselling session with her. I'd asked Amber to make the appointment, in case she recognised my name, and now I was standing at the top of a long drive staring at an impressive grand house where Esme apparently held consultations.

I'd heard of Shurland Hall, but I wasn't sure what to expect. As the building slowly revealed itself, nestled in sweeping parkland dotted with trees it was even more impressive than I'd pictured; an imposing, historic manor house that wouldn't have been out of place on the cover of a glossy magazine.

I assumed Esme Winters worked from home, not somewhere like this. I put my head down and strode nervously on, not sure how she would react to seeing me again, let alone how I was going to bring up the subject of her diary and her troubling situation with her husband. I'd have to tread carefully, build up to it, and gain her trust. It wasn't the sort of thing you could just come out with, was it? Of course, there was every chance she'd deny it. I'd have to make her see I was a friend she could trust. If things went well, we could even start planning how to get her away from Frank. Maybe I should have looked up some addresses for women's refuges before I came.

I swallowed my nerves and hammered on an over-sized wooden door, silvered with age, that was framed by a pair of crenelated towers mocking the appearance of a medieval castle. But as I waited, all the words I'd rehearsed in my mind on the bus ride over evaporated like dew on a sunny summer's morning. I counted to three, the nerves getting the better of me. Maybe I was in the wrong place after all. Suddenly it felt like a mistake to have come.

I turned to walk away. If I hurried, I might be able to catch a bus to get back in time for lunch. Michelle had been surprisingly understanding when I told her I needed the morning off to see a counsellor, and I didn't want to push my luck.

Behind me, the door creaked open.

'You must be Amber,' Esme said her voice airy. She sounded different from when I'd met her at the house. 'You found it okay, did you? Come on in.'

I thought about running, putting my head down and

sprinting as fast as my legs would carry me. Instead, I turned around and watched Esme's smile slide from her face, replaced by the slow creep of recognition.

'It's you,' she said. 'I was expecting someone else.'

'I needed to see you again. I asked my flatmate, Amber to make an appointment. I thought you'd freak if you knew it was me.'

'What are you doing here?'

'I need to talk to you alone. About your diary. I didn't have a chance to say anything at the house.' I said.

'What about it?'

I couldn't be sure, but I thought I saw her face turn a shade paler, a fleeting flicker of worry appear behind her eyes. 'Can I come in? I'd really like to talk.'

Esme stared at me, unblinking. What was she thinking? It seemed like an eternity passed awkwardly between us before she stepped back. 'It's Sky, isn't it?' she said, the initial warmth in her tone replaced with a frosty suspicion.

I stepped into a cavernous hall which looked more like a museum than the entrance to a home. It was filled with dark antique furniture, a crooked grandfather clock, glaze-cracked ceramic vases and oil paintings of pompous-looking gentlemen hanging from the walls. My pulse fluttered with nerves as Esme directed me into a drawing room which was slightly less grand than the entrance hall but adorned with an equally eclectic array of furniture.

I was so nervous I thought Esme was bound to hear

my heart thudding against my ribcage. 'This is a lovely room,' I said, for the want of something, anything, to say to break the tension.

'I'm lucky Jimmy allows me to use the house for the business,' she said, pointing me to a seat by the window.

'Jimmy?'

'Jimmy Steele. I thought everybody on the island knew him.'

'Right, yeah, Jimmy. He owns the place where I work.' Esme raised an eyebrow. 'The Golden Sands Amusement Arcade? It's on the promenade,' I said, taking a seat.

'Yes, I know it.'

'And he owns this place? Wow.' I knew Jimmy was rich, but the house must have cost a fortune. I'd never seen anything like it. A real millionaire's mansion. Not that I particularly liked Jimmy Steele. He was a sleaze, always checking me out when he came into the arcade where he had his office upstairs. He made my skin crawl.

'Apparently King Henry the Eighth stayed here once with Anne Boleyn,' Esme said.

I didn't know much about history, but even I'd heard of Henry the Eighth and his wives. Didn't he have her executed? Cut her head off, I thought. I shuddered.

'What's this all about?' Esme floated across the room to collect a notepad and pen from the desk and pulled up a chair next to mine. Her floaty green dress picked up the colour of the stunning emeralds of her necklace, but the stark, white bandage wrapped around her hand and wrist reminded me why I was there.

I folded my hands in my lap, not sure what to do with them, and took a deep breath. Now I was with her, it felt right to just come out and say what I needed to say. If I hesitated, I wasn't sure I'd ever build up the courage. 'I read your diary.' I spat the words out like they were poison. 'I didn't mean to because I know it's private and I shouldn't have been reading it. Honestly, I didn't read much. I didn't have to. But I've not been able to get it out of my head since.'

Esme watched me with dark brown eyes like orbs of chocolate, her body tense, studying me. I thought she would shout or scream, at least show some emotion. I'd read her diary, for God's sake. She must have realised what I'd seen. But she just sat there, detached. Cold. Saying nothing.

'I was going to say something when I came to your house, but Frank was there, and I didn't get the chance...' My words dribbled away as I struggled to articulate what I was trying to say. I looked down at my hands and picked at my fingers. The sunlight on the back of my neck prickled my skin and I realised I was sweating, the air in the room stuffy and oppressive.

'You came here to tell me you read my diary?'

When I looked up, a bemused grin was spreading across Esme's face. That wasn't the reaction I was expecting at all. This was turning out to be much harder than I'd thought. 'I've been so worried about you ever since, but I guess what I'm trying to say is that I'm here to help. You don't have to deal with this on your own.' There, I'd said it. It was like I'd finally let go of a thousand helium balloons. I knew she was being mistreated by her husband and now she had a friend to turn to, someone who understood and could help her escape his violence. I let out a long breath and allowed my shoulders to sag.

'Why were you worried about me?'

Was she deliberately trying to be difficult? Or was she so deeply embedded in denial that she couldn't open up to me?

'You don't have to pretend,' I said. 'I know what's been going on between you and Frank. We can work out a way of getting you out of that house,' I said.

She frowned. 'Why would I want to leave the house?'

She was putting on a good show, I'd give her that.

I sighed. 'What really happened to your hand?'

'I told you, I cut it on a wine glass,' she said, turning her bandaged hand over and flashing a set of polished fingernails. 'What's that got to do with my diary?'

I leaned forwards, reaching out for her arm, but she flinched, avoiding my touch. 'It's okay. You can tell me the truth,' I cooed, like I was coaxing a frightened child out of a hole.

'The truth?'

'Was it Frank? Did he do that to you?'

'What?'

'I know what's going on, Esme. Frank - hurts you, doesn't he?'

Esme stared at me blankly, her lips open a fraction, her mask not slipping an inch. Her eyes scanned my face. I could tell she was trying to decide whether to trust me. We were standing together on a precipice. It could go either way. She was either about to open up to me and tell me everything or step back behind her lies and deny it all.

'That's insane,' she said. 'Frank didn't do this to me. It was an accident.'

Maybe she was telling the truth after all. She certainly sounded convincing. But even if I'd jumped to the wrong conclusion about her hand, it didn't mean Frank wasn't abusing her in other ways. Physically and psychologically.

'But your diary' I said, less sure of myself now.

'What about it?'

'You said he wasn't the man you married. It's nothing to be ashamed of. This isn't your fault, but you don't have to suffer alone,' I said.

'How much did you read of my diary exactly?'

My throat tightened. This wasn't going well at all. 'Not much, I promise,' I said. 'You know there are places where you'll be safe. Places he can't find you.'

Esme made a show of putting the lid back on her pen and placing it down on a low table with her note-book. She pursed her mouth tightly shut and steepled her fingers in front of her lips. I shifted uncomfortably in my chair, my jeans sticking to the back of my legs. I'd been too direct. I'd steamed in with all guns blazing when I should have taken my time gaining her trust.

'That was my diary, Sky,' she said. 'You shouldn't have been reading it.'

'I didn't read much,' I protested.

'Enough to draw some serious conclusions.'

'Isn't it better this way? I can help you if you'll let me.'

'I don't need your help,' she said.

'Why do you keep denying it?'

'Because you've got it all wrong. Can't you see? You've dreamt up this bizarre notion that somehow Frank is abusing me, but it's simply not true.'

'What about on the beach?' I said. 'What was that all about if not about Frank and what he does to you?'

'That's none of your business.'

'Does he raise his hand to you?'

'Don't be ridiculous,' she said.

'I can't help you if you can't admit what's really going on at home,' I said.

'And I thought I was supposed to be the therapist. This is all in your imagination, Sky. Please stop.'

But how could I? Not after what had happened to Mum.

'It's not in my imagination,' I said. 'I think we found each other on the beach for a reason. No man should ever hit a woman. Never.' The fury and anger bubbled up inside me as I let the leash off years of pent up guilt and anguish. 'It's wrong. If I ever saw a man strike a woman, I'd kill him. I wouldn't even think twice about doing it.'

Esme's eyes opened wide. I think I'd shocked her with the ferocity of my rage.

'Look, she said, leaning towards me, our knees almost touching, 'I'm not a victim, Sky.'

'But your diary… '

'Yes, Frank drives me crazy sometimes. And sometimes I do want to kill him. I'm sure he thinks the same about me. But that's marriage. One day, you'll understand.'

'Let me help you.'

'I don't need your help, Sky.'

'You said you know he still loves you, but you should have left him months ago.' I threw the words from her diary back at her. I'd only read them briefly, but they'd stuck in my mind, churning over and over until I couldn't think about anything else.

'That's true,' said Esme. 'We were going through a rocky patch but really, Frank wouldn't hurt a fly. I've kept a diary for as long as I can recall. I've always found it helpful to write down my thoughts and feelings. It helps me process things, and it's so much better than keeping them pent up inside. But it only works if I'm truthful with myself. It means I write things in my diary I would never say to anyone else, even Frank.'

'But I thought — '

'You thought wrong, Sky. I appreciate your concern, but it's totally misplaced.'

Nothing I said seemed to bring her any closer to admitting the truth to me. Unless she *was* telling the truth and I'd horribly misread everything. I shrunk into my seat. What if it *was* all in my imagination? I was so desperate to make amends for Mum's death, had I been blinkered?

Esme grabbed my hands, wrapping them up in her own. 'I suppose I should be grateful,' she said. 'It's nice to know you care, but it's not what you think. Don't feel bad, but you have to let it go.'

'Why did you write that sometimes you want to kill him, then? If he wasn't being abusive, why would you say that?' I asked.

'You wouldn't understand.' Esme withdrew her hands. 'You're not much more than a child. You know nothing about the world.'

'I know more than you think,' I said. Living on the streets, fending for myself, even for a few months, had been a brutal education. 'And I know when someone's in trouble.'

'You're talking nonsense.'

I shook my head. 'I know because I watched the same thing happen to my mother,' I said. I hesitated for a second. 'She was just like you and in the end, she died because of me.'

CHAPTER THIRTEEN

Hanlon drummed the steering wheel with both hands, his excitement mounting as he approached what looked like an impossibly steep road bridge. He loved the thrill of the chase and there was no better feeling than closing in on a target. In less than two days, he'd narrowed his search for Duncan Whittaker to the Isle of Sheppey on the north Kent coast, the hard work done. The rest should be easy.

If he was lucky, he could have the job wrapped up well before the weekend. He might even take a few days to enjoy his finders' fee. Kick back, sink a few beers and take it easy. He deserved a break, and the money he'd pick up from this job alone would keep him going for a few months.

As he crested the bridge, he glanced down at the island below. Barren, wild wetlands dominated the landscape to the south, while the north was more industrial. Beyond the housing estates, dockyard cranes stood silhouetted like sentinels against the powder blue sky.

Hanlon followed the road east onto a fast-moving single carriageway lined with hedgerows that cut through fields of cattle and sheep. He switched off the radio to concentrate on the winding road.

Why had Duncan chosen here, of all places? It was the worst of both worlds; not populated enough to hide among the masses and not remote enough to be totally off the grid. What was the betting Duncan used to come here as a kid? A place he associated with happy childhood memories? People were such suckers for sentimentality, and it was almost always the undoing of them. Not that he was complaining. Duncan had made his job ten times easier.

Hanlon shifted in his seat, adjusting his position to take some pressure off his knee. He checked his mirrors. A car approaching rapidly from behind was travelling far too fast for the narrow road. As it drew closer, the blur in the mirror morphed into a small, white hatchback. A fuckwit with an over-inflated sense of his own immortality behind the wheel. Hanlon chewed his lip with half an eye on the car behind as it predictably roared up to his rear bumper and the driver slammed on his brakes. An old convertible with its roof down. Typical boy-racer; slicked back gelled hair, big, hooped earring and music thumping. What a dickhead.

He sat behind Hanlon's van for only a few seconds before growing impatient, flashing his lights and sounding his horn, two things guaranteed to send

Hanlon's irritation levels soaring. It was as much as he could do not to jump on his own brakes and give the guy a scare. But that might end up being an expensive repair job on his rear end and he didn't have the time to look for body shop garages.

Then the guy started gesticulating over the top of the windscreen, yelling all kinds of obscenities, making it plain that he wanted Hanlon to move out of his way. It wasn't even as though Hanlon was driving that slowly, but he didn't know the roads and he wasn't going to take unnecessary risks for the sake of a kid who needed to learn some respect.

On the other side of a tight corner, the road rose and straightened out. An obvious place to overtake, apart from the blind brow of a hill which meant there was no way of telling if anything was coming from the other direction. Hanlon predicted the kid wouldn't think twice about snatching the opportunity to pass him.

Time to teach him a lesson.

Hanlon dropped a gear. Squeezed the accelerator. The car behind jumped out of his slipstream, engine screaming. Hanlon pushed a little harder, anticipating the drag of the rise. Revs high. Low gear. Plenty of torque under his foot. Easy on the speed. Letting the kid think he had the better of him.

The white convertible eased up alongside, on the wrong side of the road, the brow of the hill looming. Hanlon relaxed his shoulders and tightened his grip on the wheel. Glanced across as the vehicles drew level.

The kid's face was taut with rage. Still swearing. Still gesticulating. Arsehole.

A squeeze on the accelerator. Pushing the van on. Nudging ahead. Putting doubt in the kid's mind. Had he even seen the car that had crested the hill ahead?

Hanlon fixed him with a stern glare. The kid flicked two fingers up at him and tried to accelerate away. Hanlon dropped his foot, let the revs scream, felt the punch in his back, closing off the space ahead where the kid wanted to be.

The approaching car flashed its lights. Blasted its horn. But incredibly, the kid in the convertible still seemed to think he could make the pass. With a grin spreading across his face, Hanlon kept his foot down. Not giving a single inch.

Then, as it looked as though the two cars were heading for an inevitable head-on collision, the kid stood on his brakes, swerving back behind Hanlon. But he lacked skill and experience. The ineptitude of youth. His wheels locked, and the car slewed off the road in an oily plume of tyre smoke and squealing rubber.

The other car flashed past with its horn blaring as the convertible pirouetted through a full three-hundred-and-sixty-degree spin. In his mirrors, Hanlon watched it come to an abrupt halt on a wide grass verge and allowed himself a self-satisfied smile. He pulled over, grabbed his jacket and reached for the knife he kept stowed under his seat, concealing it up his sleeve.

The young driver had turned a pasty shade of pale.

He was desperately trying to restart his stalled engine as Hanlon approached.

'Hey kid, was there something you wanted to say to me?' he asked, leaning over the driver's door, right up in the guy's personal space. Years in the force had taught him a few tricks about intimidation.

The kid's rage and bravado all but evaporated as he came nose-to-nose with Hanlon.

'I said, did you have something to say to me, boy?' Hanlon repeated, raising his voice.

'No - I'm...' the kid stammered.

'That's funny because two minutes ago you were screaming all sorts of things at me. How old are you?'

'Twenty-one.'

'And no one's taught you any manners yet?'

'I'm sorry, man, I didn't mean — '

'Shut up.' Hanlon reached into the car, snatched the keys from the ignition and tossed them into the hedge.

'What the fuck, bro? What am I supposed to do now?'

'Bright lad like you, I'm sure you'll figure something out,' Hanlon said.

'You're kidding me.'

'Maybe it'll make you think twice in future about being such a dick.' Hanlon let the knife slip out of his sleeve and into his hand. He pressed the tip into the kid's stomach, out of sight of passing traffic.

The lad's eyes opened wide. 'What are you doing?' he said with a tremor in his voice, clutching the sides of his seat so tightly his knuckles paled. 'Please,' he gasped, 'don't hurt me. I'm sorry.'

Hanlon could almost taste his fear. The guy was bricking himself and that was satisfaction enough. It was a bonus that he'd probably have to abandon his car and walk home. 'What was the hurry?' Hanlon asked, drawing out his discomfort, not quite ready to let him go.

'N - n - nothing,' he stuttered.

Hanlon cocked his head. 'Wrong answer. Try again.'

'What?'

'Simple question. Why were you in such a hurry?'

'I - I guess I needed to be somewhere,' he said.

'And now you're going to be late, all because you were being a dick.'

The lad looked like a little boy lost. 'It won't happen again.'

'No, it won't. Where were you heading?'

He mumbled something incomprehensible as his gaze settled on the hunting knife at his stomach. Maybe he'd realised it wouldn't take much more than a twitch of his wrist for Hanlon to gut him.

'Speak up. Where are you going?'

'Leysdown.'

Hanlon grinned. 'That's a coincidence. So am I. What's it like?'

The kid frowned, apparently thrown by Hanlon's sudden change of tone. 'It's okay.'

'You live there?' The guy nodded. He was shaking now. 'Is there much to do?'

'Not really. It's mostly full of holidaymakers.'

Hanlon stroked his chin. It was still early in the year. The holiday parks wouldn't be full yet. 'You grew up there?'

'Yeah.'

'You ever heard of a guy called Duncan Whittaker?'

'No.'

Hanlon pulled out the photo he'd taken from Duncan's mother's room. 'Recognise this guy?'

The lad studied it for a second or two. 'No.'

'Okay.' Hanlon retracted the knife and concealed it back in his sleeve as a coach struggled up the hill belching black diesel fumes. The driver eyed them warily and as he passed Hanlon gave him a cheery wave. No point attracting suspicion so soon after his arrival on the island. 'I'm going to be around for a few days. If I see you again or hear you've been causing trouble, I'll kill you. Understand?'

The kid blanched an even whiter shade of pale. The look on his face was priceless.

'I'm kidding,' said Hanlon. 'Unless you piss me off again.'

'I won't. I promise.'

CHAPTER FOURTEEN

I'd never talked to anyone about what happened the night my mother died. Most of the time, I tried to forget. I pushed the parcel of guilt and sorrow to the back of my mind. If I didn't think about it, I didn't have to confront the pain and regret which I knew would eat me up. But reading Esme's diary had dredged up those bad memories, reminding me of what I'd done. Afterwards, there were people who tried to make me talk. Child psychologists at first, and then the foster parents they sent me to live with. But I didn't want to discuss it with anyone. Maybe because I was scared they'd find out what really happened.

Esme stared at me, eyes wide with surprise.

'I was as guilty of my mother's death as the scumbag who attacked her,' I said. 'She was convinced he loved her, but she was in denial, too.'

'Sky, I'm so sorry. Were you close to your mum?'

What a stupid question. 'I don't know, were you?' I

fired back, tears pricking my eyes. I didn't want to cry in front of Esme, but the swell of emotion building in my chest was too strong to hold back.

'And you blame yourself for her death?'

'Well, it wasn't me who punched and kicked her so hard that she bled into her own brain. You know, they had to sweep her teeth up off the kitchen floor,' I said, the rage ballooning inside me. I lowered my head, ashamed. 'But yes.'

Esme remained unfazed by my outburst, her voice calm. 'Were you in the house when it happened?'

'House?' I laughed. 'We lived fifteen floors up in a flat probably smaller than your kitchen.'

'But you saw what happened?'

I shook my head. 'I locked myself in my room. While my mother was being murdered, I hid under the duvet trying to drown out her screams. I didn't even try to stop him.'

A tear dripped from my chin onto my thigh and soaked into the denim. Esme reached for a box of tissues on the window ledge and placed it on a table next to my chair. 'How old were you?'

'Fourteen.'

'And you've been carrying all this hurt and anger around ever since?'

I shrugged. How could I admit the hold the past had over me, how weak I was to be enslaved by guilt and regret? It sounded pathetic.

'You poor girl.' Esme picked up her pen and scribbled something in her notebook.

'What are you doing?'

'Taking a few notes. Is that okay?'

'Why?'

'If you're not comfortable with it — '

'No, it's fine,' I said, although I wasn't sure why she felt the need to write it down. I hadn't come to talk about me. Perhaps it was so she could write it up in her diary later. I'm not sure how I felt about that.

'I'm glad you came to see me today. This has been eating you up for a long time, hasn't it?'

I nodded, biting the inside of my lip to create a physical focus for my pain. I wanted to put those memories back in the box and seal down the lid, but they kept floating around inside my mind.

'It's not healthy to keep painful emotions bottled up,' Esme continued. 'They need a vent. It's why I keep a diary, but it's good to talk about these things, too. Get them out in the open. Set them free.'

Is that what I was doing? Setting the bad memories free? Then why did I feel so wretched? A blackbird shot past the window, sounding a noisy note of alarm. Outside, everything looked so peaceful and serene under the weak April sun. And yet inside my head, there was a rampage of emotions. I didn't know what to feel or think.

'His name was Stefan,' I said after Esme allowed a long silence to fill the space between us. 'He was a truck driver. I think he travelled all over Europe, but he always came back, turning up whenever it suited him. He seemed alright at first. Mum had been on her own for a while, so I was pleased she'd found someone. But she didn't really love him. She was just grateful not to be on her own.'

I tugged at a snag of skin around my thumbnail as I opened the floodgates to the terrible memories I'd kept hidden for so long.

'She always seemed to pick the bad ones,' I continued. I'd started, so I might as well tell Esme the whole story. 'After a few months, things changed. He was moody and always seemed to be angry at something, although mostly me or Mum. He was hardly ever sober, and they were always arguing. That's when he first started to... ' My words drifted away like smoke rising from a beach fire.

'Go on,' Esme urged, her tone warm and silky. 'Take your time.'

I took a deep breath, filling my lungs, building the strength to say it out loud. 'That's when he hit her.' My tears flowed freely. 'No matter how loudly I turned up my music, I always heard everything. His yelling. Her screams. And there was nothing I could do about it. It was the same on the night she died. We'd not seen him for a while, and I'd prayed he might not be coming back. We didn't need him. We were alright on our own. But then he turned up again. It was late. He was drunk, banging on the door, and of course, Mum let him in. The shouting started almost straightaway. I couldn't stand it, so I curled up in bed, trying not to listen, hoping it would stop soon.'

Esme listened in silence, nodding as she scribbled notes, her expression inscrutable.

I raised my eyes to the ceiling, hoping gravity might stop my tears. I couldn't believe I was telling her all this stuff. But now I'd started, I couldn't stop. 'I lay there with my hands over my ears and did nothing as he beat my mum to death. I could have stopped him. But I didn't.'

'You can't blame yourself, Sky. You were only a child.'

But I did blame myself. 'I should have done something, but I was so scared. And I let her down.'

'That's not true.'

'Sometimes I don't think I deserve to live after what I did,' I said.

'There's no one to blame for your mother's death other than the man she invited into your home,' Esme said.

I wished it was true, but it wasn't. If I'd been braver, not acted like a coward, I could have stopped him. I could have distracted him or made him turn his anger on me or called the police. Anything. There were a million and one things I could have done. And Mum might be still be alive.

'They said he threw himself under a train,' I said. 'I don't know if that's true. To be honest, I don't care. He meant nothing to me and whether he's alive or dead, it won't bring Mum back, will it?'

'And what do you think your mum would say if she

could hear you, if she was sitting in that chair over there, listening right now?' Esme asked.

I stared at the empty, scuffed leather armchair and the tartan throw draped over one of its arms. I blinked, trying hard to imagine Mum, a glass of vodka in one hand, the bottle at her feet and a smouldering cigarette on the go.

We didn't spend evenings together on the sofa watching TV or chatting about clothes and fashion. Not that we weren't close, we just weren't good at showing it. I wish now I'd worked harder at my relationship with her, appreciated her more, argued with her less and been less of a pain in the arse. If I'd known I was going to lose her when I was only fourteen, I'd have made the most of every second, every minute, every hour with her. I missed her so much. I missed the sound of her laugh, the stupid jokes she used to tell, even how she used to make me run to the shops for fags, even though I was underage.

I never knew my father. He buggered off when I was only a baby. Mum was the only family I had, and she was taken from me far too young. I'd give anything to have her back. 'She'd probably tell me how disappointed she was that I did nothing to help her when she needed me most,' I said.

'I doubt that very much. You know what I think? I think she'd be proud of you and she'd want you to stop beating yourself up over something that wasn't your fault,' Esme said.

It was a small crumb of comfort, but I couldn't see

how Mum could be proud of anything I'd done. I shook my head. I hadn't come to the house for Esme to pull a Dr Freud number on me.

'She was like you,' I said. 'She was convinced Stefan loved her even when he beat her. I can't stand by and watch the same thing happen to you as happened to my mum.'

'Alright,' said Esme. 'I think that's enough for now. We're in danger of going around in circles.' She checked her watch on a slender wrist. 'Let's leave it for today. We've covered lots of ground and it's good you've been able to talk about your past, as painful as it must have been.' She snapped her notebook closed and stood. 'Let's pick this up again next time. I'm afraid I have another client.'

'Next time?'

Esme crossed the room to her desk and opened a laptop computer. 'I think it would be good to delve deeper into your relationship with your mother,' she said. She glanced at me and smiled. 'How would you like to pay today?'

'Pay?' What the hell?

Esme frowned. 'It's thirty pounds for an hour. I prefer cash, but I can take a card.'

I hadn't even thought she would try to charge me for her time. It was supposed to be me doing her a good deed, not the other way around. 'I'm not sure if… ' I stammered, hunting in my bag for my purse.

'I'm not operating a charity here, Sky.' She smiled without humour.

'I came because I wanted to help you.'

'But I don't need your help, Sky. I know it must have taken a lot of courage for you to come here today, but we've made excellent progress. Let's not end on a sour note. Just confronting what happened is a big step in the right direction.'

My head was in a whirl as I found my purse and looked for some cash. 'It'll have to be a card,' I said, holding up my credit card. I'd have to worry about how I was going to afford a wasted thirty-pound counselling session later.

'Contactless?' Esme held out an electronic reader with a smug smile. When the payment had gone through and she handed me a thin slip of a receipt, she asked, 'Shall we book another appointment now?'

'I think I'll leave it,' I said. I couldn't afford it, apart from anything else.

'Well, you have my number. Call me when you're ready and I'll do my best to slot you in.' She led me out of the room and back through the entrance hall, tugging open the heavy door with both hands.

I walked out with my head bowed, my shoulders hunched and my hands in my pockets. Esme Winters had run rings around me, manipulating me to talk about my mother when that's the last thing I had on my mind. I was strung out and drained, my eyes heavy and my mind numb.

'Thanks again for returning my diary,' Esme said, cheerily. 'I enjoyed our chat today.'

CHAPTER FIFTEEN

After his encounter with the boy racer on his way into Leysdown, Hanlon had spent the rest of the day trawling every holiday park on the eastern end of the island, hoping to find someone who'd seen Duncan Whittaker arrive, checked him in, or remembered his face. But he'd had no luck.

He'd put himself in Duncan's shoes, trying to think like him. Why choose somewhere like Leysdown, other than for sentimental reasons? The only other thing going for it, if you were trying to disappear, was that caravans and mobile homes outnumbered bricks and mortar houses in the town by about five to one. And that meant lots of strange faces coming and going without attracting any attention. Most of the population was transitory. Duncan could have easily passed himself off as a tourist, even if it was a little early in the season. And yet nobody had apparently seen or heard of him. It was the same in all the cafes, fish and chip restaurants and shops Hanlon had tried so far.

Tired and hungry, and with the evening closing in, he'd switched his attention to the town's pubs and chose the Britannia, close to the centre, as his starting point for no other reason than it was in a prime location and likely to be well frequented. Pubs were such a great source of information and gossip, especially in such a small town.

Inside, the clientele was mostly male. Regulars too, from the way they occupied the bar. The vans in the car park suggested they were also predominantly tradesmen; builders, bricklayers, plumbers, electricians and plasterers, turning the air blue with ripe language and boisterous laughter. The perfect place to ask about Duncan Whittaker.

After finishing a pint and an unappetising soggy steak and kidney pie, Hanlon sidled up to the bar, squeezing past a small group of men in paint-splattered overalls. He caught the barman's attention and slipped the photo of Duncan onto the counter.

'I'm looking for a friend of mine I was supposed to be meeting, but I've lost his number. Do you recognise him?' he asked.

The barman eyed him suspiciously. He studied the photo briefly and shook his head.

'His name's Duncan Whittaker. Mean anything to you?'

'Nope.'

'Alright, thanks anyway.'

Squeezing information out of bar staff was usually like mining for gold on the moon, but always worth a try. They never liked to give up intelligence easily. Not good for business. Hanlon turned his attention to the men at the bar and posed the same question. They were in good spirits and happily passed Duncan's photo between them, but none of them recognised him. It was becoming a depressingly familiar pattern.

He moved onto the next group and the next, ignoring the curious stares as he made a circuit of the bar. When you'd been in the force, it was hard to shake off the stench. Something about the way he walked or talked or both. Whatever. It didn't matter. If anyone knew Duncan Whittaker, they certainly weren't saying, whether or not they suspected Hanlon was a cop.

Finally admitting defeat, he walked out, heading for the car park. The door shut behind him, dulling the hubbub from inside. But a few seconds later, it opened again, the sound of alcohol-fuelled chatter and laughter rising in volume.

'That bloke you're looking for. I recognise him,' a gruff voice called out.

Hanlon stopped and turned slowly, appraising the guy who'd followed him. Shaved head. Thick stubble and tattoos up both muscled arms. From the calluses on his hands, he was probably a builder or a bricklayer. A manual labourer of some sort. He'd been in one of the groups at the bar, but like the others had denied any knowledge of seeing Duncan Whittaker around.

Strange he'd offered information now, out of sight of his mates. What was his play?

'Can I see the picture again?'

Hanlon showed him the photo. The guy took it and studied it, nodding.

'I'm pretty sure it's him. What did you say his name was again?'

'Duncan Whittaker. We lost touch a while back. Where did you see him?'

The guy glanced up at Hanlon. Handed the picture back. 'Are you a cop?'

'Like I said, I'm looking for my friend. That's all.'

The guy rolled his tongue behind his bottom lip and over his teeth like he was contemplating whether it was worth his while divulging what he knew.

'I've been working on a property up at Warden Bay. Pretty sure this is the guy who lives opposite.'

'Got an address?'

'How badly do you want to find him?'

'It's been a while since I've seen him,' Hanlon said. 'Thought it would be nice to look him up, that's all.'

'Does he owe money?' the guy asked.

'He's just a friend.'

'If you say so.'

'Could I have the address?'

The guy breathed in through his nose, lifted his chin and crossed his arms over his bulging chest. It wasn't the muscle you built solely on a building site. He must work out. And from the look of arrogance on his face, fancied himself as something of a player. 'What's in it for me?'

And there it was. The guy wanted money. Hanlon's fists clenched tightly. Why was everyone on the take these days? 'What did you have in mind?'

'Depends on how badly you want to find your friend.' He hesitated as he sized Hanlon up. 'Let's say two hundred quid.'

Hanlon snorted a laugh and the guy's face darkened.

'If you're not interested, it's no skin off my nose, mate,' he said.

'It's a lot of money. What guarantee do I have that I'm not being fleeced?'

'You don't,' the guy said. 'You'll have to take my word. It's up to you.' He shrugged and when Hanlon didn't reply, turned away, reaching for the door as he made to go back inside.

Hanlon unclenched his fists and glanced up at a rusty security camera on the wall. If the information was accurate, it was worth a couple of hundred quid. He'd get that back on expenses. But if the guy was pulling his chain, or he was mistaken, the money would have to come out of his own pocket. There was an alternative. He could force the information out of him. There were plenty of dark corners around the car park that looked as though they weren't covered by the camera, but he was tired, time was running short, and it could open up a whole new set of problems that he didn't need. And besides, the guy was built like a brick shithouse.

Reluctantly, Hanlon reached for his wallet. He plucked out four fifties and held them between his fingers, out of the guy's reach. The man let the door go, silencing the din coming from inside.

'If you're jerking me around, I will come and find you,' Hanlon said. 'And trust me, you don't want that.'

The guy snatched the money, folded it, and shoved it in his back pocket. 'The place you're looking for is in Cliff Road. It's a white bungalow. Number seventy-six. That's where you'll find him.'

Hanlon nodded. The guy slipped back inside the pub. No doubt he was going to have a good night on his earnings. Hanlon blipped open the doors of his van with his heart beating a little faster, his palms damp with sweat and anticipation.

CHAPTER SIXTEEN

W*hat he did was unforgivable.*
  Is it so terrible that I want to kill him?

The words in Esme's diary continued to worm through my brain, consuming my thoughts. I pictured her locking herself in the bathroom, sobbing as she nursed another black eye, Frank hammering on the door. I shuddered, partly at the awful images in my mind and partly because I was helpless to prevent her suffering.

I'd never believed in God or any other celestial being, but I couldn't help but think I was being tested by some greater universal force. I'd failed my mother when she needed me most. Esme's dire situation was a shot at redemption. Had our paths been destined to cross on the beach that night? Had Esme dropped her diary, subconsciously intending for me to discover it? A cry for help? I could never bring Mum back, but at least if I could save Esme, some good might come from her death.

The only problem was that she'd shut me down when I tried to confront her and going to the police with no evidence seemed extreme. It would be easier to walk away, to forget Frank and Esme Winters, but my conscience niggled at me constantly, like a devil on my shoulder whispering in my ear.

To clear my head and think things through, I headed to the beach as the sun was going down.

I picked my way along the water's edge, watching my step on the slippery rocks. The sound of the waves hitting the beach soothed my mind, and the jacket of impending darkness helped me to think.

'Hey, fancy joining me?'

I stopped in my tracks, my heart lurching. I'd been so lost in my thoughts I hadn't noticed the solitary figure sitting on the sand. 'Gavin?'

'I didn't mean to scare you. I thought you'd seen me.'

'I was miles away,' I said. I had a sudden shameful recollection of what Amber had said about the night of the party when I'd disappeared off with him. A spike of nausea rolled around my stomach and I felt my face burn with shame. What had I been thinking? Clearly I *hadn't* been thinking at all, and that was the problem. God, what must people have thought?

'Want to sit with me for a bit? I could use the

company,' Gavin said, holding a bottle of beer by its neck.

'Are you here on your own?'

'I needed some head space.'

'Me too,' I said. Alone, Gavin had lost his bravado. 'Everything okay?'

'Yeah, I'm fine.' He took a swig of beer.

'Look, about the other night — ' I had to mention it otherwise it was going to sit awkwardly between us, like an angry boil.

'We were both drunk,' he said, before I could finish my sentence.

'It's just that normally, I don't, you know.'

'It's okay. We don't have to talk about it. Please sit with me?' he asked.

I shuffled my boots in the sand. Oh God, he wasn't thinking we could pick up where we'd left off, was he? I shuddered at the thought. I had no desire for a repeat performance, especially sober.

'I only want to talk,' he said.

If he tried anything, I'd scream. There were houses on the cliff top behind us. Someone would hear. I found a dry patch of sand and sat. He offered me his beer, but I wanted to keep a clear head.

'I was watching the moon,' he said. 'It's so beautiful tonight.'

Gavin was the last person I expected to notice, let alone comment on the beauty of nature. But he was right. It was a stunning half-moon, hanging low and heavy over the horizon, shining brightly, spilling silvery light across the spindly turbines of the wind farm off Herne Bay.

'It's hard to believe they actually put men up there,' I said.

Gavin glanced at me. 'You don't believe that, do you?'

'What, that they put men on the moon? Of course I do. Why wouldn't I?'

'Fake news.'

I groaned inwardly. 'Come on, seriously?'

'A total hoax. Everybody knows they faked it in a TV studio.'

'And why would they do that?'

'So the Americans could prove they were ahead of the Russians. There's loads about it on the internet. Nobody believes it really happened.'

'I do,' I said, startled that anyone would doubt it.

'Even though all the evidence proves it was faked?'

'What evidence?'

'You've seen the pictures, right? Did you ever notice there were no stars? And what about the flag they planted? It was fluttering in the wind, even though there's no wind in space. And don't even get me started on the technology. It was like the nineteen sixties. They didn't even have computers, so how are you supposed to believe they had the technology to land on the moon? It was all made up to brainwash us.' He sipped at his beer and wiped his mouth with the back of his hand.

I glanced at him, half expecting to see a wry smile

appear across his lips, that he was winding me up. But no, he was deadly serious. 'Do you really believe that?' I asked.

'The US government's been pulling the wool over people's eyes for years. And you know, if you really want to convince people, you need to do a bit more than produce a bit of grainy film.'

'You mean like all the moon rock they brought back?' I vaguely remembered them telling us about it at school and how there was even one piece in a museum in America that people could touch.

'They probably faked that, too.'

I sighed. 'You'll be trying to tell me the earth's flat next.'

Gavin's bottle stopped halfway to his mouth. 'Funny you should say that.'

I was about to despair of him when he smiled.

'Nah, that's just a crazy conspiracy theory. You can prove the earth's round. People fly and sail around it all the time,' he said.

'Have you ever done either of those things?'

Gavin laughed. 'Nah, course not.'

'So how do you know for sure? You're happy to accept the earth is round even though you don't have any direct proof, but you think the moon landings were faked.'

'It's different.'

'How?'

'I don't know,' Gavin said, his jaw tensing. 'It just is.'

That killed the conversation. Along the shore the lamps of at least three night anglers, their long poles anchored in the sand, twinkled in the dark. I listened to the sound of the waves and the wind tickling the soft, muddy cliffs behind us.

'I've had a shit day,' Gavin said, breaking the silence between us.

'What happened?'

'Some bloke ran me off the road then pulled a knife on me.'

'Are you serious?'

'Yeah, the guy was like a total psycho. Honestly, I thought he was going to kill me.'

'Where? On the island?'

Gavin nodded. He tossed his empty bottle over his shoulder into the scrub. I heard it land with a crack and made a mental note to collect it later. I hated seeing rubbish spoiling the shoreline.

He told me about how he'd been run off the road by a driver in a campervan who'd then threatened him with a knife and thrown his keys in a hedge. He showed me the lacerations that criss-crossed his lower arms where he'd been hunting for them.

'Oh my God, did you call the police?'

'What's the point?'

'He could have killed you,' I said.

'What are they going to do? I don't know who he was, and I didn't get his number plate. I'm thinking about getting one of those dashcams now, though.'

'Did anyone see what happened?'

'I don't know,' he said, drawing circles in the sand with his finger. 'Anyway, what about you? Your day can't have been as bad as that. Come on, cheer me up.'

Compared to what had happened to Gavin, my chat with Esme seemed pathetically trivial. 'I tried to help someone I thought was in trouble and they threw it back in my face,' I said. 'Not quite a crazed maniac with a knife. So you win.'

'Some people don't want to be helped, I guess. What kind of trouble?'

'A woman whose husband's abusing her, but she's denying it.'

'At least you tried.' Gavin glanced up at me.

'But I can't pretend everything's alright. He could end up killing her.' It sounded melodramatic, but I knew how easily violence at home could escalate.

'Go to the police then.'

'I can't.'

'Why not?'

I opened my mouth to reply, then clamped it shut. I couldn't go to the police because since I'd handed back Esme's diary, I didn't have any evidence. 'I need to find some proof,' I said, the realisation of what I needed to do finally hitting me.

If Esme continued to deny anything was wrong and couldn't even admit there was a problem, I needed to prove what was going on, find something that couldn't be disputed, even if she denied it all.

The police would have to take me seriously then. They could get her away from Frank to somewhere safe, stop him before it was too late. I should have thought of it before. If Esme wouldn't help herself, I needed to act myself.

CHAPTER SEVENTEEN

C liff Road was one of those streets where no two houses looked the same, an eclectic mix of detached buildings of different sizes and ages like a line-up of mongrels at a dog pound, built in a modern-day land grab with no uniformity of style. It made the street look messy. Disorganised.

Hanlon pulled up to the kerb and killed his lights. Number twenty-six was exactly as the builder at the pub had described; a little white bungalow set back from the street. Greyed with age and the elements. Compared to the house Duncan had abandoned in the country, the bungalow was a hovel. The grass in the front garden was knee high and the paint on the window frames flaking. He was definitely slumming it in his efforts to vanish.

Hanlon stepped out of the van and reached under his seat for the knife he'd had to pull on that idiot boy racer earlier. He slid it up his sleeve out of sight of any nosey neighbours who happened to glance out of their windows. A silent insurance policy in case things turned nasty. He wasn't sure how desperate Duncan was not to be found, but if he had any sense, he'd have taken precautions. Maybe a knife wasn't enough. Hanlon crawled into the back of the van, unlocked a hidden cupboard under the rear seats and pulled out a small, black case. Flipped it open. The Glock 9mm shadowed in the darkness, a familiar friend. He checked the magazine and chambered a round, savouring how it balanced perfectly in his hand. A beautiful piece of engineering. He attached a long-barrelled silencer, screwing it firmly into place, and slipped the weapon into the waistband of his trousers. For emergencies only. But better to be safe than sorry.

Thankfully, the street was deserted. Hanlon nipped through a rusty gate and followed a path through the overgrown garden. A light was on behind the curtains in a room at the front. Somebody was home. Hanlon took a breath and knocked on the door. He'd only been tasked to locate Duncan at this stage. To report back and wait for further instructions. But he had to be sure he'd found the right guy. And anyway, he was fairly certain what they'd ask him to do next. Whoever was paying him wanted their money back. They'd want him to put the squeeze on Duncan. It's what he did. And he was bloody good at it.

A light came on in the hall. Movement inside. A shadow appeared behind the frosted glass. Hanlon readied himself. Sometimes it was fun when they put up a fight or tried to run. But not tonight. It had been a long day and it would be better all-round if Duncan simply accepted he'd been caught and gave himself up easily. Hanlon could do without the drama. He reached behind his back and slipped a hand under the tails of his jacket, his fingers brushing the grip of the Glock. Readying himself, just in case.

A bolt clicked back and as the door cracked open, Hanlon shoved it with a burst of energy, knocking an old lady backwards.

Shit. Wrong house.

Hanlon clamped a hand over his mouth. 'I'm so sorry, I was looking for my friend, Duncan. I was told he lived here.'

That builder had lied to him after all. He was going to kill him.

The woman stared at him wide-eyed through smeary glasses, clasping her hands to her chest. It was lucky she hadn't keeled over with the shock.

'I take it you don't know him?' he said, smiling but aware he had a face that didn't exude a natural friendliness.

The woman shook her head, terrified. 'Who are you?' she asked, finally finding her voice.

'I'm Harry. An old friend.'

'I don't know anyone called Duncan.' Her voice trembled.

'No, of course. My mistake. I hope I didn't frighten you.'

She edged towards a telephone on a table in the hall.

'I wouldn't do that,' Hanlon said, retreating from the door. 'We don't want any trouble, do we? It was an honest mistake. I'm sorry again if I startled you. I'll leave you in peace. Goodnight.'

She slammed the door in his face and as the locks and bolts clicked into place, he sighed. The last thing he needed was the police turning up asking awkward questions. He had enough on his plate trying to locate Duncan.

Cursing the wasted hour, and the two hundred quid down the drain, he trudged back to his van and packed the gun away in its case, his anger simmering. After a frustrating day trawling the island, he could have done without the wild goose chase. He slammed the side door closed, kicked the front wheel and climbed into the driver's seat, tossing his knife onto the dashboard.

What kind of idiot did that builder take him for? No one played Garrett Hanlon for a fool, especially someone like that low-life meathead. He thumped the steering wheel with his fist, imagining it was the guy's head, picturing how he was going to make him pay, once he'd got his money back. Time to recoup his losses and teach him a lesson he'd never forget.

Hanlon ignored the speed limits on his way back to the Britannia, his mood darkening with every mile. He pulled into the car park and reversed into a space in the shadows, out of the direct line of the security camera he'd clocked earlier. He crept to the front of the building, glancing through a casement window to confirm the builder was still inside, part of a small group by the bar, no doubt enjoying his cash windfall, having a laugh at Hanlon's expense. The group was even more raucous than earlier, their drunken laughter clearly audible from outside.

He resisted the urge to march in and confront the guy there and then. It was a bad idea, no matter how much of a rage he'd worked himself into. Taking down one guy was one thing. A mass brawl with his mates was suicide. And he couldn't take the risk of causing a scene. He'd have to wait for him to come out where he could tackle him on his own. He'd have to be patient for once.

Reluctantly, Hanlon returned to his van and made himself comfortable, watching the entrance, waiting for movement. He breathed in through his nose and out through his mouth, calming himself, ensuring the knife was within easy reach. He wasn't sure yet whether he was going to use it. It depended on the guy's attitude, whether he was contrite, and ready with an apology and the money.

Two long hours passed before the builder appeared, unsteady on his feet but thankfully alone. Hanlon sat up straight, his muscles coiled like springs, alert and attentive to the job in hand. Blood pumped hard through his veins, his anger reignited.

As the builder stumbled across the car park, he

stopped briefly to light a cigarette. On the main road, opposite the pub, a car pulled up. Someone jumped out and ran into the Chinese takeaway, paying no attention to the drunk guy struggling with his lighter.

Hanlon picked the knife off the dashboard with one hand and silently opened his door with the other. He was going to enjoy this.

The builder pulled a key out of his pocket, aimed it at a white van and blipped open the locks. Orange lights flashed three times, illuminating the darkest recesses of the car park. Hanlon shouldered his door wide open and slipped out a leg, his gaze focused on his man, hardly able to believe, given the state he was in, that he was about to climb into a vehicle and drive. Still, a few more steps and he'd be in the shadows. Time to get reacquainted.

As Hanlon glanced back to the entrance to the pub, double checking no one else was coming to disturb his fun, a motorbike with a noisy exhaust roared past, catching his attention. The car was still parked opposite the takeaway, hazard lights flashing. Hanlon hesitated, something about the vehicle triggering a hazy memory in the back of his mind. Nothing particularly unusual about it. One of those big 4x4s that were popular these days, especially with mums on the school run. A Range Rover, its paintwork splattered with mud and dirt. What the hell was it? And then he saw the number plate. Or at least part of it. From the angle the car was parked, it was difficult to see the whole plate. Only the first few digits.

DW1.

Shit. He almost dropped the knife. It couldn't be, could it? A figure emerged from the takeaway carrying two paper bags, too far away to be distinguishable. Or even if it was a man or a woman. They jumped in behind the wheel, killed the hazard lights and pulled away. Surely a man who was trying to vanish wouldn't have kept his car, let alone one with a personalised number plate. Could Duncan Whittaker be that arrogant? It seemed unlikely, the coincidence too great. But Hanlon couldn't ignore it, especially as he'd run out of leads. The builder was going to have to wait.

He was already clambering into his van. With any luck, he was so drunk, he'd wipe himself out on the way home. No more than he deserved, but Hanlon would have to leave that to fate. No matter how small the chances were that he'd watched Duncan Whittaker climb into his car and drive away, he couldn't ignore it.

He pulled his door shut, snatched at the ignition and pulled out with his wheels spinning. He swung out onto the main road in the direction the Range Rover had headed and almost tail ended a taxi that had stopped at a red light on a pedestrian crossing. Hanlon blasted his horn in frustration. Duncan was getting away.

He swerved around the taxi, onto the opposite side of the road and straight through the red light, frightening a young couple who were crossing. Ahead, he saw taillights disappearing into the distance. He put his foot down and accelerated aggressively, snatching through the gears despite the whining protestations of the engine. If it was Duncan, he couldn't let him slip through his fingers. He had to catch him.

The vehicle turned right. Into a side road. Hanlon followed a few seconds later. Getting closer. His heart pounded as adrenaline flooded through his body, his palms damp with sweat at the anticipation of the catch.

A sharp left-hander and Hanlon was right on him. Less than a couple of car lengths off his bumper. But it wasn't a Range Rover ahead. It was an old Japanese saloon. What the hell? He slowed down, dabbing his brakes, checking his mirrors, replaying the last few miles in his head. He'd locked onto the first set of tail-lights he'd seen and followed glibly, but somehow lost the Range Rover, somehow lost Duncan Whittaker.

'Shit,' he screamed, thumping the steering wheel as he slowed to a crawl. 'Shit! Shit! Shit!'

CHAPTER EIGHTEEN

A fter my chat with Gavin, I began thinking about how I could collect evidence against Frank. I needed something conclusive to convince the police that Esme was in real danger and that my concerns weren't just the product of a vivid imagination. All sorts of ideas wheeled through my head, each more absurd than the last. And no matter what plan I came up with, it seemed hopeless.

Twice that morning Michelle had caught me staring vacantly into space, lost in my thoughts while customers were waiting. By late afternoon, I still hadn't come up with anything and was so distracted I didn't notice the young boy still in his school uniform who'd wandered in alone until he'd started playing the penny drop machines.

He was too young to be in the arcade without a parent or guardian. Michelle was quite clear about the rules on letting underage children in on their own.

She'd even put posters up around the place about the age restrictions. But what the hell. He wasn't doing any harm. I let him be.

He pushed a coin into a slot and watched it dance and jig over a maze of pins, hit the top shifting shelf, roll on its thin edge and finally come to rest, nudging a flat pile of two-penny pieces. He dropped half a dozen more coins into the same machine with studied patience and was eventually rewarded with the clink and clatter of a big pay-out. He looked up at me with a grin that reached from ear to ear as if he couldn't believe his luck.

I smiled at him, happy for the diversion. His winnings probably amounted to less than the cost of a chocolate bar, but I could see it wasn't about the cash. He'd go home that night feeling like a winner. And sometimes it was the minor triumphs that made the biggest difference to your day.

By a quarter to five, he was done. He'd gambled everything he'd won, but not lost the big grin on his face. As he left, my attention was caught by a group of three teenage boys who looked like they might be trouble. The difficult ones always came in groups, never alone, acting like they owned the place and never had to answer to anyone. These three were already larking about as they ambled in, laughing and shoving each other around. One of them bumped heavily into one of the slot machines, which they all found hysterical.

'Behave in here or you'll have to leave,' I shouted.

For a second, they looked chastened by my raised

voice. But then one of the lads, a skinny kid with the faint trace of a pubescent moustache, mocked my words in a silly voice to the delight of the others and they sauntered off towards the video games at the back. It was nothing unusual. The arcade attracted boisterous teenagers. Most of them were just letting off steam and only needed a reminder to mind their manners. They were rarely any real trouble.

I pushed back my stool and stretched, glad my shift was almost done. Outside, the young boy who'd been playing the penny drop machines was standing with a group of bigger lads in identical school uniforms. One boy stepped up to him and prodded him aggressively in the chest. The boy's head dropped as he staggered back, catching his balance. And then the others swooped in, crowding around him, shouting and jeering, pushing and jostling. His big grin had vanished, and he looked on the verge of tears. My stomach tightened.

One kid grabbed his rucksack and tried to pull it off his shoulder, but to his credit, the boy didn't give it up easily. He held on, fighting back. Until a fist flew, catching him on the side of his head, and he landed flat on his back.

I desperately wanted to run to him, to shoo the bigger kids away, but I couldn't abandon my booth and the trays of cash. It was one of Michelle's golden rules. She'd even made up some laminated signs which she'd taped onto the counter to remind us.

I scanned the room looking for another staff

member to cover for me, but typically there was no one around. I was on my own.

Screw it. Some things were more important. I rushed out, sending my stool flying. 'Leave him alone,' I roared.

The boys scattered like pigeons, leaving the boy sprawled out on the pavement in tears, still clutching his rucksack, his glasses askew.

I picked him up, dusted him down and checked him over. He had a red mark on his cheek where he'd been hit. He pulled away from me, nudging his glasses up the bridge of his nose. I guessed he was embarrassed.

'Are you okay?' I asked.

'Yeah, I'm fine,' he said.

'Do you know those boys?'

'They're just kids from my school.' The way he said it gave me the impression it wasn't the first time he'd been picked on by them.

'Come back inside for a bit until they're gone,' I said. 'Is there someone who can come and pick you up? I could call your parents.'

The boy shook his head. 'It's okay. Thank you.' All trace of the happy little boy who'd been delighted to win big only a few minutes earlier had vanished.

I ushered him back into the arcade and reached into my booth for my bag, thinking I could find him a couple of quid in my purse to keep him occupied for a while.

But something was wrong. I flushed hot and cold, my stomach knotting. The counter was bare. Three trays of coins were missing. Neat rows of coins separated into different denominations. Almost a hundred pounds worth of change. I'd turned my back for less than a minute. But it was all gone. Fuckity fuck.

Michelle was going to kill me.

CHAPTER NINETEEN

Hanlon finished the last mouthful of a dry slice of carrot cake and pushed the plate away. It had been another frustrating day, and he was still angry with himself for the two stupid mistakes he'd made the night before. Not only had he lost the Range Rover he'd seen speeding away from the centre of town, but a builder he should have known better than to trust had fleeced him. And time was running short. He only had another twenty-four hours to locate Duncan Whittaker, and so far he'd remained tantalisingly out of reach. The Range Rover, with what looked like Duncan's personalised number plate, had been his best lead, but he'd blown it. Now he was back to square one, hoping his luck would change, that someone somewhere in this poxy town knew where he could find Duncan.

He'd visited most of the pubs within a ten-mile radius of the town, all the caravan parks and a dozen or more shops and drawn a blank in them all. It was time to think more laterally.

'You finished, darling?' a waitress asked.

Hanlon drained the last mouthful of coffee and nodded, handing her his mug. Across the street from the cafe, a group of kids was larking about outside an arcade. Half a dozen of them flocking around a smaller boy with glasses. One shoved him in the chest, and another felled him with a clobber of his fist. Hanlon watched on, amused. Once, he'd been that kid in the middle, the one being pushed around and picked on. Until he'd learned to fight back. No one pushed him around anymore. A girl with long black hair and a baggy t-shirt rushed out of the arcade, waving her arms, shooing the bigger kids away. She picked up the small boy and dusted him down. Hanlon shook his head, sadly. The kid needed to learn how to stand up for himself.

He was getting distracted. Hanlon turned his attention back to more pressing matters. How to find Duncan. He'd tried calling the takeaway opposite the Britannia pub to see whether they had a number or even an address for the Range Rover driver, but there had been no reply and they didn't open until six. He'd called in at two garages and a barbers' shop. But where else was Duncan likely to have been? A Gym? The local library? And more to the point, where was he living? Hanlon had ruled out all the caravan parks and holiday lets, which must mean he'd rented or bought a property.

He checked the internet on his phone and discovered there were only three estate agents in the town. It was worth a shot. He pulled on his jacket, left some coins on the table.

His first port of call was a national chain on the high street. But no one showed even a glimmer of recognition when he showed them Duncan's photograph. Plenty of blank looks and shaking of heads. It was the same in an independent agency on the opposite side of the road.

The breakthrough he'd been waiting for finally came at a down-at-heel rental agency in a tatty building on the outskirts of the town centre. The office was small and dated, with cheap carpet and even cheaper furniture. A young, blonde woman with thick, fake eyelashes smiled when he walked in. She stood up from her desk and met him at a counter at the front.

Hanlon flashed his fake police warrant card. 'DC Barraclough,' he said, pulling out the photo of Duncan. 'I'm looking for this man. Do you recognise him?'

The woman took the picture and held it up to the light, showing off long, painted fingernails.

'He moved to Leysdown fairly recently and might have been looking for somewhere to live,' Hanlon added. 'His name's Duncan Whittaker.' He studied her face, looking for any flicker of recognition.

The woman frowned. 'He looks familiar,' she said.

'Are you sure? Take your time.'

'Yeah, I think that's the bloke who took the place up in Warden Bay. Is he in trouble or something?'

'We need to speak to him as part of our enquiries into a serious crime,' Hanlon said.

'Duncan, did you say?' the woman asked.

'Duncan Whittaker. He moved here from Essex.'

The woman chewed her lip and shook her head. 'No,' she said. 'He wasn't called Duncan. I've got an Uncle Duncan. I'd have remembered.'

'What was the address of the property he moved into?'

'Hang on, let me get the file. It was that big, detached house up on the cliffs, I think from memory.'

A guy with thinning hair and a crooked nose appeared from a side office.

'Phil, do you remember that guy who rented the big house up in Warden Bay a few weeks ago?' the woman asked. 'Can you remember his name?'

'What's this about?' The guy eyed Hanlon suspiciously.

'DC Barraclough. I'm with the Met Police. Your colleague was helping me with an inquiry concerning a serious crime we believe involved this man.' Hanlon held up the photo of Duncan. 'And you are?'

'Phil Huxley. Manager.'

Huxley walked slowly to the counter, distrust painted across his face. He took the photo and examined it.

'I just need the address of that house,' Hanlon said.

'Here we go.' The woman pulled a cardboard file from a drawer at the back of the office. 'I remember now. Nice guy. Came in with his wife. They paid six months up front in cash. Who pays for anything by cash these days?'

'What name was he using?' Hanlon asked.

'He told us he was called — '

'Thank you, Katie. That's enough,' Huxley said, cutting her off. 'We're not at liberty to give out those details, I'm afraid. We obviously have a duty of confidentiality to our clients.' He gave Hanlon a wan smile.

'Yes, of course.' Hanlon countered with his own polite smile that masked his irritation. Jumped up jobsworth. 'You understand I'm investigating a serious criminal matter though? If you don't cooperate, that could be construed as obstruction of a police officer in his lawful duty.' It was nonsense. Huxley had every right to demand a warrant, but Hanlon was banking on the threat to intimidate him into complying.

'What was your name again?'

'DC Barraclough.'

'I'm afraid you'll have to make a formal application if you want access to any of our files, Detective,' Huxley said.

'It's only an address.'

Huxley shoved his hands in his trouser pockets. A gesture of defiance. A look that said he couldn't care less. 'Can't help you, sorry. Not without the right paperwork.'

CHAPTER TWENTY

I grabbed my bag and with a deep breath headed for the back office, noticing the rowdy teenagers who'd been playing on the video games had vanished. If they'd taken the money, the security cameras should have picked it up. It didn't stop my hands from shaking as I knocked on the office door and let myself in. Michelle was at her desk. She put her e-reader down and sat up straight.

'Are you done for the day?' she asked. 'How's it been?'

'Someone's taken some cash from the booth.'

'What?' She scowled. 'How?'

'There was a disturbance outside, and I only popped out for a second — '

'You left your booth unattended?'

'Only briefly,' I said. Thinking about it, it could only have been for less than a minute. Someone must have been watching me.

'Jesus, Sky. You know the rules. You never leave money unattended. How many times have I told you?' Michelle stood slowly and put her hands on her hips.

'I know.' I hung my head. She'd told us so many times. But it had been an emergency. Not that she would understand.

'How many trays?'

I drew a circle with the toe of my Doc Marten. 'All of them,' I croaked.

'You're kidding?' Michelle's voice went up an octave. 'Did you see who took them?'

'I think it might have been a group of teenagers who were hanging around by the video games.'

'How much did they take?'

'Seventy. Maybe a hundred quid. I'm not sure. It's been a busy afternoon,' I said.

'You know it'll have to come out of your wages.'

'Seriously?' It barely covered my rent. I couldn't afford to lose that kind of money.

'That booth was your responsibility. You should never have left it unattended,' Michelle went on.

I understood that. It's not like I'd asked someone to steal the bloody money. 'But this kid who'd been in earlier was being bullied outside.' I stopped myself, but it was too late. I'd said too much.

'What kid?'

'I don't know. I've never seen him before.'

'An underage kid?'

I nodded mutely.

'What have I told you about letting children in here without a parent?' Michelle said, looking exasperated.

'I know, but that's not the point. He was being picked on by a load of bigger kids outside,' I said.

'So you thought you'd leave your booth unattended? Sky, he wasn't your responsibility. The booth and the float are your responsibility.' Michelle sat back down, shaking her head. She clicked her mouse and her computer blinked into life. 'I'll have to file a report and let Mr Steele know.'

'Jimmy? Please, Michelle. Give me a break. Don't tell him.'

'Company policy.' Michelle tapped at her keyboard. 'I don't have any choice.'

'You could check the security cameras,' I said. 'I'm sure they'll have caught whoever did it.'

'Yes, thanks for pointing out the bleeding obvious. Of course we'll check the footage.' I hated the way Michelle spoke to me when she got like this, all officious and patronising. 'That won't get the money back though, will it? You know, this is typical of your behaviour of late. You turn up most mornings stinking of stale booze and cigarettes, and even when you are here, your head's in the clouds most of the time. You show no interest in the job. You're rude. You're lazy. I think we're going to have to give serious consideration to your future here.'

I'd been trying hard not to cry. I didn't want to appear weak in front of Michelle or give her the satisfaction of knowing how badly her rebuke had stung, but with every word the pressure of my tears built until I couldn't hold them back. 'I'll make it up to you,' I said. 'I need this job. Give me another chance.' I hated having to beg her, but it was time to swallow my pride.

'I've given you chances before, and you've thrown them back in my face.'

She could be a hard-nosed cow.

'Ultimately, it'll be up to Jimmy, so you can stop your blubbing. It won't wash with me. There'll be disciplinary action, of course, and because it was a dereliction of duty, I ought to warn you it could result in the termination of your employment.'

'You're sacking me?' It wasn't as if *I'd* stolen the money.

'Yes, that's a possibility if, when we've reviewed the evidence, we find you were guilty of gross misconduct.'

Gross misconduct? What the hell? Was she serious?

'I'll pay the money back, but please don't sack me. I'm begging you, Michelle.' I hated myself for even thinking the words, let alone saying them out loud, but I was desperate. I couldn't lose my job.

'Go home, Sky, and take a long hard think about your attitude. We'll talk in the morning.'

'That's it?'

'Go home.'

CHAPTER TWENTY-ONE

The woman in the estate agent's office was caught in a no-man's-land, the file with Duncan's address in her hand, almost within Hanlon's grasp. Her boss was being a prick, but perhaps he could persuade her to give him the information.

'Maybe you should call my DI and have a word with him,' Hanlon said, as the office manager, Huxley, stood staring at him defiantly.

Huxley sniffed and looked Hanlon up and down as if he was mulling over his options. 'Alright then. Give me his number.'

Hanlon rattled off a fictitious mobile number from the top of his head. Huxley scribbled it down on a scrap of paper. 'His name's Collins,' he added, spotting the name on a paper calendar hanging on a wall over Huxley's shoulder.

'Give me two minutes. Stay here,' he said, turning to march back into his office. In all honesty, it probably wouldn't take him two minutes to discover Hanlon had given him the wrong number. Not much time at all.

Hanlon drummed his fingers on the counter and smiled at the woman still clutching the folder. She was looking increasingly uncomfortable. 'You know, it's going to take time to get the paperwork for a warrant sorted. And if our man gets wind we're onto him, he could disappear like that.' He clicked his fingers. 'But you're a smart woman. You know the right thing to do. You could pop the folder on the counter and turn your back for a second or two. Nobody would know. It would be our little secret.'

'I'm not sure,' the woman said, glancing at Huxley's office.

'This is a police investigation,' Hanlon said. 'Come on. Do the right thing. Give me the address.'

Still she didn't budge. It was as if she was glued to the spot. 'Phil said we shouldn't.'

'You know what management's like. Always got to play by the rules.' Hanlon rolled his eyes.

'Tell me about it.'

'But just because he's the boss, doesn't mean he's always right. You know the penalty for obstructing a police officer in the execution of his lawful duty, don't you?'

The woman's forehead creased with worry. She was cracking, but Hanlon could already hear Huxley talking to someone who'd answered his call.

'One quick glance at that paperwork. It's all I need and then I'll be gone,' Hanlon said, willing the woman closer. He was half-minded to vault the counter and snatch the file.

'I want to help but… '

'Do the right thing. Let me see the file.'

'I'm sorry,' she said as Hanlon heard a phone being slammed down.

'Alright, thanks anyway,' he said, moving swiftly for the door.

He was already out on the street, head down, when he heard Huxley's voice shouting behind him. 'Hey, Detective, wait! Come back. You gave me the wrong number.'

But Hanlon kept walking and didn't look back.

CHAPTER TWENTY-TWO

I wasn't in the mood for a party, but Amber had insisted I go with her after I told her about the stolen money and how Michelle had threatened to sack me.

'If nothing else, it'll take your mind off everything for a while,' she said.

We pre-loaded on half a bottle of vodka in the caravan before walking to the party in a house overlooking the estuary. It belonged to the parents of Amber's new boyfriend, Marc. They'd apparently gone away for a few days.

'Am I going to know anyone?' I asked, predicting how the evening would pan out. Amber would disappear off with Marc the moment we arrived while I was left to look after myself. It was no wonder I drank so much. It was the only way I could cope.

'You'll meet new people, and you might actually

enjoy yourself,' Amber said, grabbing my hand and tugging me along.

The house was an impressive detached new-build with grey weather-boarding and enormous windows. The garden was already full of people chatting and swigging from bottles of beer.

'Wow, Marc's parents must be loaded,' I said.

'Wait until you see inside. Come on, let's get a drink.' Amber pulled me inside.

The entire house was spectacularly spartan and lacking any homely touches, apart from a carefully positioned bunch of pristine white lilies in a vase on a credenza in the hall. If it had been in a magazine, it would have been described as fashionably minimalist.

'Hey, babe, you made it,' Marc said, appearing from nowhere and swooping in to kiss Amber. He wrapped a possessive hand around her waist and pulled her close.

'You know Sky, my flatmate, don't you?' Amber said. 'I hope you don't mind her coming, but she's had a shit day at work.'

'No problem,' he said, not even looking at me. He only had eyes for her. 'Come through. Everyone's in here.' He guided her into a lounge at the back of the house. It was crowded with people, none of whom I recognised. I'd have felt like a proper gooseberry tagging along with them, so I split off into the kitchen looking for a drink and found even more people I didn't know.

I helped myself to a beer from a tin bucket of ice on an island in the middle of the room and drank half of it down in one go. I'd give it half an hour and if things didn't pick up, I'd head home. If I was going to be on my own for the night, I might as well enjoy the comforts of the caravan rather than being lonely among strangers.

The beer didn't last long. I put the empty bottle on the side and regretted not bringing something stronger. Maybe I could find something in the house. I pushed past a couple in a tight clinch and threw open a cupboard filled with cereal packets, bags of flour and sugar. In the next cupboard along were cups, mugs and glasses. But nothing to drink.

Someone turned up the music a couple of notches and the din of people enjoying themselves became that bit more boisterous. It was going to be a riot. It had that vibe. Young people letting their hair down and having a laugh in the luxury of someone else's home.

I bent down to check the cupboards under the counter and bumped against a guy standing with his back to me in conversation with two hipster types. 'Sorry,' I said, glancing over my shoulder with a smile of apology.

The last person I expected to see was Cam, the guy from the store, all floppy hair and blue eyes.

'What are you doing here?' I'm sure he hadn't been in the kitchen when I first walked in. I would have noticed.

'Hi,' he said, glancing down at his feet. 'I could ask you the same thing.'

'What?'

'What are you doing here?' he asked.

I shook my head, trying to get a grip of myself. He'd got me all flustered and I couldn't think straight. 'Umm… I heard there was a party,' I said. Stupid thing to say. 'Amber dragged me along. She thought it might be fun.'

'And is it?'

'Not really.'

He laughed. 'Not feeling it tonight?'

'You could say that.'

'No, me too.' He turned, as if to introduce me to the two guys he'd been chatting to, but they'd already wandered off, leaving us alone. Awkward. I could hardly walk away now. I was trapped with him and I hardly knew him. 'You've not got anything to drink. Do you want a beer?' he asked. He grabbed a bottle from the ice bucket on the island and cracked it open for me.

'Thanks,' I shouted over the music and the raucous crowd, grateful to have something to do with my hands. 'I don't think I'll stay long.'

'Me neither. Got to be up early for the shop.'

'At least you have a job. I might be unemployed by tomorrow.' I don't know why I felt the need to tell him that.

By now the kitchen had filled with people and it was almost impossible to hear myself over the rising noise.

'What?' Cam leaned closer and cocked an ear towards me.

'I said, I might have lost my job. Some kids stole some money from my booth today.'

'Someone stole some money from you?' Cam frowned.

'From the arcade.'

'I can't hear you.'

'Do you want find somewhere quieter?' I mouthed.

Cam nodded enthusiastically. We pushed our way out of the kitchen and into the hallway. There were people everywhere. A few faces I recognised. A lot more I didn't. I needed some space away from the crowds and the noise. I headed for a spiral staircase that wound its way artfully up to the next floor and stepped aside to let a guy pass. His eyes were glazed, clearly the worse for wear. There was always one who hit the booze too hard and too fast, who didn't know their tolerances. At least I usually made it through to the end of the evening.

The stairs led to a wide landing with a picture window and stunning views of the estuary, the dim lights of Southend twinkling in the distance.

'This house is something else,' Cam cooed.

'Architect designed, apparently,' I said, making inverted comma signs in the air with my fingers, mimicking what Amber had told me on the way over. 'How the other half live, eh?' I threw open a door on an enormous, tiled bathroom with a walk-in shower and an arrangement of expensive looking soaps and hand creams in a wicker basket by the sink. 'Look at this.'

We giggled as we tiptoed around the rest of the floor like naughty schoolchildren, inspecting every room while poking fun at the ostentatious opulence of it all.

'You know, this is what I thought I was going to do when I left school,' I said.

'Interior design?'

'No, dummy. Architecture, but not designing houses. I wanted to create places for ordinary people to live. You know, like flats and tower blocks, but really cool ones where people are actually proud to live and the buildings make everyone happy to be there.'

Where I'd grown up in a crumbling tower block in Tower Hamlets, everyone always seemed to be miserable. The lifts never worked, the staircases stank of piss and no one knew their neighbours. I always thought there had to be a better way.

Eventually we found what appeared to be the master bedroom. I pushed open the door and peered in. A huge double bed faced sliding glass doors out to a balcony with more amazing views over the water.

'Come on,' I said, stepping inside and urging Cam to follow.

'I'm not sure,' Cam said, hesitating in the doorway. 'We shouldn't be in here, should we?'

'Don't be such a killjoy.' Although I wasn't drunk, I was feeling the effects of the alcohol and the first flush of awkwardness I'd felt when I bumped into Cam had evaporated.

He wasn't bad looking now I thought about it. And I had a feeling he was into me. I took his hand and pulled him into the room, shutting the door behind us. Maybe the party wouldn't turn out so badly after all.

We perched on the end of the bed and I imagined what it must be like waking up to the view with yachts and container ships drifting past under a rising morning sun.

'What stopped you?' Cam asked.

'Stopped me what?'

'Becoming an architect.'

I laughed. 'It was a stupid dream. I could never do something like that.'

'Rubbish.'

'Says the man working in his parents' shop.'

'That's my choice.'

'I enjoy working in the arcade. At least, I did.' I told him about the stolen money and how I'd been threatened with the sack.

'Look, I can't promise anything, but I could have a word with Dad and see if we could offer you some hours in the shop.'

'Thanks, Cam, but I'm not that desperate.'

He winced and I felt a distance open between us. My stupid mouth. What did I say that for?

'Yeah, well, there are bound to be other jobs,' he said. The hurt in his eyes made me feel bad. 'What about going back to college?'

'Nah, I don't think so.'

'Why not? It's not too late. You could still become an architect if that's what you really want.'

'Do you have an idea how long you have to study?

And anyway, I can't afford to go back to college, even if I had the qualifications.'

'Well, what are you going to do? You can't work in the arcade for the rest of your life. You're too good for that.'

My cheeks burned. Nobody had ever been this nice to me before. I'm sure he must have noticed, even in the gloom. 'I can't,' I mumbled.

'Okay, tell me where you see yourself in ten years. Surely not still stuck on this island?'

'What's this, a job interview?'

'Answer the question,' he said, putting his fist up to my mouth like he was holding an imaginary microphone. 'Where do you picture yourself?'

'Stop it,' I said, batting his hand away. 'I don't know.' I didn't want to play this game. 'Life's short. I want to have some fun for now. What about you? You still going to be running the local shop when you're thirty?'

'I want to travel and see the world,' Cam said.

'So why don't you?'

He frowned. 'The shop? My mum? I can hardly just pack my bags and leave, can I?'

I'd done it again. Opened my big mouth without thinking. 'Sorry,' I said. 'Silly thing to say.'

'It's alright.' Cam picked at the label on his bottle, scratching it with his thumbnail until it was half hanging off. In the dull light, he looked so sad. Out of nowhere, I had the urge to kiss him. Why not? We were young. Single. Independent. We could do what we wanted. It was only a bit of fun and there wasn't much other reason to stay at the party.

He looked up and caught me examining his face. I glanced away, but not quickly enough.

'What?' he asked.

'Nothing.' I leaned in closer until I felt his warm breath on my cheek, willing him to take the hint.

He put a hand on my arm and our lips locked, gently, unsure at first. I kissed him harder and initially he didn't respond, as if he couldn't believe what was happening. But then his hunger for me grew, his hands on my back, stroking my neck, his fingers in my hair, and I knew I wanted this. I really wanted this.

I put a hand on his thigh, sending him a signal. No ambiguity. I wanted more. I was his for the taking.

CHAPTER TWENTY-THREE

I let my hand creep higher, my mind on one thing. My skin tingled at his touch and a gaping hole chasmed inside me. His touch thrilled me. The feel of his muscular arms around me, his chest bearing down. I wanted this more than anything.

'Sky, what are you doing?' Cam said, pushing my hand away as I moved it up his thigh. He pulled away, breathless, and with an odd look in his eye I couldn't interpret. It was weird. I'd never had a guy react like that before.

'Don't you want to?' I cooed, trying to kiss him again.

He pushed me back by my shoulders. 'Not here. Not like this,' he said. 'I don't want to be just another one of your conquests.'

Conquests? Did he have that low an opinion of me? I was no angel, but that didn't make me a slut. I pulled away from him, wrapping my arms across my chest, hugging my body. 'Is that what you think?' I said, recoiling as he reached for my hand.

'Sorry, that came out wrong. I didn't mean it to sound — '

'What did you mean?' The shock that he'd rejected me, accused me, gave way to anger. How dare he talk to me like that.

'I meant you're worth more,' he said.

'I thought you wanted it.'

'I do,' he said, burying his head in his hands. 'But not like this.'

'What did you expect? Candlelight and roses? Get real, Cam.'

'Please, don't be like that. I do like you,' he said. 'I mean I *really* like you.'

'You've got a funny way of showing it.'

'Can we start again?'

What had I been thinking? I didn't even fancy him that much. It was only the booze talking. Oh, well, his loss. 'You don't know what you're missing,' I shouted at him.

'Don't leave,' he said, as I jumped off the bed, heading for the door.

I had to get out. Away from him. Away from this party. He tried to grab my arm, to stop me, but I wriggled free of his grasp. What a loser.

'Sky!'

I slammed the door and stumbled towards the stairs, bouncing off the wall as I lost my balance.

My way out was blocked by a crowd of people at the

bottom of the stairs, their attention drawn to something going on in the lounge. They were baying and cheering as if they were at a sporting event, a frisson of tension in the air. I stood on the bottom step and peered over everyone's heads.

In the lounge, two men were squaring up to each other, chests pumped up, chins out. Marc and another guy I recognised. Aaron. The guy Amber had been dating before she'd met Marc. Two stags fired up with jealously and hatred. Christ, were they fighting over Amber? I really didn't have the headspace to deal with this right now.

Aaron shoved Marc in the chest, sending him staggering backwards. 'Come on then, big man. Let's see what you've got,' Aaron snarled.

The music stopped. Marc caught his balance, his nostrils flaring. 'Get out!' he yelled at Aaron. 'Get out before I fucking kill you.'

'And you're going to make me, are you?'

My heart pounded. They looked like they were prepared to murder each other. A gut-wrenching display of testosterone and aggression. But as much as I hated seeing it, I couldn't tear my eyes away.

Now Marc was up in Aaron's face, his head bobbing like a boxer's, his eyes wide and black. Where the hell was Amber?

I scoured the room, hoping she'd had the sense to make herself scarce. We used to joke about what it would be like to have two men fighting over us, but I never imagined it would be anything like this. It was brutal. Grotesque.

And then Amber appeared from nowhere, mascara streaking her face. She threw herself between the two men, attempting to push them apart. 'Stop it!' she yelled, her voice cracking with emotion. 'That's enough!'

'Amber!' I shouted, trying to push through the throng, but they were too drunk, too excited. I couldn't reach her.

A blonde woman I didn't know took Amber by the arm and pulled her away, as Aaron stepped back and swung a fist. It connected with Marc's head with a repugnant thud. He wobbled on weak legs.

Marc dabbed his lip, wiping away a pearl of blood, and jabbed a stinging fist in Aaron's face. A single punch, but a decisive blow. Aaron keeled backwards and his eyes rolled up as he collapsed unmoving on his back, felled like a tree. A hushed shock reverberating around the house.

I couldn't stand to watch a second longer. My hands were shaking and my lungs tight. I wanted to stay, for Amber's sake, but I needed some air. And I knew I couldn't reach her anyway. She had other friends. She'd be okay.

I heard footsteps on the landing. Cam was coming. I pushed my way out into the garden where the chill hit me like a restorative tonic, cooling my flushed face. I drew in a salty breath, savouring the taste of the sea, and vomited all over the lawn. I doubled over, retching and coughing until my stomach was empty.

A hand lightly touched my back.

'Sky, are you okay?' Cam's voice, full of concern.

'Leave me alone,' I yelled, my mind a turmoil of emotions. I needed to be by myself. His rejection still stung, and the image of Marc and Aaron fighting was burned into my mind. Their raw brutality had left me trembling with shock. Poor Amber, having to deal with those two arseholes. She deserved better, and I knew I should be in there, comforting her, like she would have been there for me. But I couldn't be in that house. The atmosphere was toxic. I had the urge to run, to put my head down and keep going, away from Cam. Away from the house. Away from everything.

I pushed Cam away and hurried out into the street, not caring where I was going, not slowing until my feet sank into the sand and the hiss of surf rushing along the shore filled my ears. I let the darkness consume me, vanishing into its belly.

When the party was far behind me, I slowed down, panting for breath and tasting the foul, acidic burn of vomit at the back of my nose and throat.

Although I'd been upset by Cam's behaviour, it was the violence that had really shaken me. That single, brutal punch. Why did men always seem to think they could solve their problems with their fists? I tried to hold the tears back. But they wouldn't be quelled. They came in sobbing, gigantic waves, like my body was purging itself of the terrible things in my head. And suddenly I knew what I had to do.

CHAPTER TWENTY-FOUR

One foot led in front of the other. I tripped and stumbled through the dark, my boots catching in the sand and on the slippery, hidden rocks with my focus on the headland and the vague outline of the pill-boxes in the distance. My head jumped from one bad memory to the next, of everything that had happened in recent days. But there were two faces that dominated my thoughts.

Frank and Esme.

How were they spending their evening? Was Esme cowering from Frank, curled into a corner under a brutal onslaught of his rage? Had a misplaced word or look sent him spiralling over the edge? I tried to blink away the hideous image of his hands around her throat, strangling the life out of her, his fists landing heavy blows on her head. What was he doing to her behind the veil of their apparently perfect life? I had to get Esme away from him to somewhere safe before he killed her. Somewhere she could rebuild her life. She deserved so much better. I thought about Esme's diary and my mother.

The stench of stale beer on Stefan's breath was still fresh in my mind after all these years. Rank and odious as he tried to kiss me on the cheek, pinning my arms to my sides until I could wriggle free and escape to my room. He spoke to Mum worse than you'd speak to a dog. Bitter. Nasty. Aggressive. I never knew why he was so full of venom or where his hatred came from. But it spilled from his mouth and leaked from his pores every time he was in the flat.

The last time it happened, Mum had yelled back, fuelling his temper. I pulled the duvet over my head and clamped my hands over my ears. Hummed to myself. Tried not to hear. But it was impossible. Their voices cut through, seeping into my soul.

It started with a loud thud, like someone had dropped a vase. That's when Mum stopped shouting, her screams cut short. The thudding continued. Regular and unrelenting. I squeezed my eyes shut, trying to block out the image in my mind as tears wet my cheeks. I knew what he was doing to her, but fear paralysed me. I couldn't move. I just lay there praying it would stop and that Stefan would go away forever.

When it eventually ended and I found the courage to sneak out of my room, I found the front door wide open, letting out the warmth, a chilly breeze drifting in. I pushed it closed and tiptoed into the kitchen, fearful of what I would find. Of what he'd done to her.

'Mum? Are you okay?' I whispered into the dark.

My hand searched for the switch on the wall. Harsh fluorescent light flickered on and illuminated the blood on the cupboards and the walls, and the twisted figure of my mother sprawled across the floor, her face unrecognisable. Beaten to a pulp. My legs lost their strength. I grabbed the wall, a hard lump balling in my throat.

'Mum!' I screamed. 'Wake up!'

But I knew she was gone. Nothing I could do to help her now. It was too late. I'd let her down when she needed me most. I'd never be able to forgive myself for that.

I couldn't let Esme suffer the same fate as my mother. Whether or not she wanted my help, I was going to save her. And that's why I ended up back at Frank and Esme's house, standing at the top of the drive, looking through the iron gates at a single light burning in a downstairs window.

Two cars were parked outside. Frank's big 4x4 and Esme's silver Mercedes. From the outside, it was the picture of domestic normality. But I knew what went on behind those walls. The question was how could I stop it? I'd come to the house without a plan. It just seemed right. The place I needed to be.

I tested the gates, but they were locked and didn't want to budge. As if that was going to stop me. Unsteadily, with a mixture of beer, vodka and adren-aline washing through my system, I climbed them, losing my balance as I threw one leg over the top. I landed heavily on my ankle on the other side and stifled a cry of pain.

I rose gingerly, wincing. My ankle was sore, but at least I could put weight on it.

I hobbled on, running on pure instinct, my courage driven by the alcohol. If I'd have been sober, I'm sure I would never have been so bold. But I was feeling unstoppable. I picked a wavering path to the house across the unkempt lawn, my heart hammering way too fast and my ankle throbbing. I hesitated when I heard barking, but it was coming from a neighbouring property. Frank and Esme didn't have a dog, as far as I was aware. Just as well, really. But my biggest concern wasn't a dog. It was being caught by Frank. How could I possibly explain what I was doing at the house again? I'd have no explanation other than the truth. But maybe that wasn't a bad thing. What was he going to do? Hit me? Like he hit Esme? We'd soon see how that ended. It would be the perfect excuse to call the police and have him arrested. And then his whole sorry story would have to come out.

I reached the front of the house and crouched at the window with the light, peering in like a voyeur. The room was empty. No one on the big sofas watching TV. No one curled up with a book or a glass of wine. But there was something. Angry voices. Two people yelling. First, Frank's deep growl, answered by Esme's frightened retort. I gasped, hardly able to believe I'd caught them in the middle of a blazing row. Frank's staccato outbursts brought back terrible memories of the way

Stefan used to scream at my mother. A burning anger flamed in my chest. I knew how a few cross words could quickly end in violence.

As the voices became louder, I closed my eyes and sucked in a deep lungful of air, grounding myself, trying to control my emotions. It was all so painfully familiar. It brought back visceral memories that raised the hairs on my arms and the back of my neck. Frank was winding himself up into a fury. How long before he settled it with a slap? Or worse? Just like Stefan used to do. An awful image of him cracking Esme's head casually against a wall spilled into my head.

I had to stop him.

But how? Maybe I could create a diversion. Frank's car was right behind me. No doubt an expensive vehicle like that would be alarmed. If I tried the doors, would that set it off? But then what? When he'd found his car was safe, he'd surely just return to what he'd started with Esme. But at least it might give her the opportunity to lock herself in the bathroom. Or maybe I could sneak in while he was distracted and help her to safety. But what if she wouldn't come? What if she persisted with the lie that Frank had never laid a finger on her?

There had to be something else. But my mind was blank. I had no real idea how I could stop the horrors being perpetuated inside their home. I was helpless. Whatever was I thinking coming here in the first place? I couldn't help Esme.

The splintering sound of smashing crockery and an

ear-splitting scream were so unexpected, I jumped and let out a little scream of my own. I pressed my nose to the window, shading my eyes to see beyond the reflection of my face, and saw a darting shadow like a disturbed songbird taken to flight. Esme, with a tissue to her mouth, sobbing. She raced up the stairs, disappearing from my narrow view.

Frank appeared after her, his face clouded with anger. 'Esme!' he yelled. 'Get back down here!'

Upstairs a door slammed shut. Frank charged after his wife, his footsteps on the stairs thudding through the house.

This was it. My chance to catch Frank in the act of attacking his wife. The proof I needed. I crept around the outside of the house into the rear garden and peered into the conservatory where the argument had most likely started.

Inside, the worktops were cluttered with the remains of a meal; dirty pots and pans, a bottle of wine and two glasses, a knife on a wooden chopping board next to an upturned basil plant, soil spilt over the counter. And on one of the cream walls, a red smear. I clamped a hand over my mouth, silencing a gasp. It was splattered at head height with three ominous drips of differing lengths in a slow-motion race to the floor.

My legs shook and my pulse thrummed through my veins. Bastard. Total bastard. I could have killed him.

The glass was cold to the touch as I pressed my hand to it. Was he upstairs with her now finishing what he'd started? Maybe I should call the police after all.

169

Surely Esme's blood on the wall was all the evidence they'd need to believe Frank had attacked her. I couldn't see either of them explaining that away in a hurry.

But as I plucked my phone from my pocket to make the call, my mind made up, something made me hesitate. I saw a plate on the floor, smashed into three pieces, covered in the remains of a tomato sauce.

Not blood on the wall then. But even so, evidence of Frank's abuse. When he'd lost his temper, he must have thrown the plate. I imagined Esme ducking, it narrowly missing her head. It was the sound of splintering crockery I'd heard a short while ago.

But was it really enough to justify calling the police? My fingers hovered over the number pad of my phone. It proved nothing. Instead of making a call, I flicked on the phone's camera and tried to frame the mark on the wall with the plate in shot. But I was too far away. All that came out was an indistinct splodge. I needed to move closer.

I stepped silently out of the shadows and into the carpet of light cast out from inside, now dangerously exposed. Anyone looking out from inside the house was sure to spot me instantly. But what choice did I have? I crept around the outside of the conservatory, held my phone up and fired off three more shots. The results were better, but not great. At least you could see the broken plate even if the mark on the wall wasn't all that clear. I tried again.

With my free hand, I tapped the screen. Adjusted the brightness. Centred the focus. I had to hurry, but I needed a clear shot. And it was proving harder than I'd thought. I checked the results. One more try.

A shadow flashed across the door from the hall. Frank returning. His face set in a black scowl. Every muscle in my body went rigid. I dared not move. If I made the slightest twitch, I was sure he'd see me, framed in the window. The darkness of the garden beckoned behind me. But I couldn't move. My shoulders tight. My mouth dry. I willed him not to look. Not to see me. God knew what he'd do if he found me and saw I'd been taking pictures.

Thankfully, he was preoccupied to notice me. I hoped Esme had locked herself away somewhere safe where he couldn't get to her and he'd given up. He threw open the dishwasher and turned his back on me to load it. This was my chance. I took a step backwards, away from the glass, not rushing it. All my senses dialled up.

Another step, fighting the urge to run, sliding my foot over the smooth patio tiles.

And then he turned. Out of the kitchen and into the dining area. Moving closer to me. I stopped dead, as motionless as a statue with my phone still raised up in front of my chest. Frank strode across the room and gathered up the pieces of the broken plate, collecting them gingerly, careful not to cut his fingers.

While Frank was distracted, I lowered my phone. I was so close now to the security of the darkness. Another couple of steps and I could slink away. He'd never have to know I'd been there.

My heel brushed the edge of the lawn and I let out the breath I'd been holding. One last slow, controlled step back and I was finally out of the light and out of danger. Even if he looked up now, I was sure he wouldn't see me. I let my muscles relax as a wave of relief washed over me. Maybe it was my anxiety to escape, rushing it when I should have taken my time, but as I turned my foot snagged in a divot. I lost my balance and threw up my arms. The entire garden was suddenly awash with a searing, bright light. Shit. I'd triggered a security lamp, so harsh it blinded me, lighting up the lawn like it was day.

Frank looked up, surprised. His eyes opened wide as he saw me staring back at him through the glass. A few shocked seconds seemed to last minutes as we stood watching at each other, equally horrified.

Frank reacted first, the astonishment on his face turning to something like anger. He yelled at me, gesticulating aggressively, before racing out of the kitchen. My instinct told me to run. But which way? He was coming for me. I was sure of it. Was there anywhere I could hide? It was too far to make it back up the drive and over the gate, but it was the only way out I knew. Too late. He was there, in the garden, running towards me with a shotgun in his hands.

What now? Was he going to shoot me?

'Don't move!' he screamed.

I focused on the two gaping holes at the end of the barrels of the gun, and I was convinced from the look in his eye that he was going to kill me. He knew I'd seen the broken plate. Now he was going to silence me. I turned away and tried to run, aiming for the hedge that surrounded the garden. Maybe if I could reach it, I could squeeze through. Find another way out. Maybe down the cliff and onto the beach.

But as soon as I put weight on my ankle, it gave way with a stab of pain. I stumbled, my body tumbling towards the ground. The grass came rushing up to my face and as I put my hands down to break my fall, a single gunshot splintered the night air.

CHAPTER TWENTY-FIVE

Hanlon parked on a bend in the road to watch the house across the street, conscious that an unfamiliar campervan was likely to attract the notice of the neighbours in a tight-knit residential area. But it was a Friday night. People had other things on their minds. He trusted he'd be left alone.

Stakeouts were a boring but essential part of the job, hours spent sitting in vehicles, watching and waiting. He'd never enjoyed them, even when he was in the force. Trying to maintain concentration during hours of sitting doing nothing was exhausting. His back was already aching, and his knee was stiff and sore.

He'd watched Phil Huxley lock up the estate agent's office at around six and followed his BMW three-series at a discreet distance as he'd driven home, stopping only briefly at an off-licence to pick up some cans of lager. Now it was a waiting game. Maybe another three hours? Four to be on the safe side.

There had been only three realistic options for laying his hands on Duncan Whittaker's address. The first, to break into the rental agency, was the most direct option and one he'd seriously considered. Three narrow windows set high in the wall at the back of the office above a row of filing cabinets, designed to let in light rather than provide views, would have been an easy entry point. The windows overlooked a dingy courtyard full of wastebins. No CCTV cameras. No neighbouring properties. But there was the alarm to worry about. He'd noted a control panel on the inside of the door when he'd called in that afternoon. An illuminated number pad connected to invisible alarms. The unknowable factor was how long it would take the police or a security firm to respond. Five minutes? Ten? He only had to locate Duncan's file, but he didn't know how long that would take.

A second, more appealing option, was to target the woman in the office who'd almost capitulated into giving him the address. He'd seen the uncertainty in her eyes as she was caught between complying with what she thought was a legitimate police request for information and following the explicit instructions from her boss. A little more time with her and he was sure he could persuade her to give it up. He thought about intercepting her on the way home, sweet talking her into doing the right thing, maybe offering to take her for a drink. She seemed like the compliant type. But there were too many variables to control. Too many things that could go wrong. The least of his worries was that she might suspect he wasn't really a detective. His bigger concern was if she freaked out if he approached her in the street and she refused to co-operate. There was also every chance she'd not remember the address without referring to the file.

His third, and favoured, option was to focus on the office manager, Huxley, which was why he was now patiently waiting outside his house. He drummed his fingers on his knee, his stomach rumbling. He'd not had the chance to eat anything since that slice of dry carrot cake in the cafe earlier and regretted not picking up some food when he had the chance.

In his mirrors, he watched a car approach from behind, slowing as it passed, the driver taking his time to check out Hanlon hunkered down behind the wheel. Hanlon kept his eyes narrowed, feigning sleep, praying the driver wouldn't raise the alarm. How could he possibly explain to a police patrol why he was loitering on the estate, dressed from head to foot in black?

The car drove on without stopping, turning off into a connecting road, disappearing out of view. Hanlon breathed out heavily through his nose and refocused on the house opposite as his phone buzzed on the dashboard. He snatched it up after only one ring.

'Have you found him yet?' The rich, velvety tone of the Romanian woman who'd hired him.

'I'm close,' he said.

'How close?'

'I'll have his address by tonight.'

'Time's running out,' the woman said.

'As soon as I have a visual on him, you'll be the first to know.'

'You won't let me down, will you, Mr Hanlon?' A threat more than a question. He didn't need to be reminded. The sort of people who called on his services didn't stand for failure or being dicked around. Not that he was planning on either.

'Of course not. I'll call you first thing in the morning as soon as I have news.' Hanlon hesitated. 'And when I've found him, is there anything else you need me to do?'

'Just call me and don't screw this up,' she said.

'Of course — ' But she'd already hung up.

Hanlon threw the phone down, licking his dry lips. Time was short, but he was definitely getting close. He fully expected to have Duncan Whittaker cornered by the morning. The chase was coming to its thrilling end. The bit he liked the best.

He glanced up at Huxley's house. A light flashed on in an upstairs window. Hanlon settled back in his seat, making himself comfortable, stretching his leg and his stiff knee. Not long now. He just had to be patient.

CHAPTER TWENTY-SIX

I rolled onto my back, my t-shirt and hoodie damp against my skin with what I guessed was blood. My blood. But I felt no pain. Was this what it was like to be shot? Maybe I was in shock.

'What are you doing here?' Frank barked, looming over me with the shotgun aimed at my chest, his body silhouetted against the dark sky.

'You shot me,' I gasped.

'Don't be ridiculous.'

I ran my fingers over my body, searching for a wound. But there was no blood. No ripped skin. It was the grass, wet from an earlier rain shower that had soaked through my clothes.

'Who are you?' Frank snarled, tucking the gun into the side of his stomach, his finger perilously near the trigger. 'What are you doing out here in the dark?'

I opened my mouth to speak, but the words gummed up in my throat. I couldn't think of any explanation other than the truth and lying there staring terrified at the double barrels of a gun, it didn't feel like the right moment to confront Frank with that.

I heard Esme's voice. 'Frank? What's going on? Was that a gunshot?' A second later she was standing at his side, staring down at me. 'Oh, my God. Sky?' she said, frowning. 'Is that you? Frank, you didn't shoot her, did you?'

'Of course I didn't bloody shoot her,' he snapped back. 'I put a warning shot over her head. That's all.'

'Oh, for pity's sake. Get out of the way, you stupid man.' She scowled at Frank, pushed him aside and knelt at my side. 'Are you hurt?'

I tried to sit, pushing myself up on my elbows. How the hell was I going to explain my way out of this? 'Hi,' I said, with a nervous smile.

'What are you doing here? Do you know what time it is?' Esme put a hand under my arm and helped me to stand.

I brushed off my clothes and stood sheepishly in front of them, wondering how the hell I was going to explain myself.

'Sorry,' I mumbled.

'You know her?' Frank asked.

'It's the girl who found my diary on the beach, remember?' Esme said.

Frank narrowed his eyes as he scrutinised my face. 'She was here the other night,' he said at last, tightening his grip on the gun. 'What's she doing back?'

'I don't know, Frank, why don't we ask her? God,

she's drunk,' she said, turning her head and screwing up her face as she caught a waft of my vodka and beer-laced breath. 'Let's get her into the house and sobered up. Then she can tell us what she's doing here.'

They were talking about me like I wasn't there, as if I was in a bad dream. Maybe I'd wake up in a minute and I'd be back in my bed. Esme guided me towards the house, but when I put weight on my ankle, a bolt of pain shot up my leg. Nope, very much awake.

Esme caught me and held on tightly, helping me limp towards the house. 'And put that gun away, Frank,' she said, 'before you do someone a mischief.'

Frank cracked the shotgun, expelling an empty cartridge, a sulky expression on his face like a child who'd been told to pack away his trainset by his mother. 'I don't care who she is, she shouldn't have been prowling around the garden in the middle of the bloody night,' he said.

'He tried to shoot me,' I said to Esme, her arm around my shoulder. My teeth were chattering even though I didn't feel cold.

'I know. Come on, let's get you inside.'

I allowed Esme to shepherd me into the house, the pain in my ankle easing as I walked. Hopefully, I'd not done anything too serious. Twisted it, maybe.

It was weird seeing their kitchen from the other side of the glass. A few minutes earlier, I'd have given anything to be inside the house, but now I wanted to get as far away from it as I could. Esme pulled out a chair from under the dining table for me and as I sat, stretching out my foot and ankle, she fetched me a glass of water.

'Are you sure you're not hurt?'

'I don't think so,' I said, 'apart from my ankle. I fell on it awkwardly, climbing over your gate.' Why did I say that? It was as good as admitting I'd broken into their property.

'Do you want some ice to put on it?' Esme asked.

'No, it's fine.' It felt like Esme was judging me as she looked me up and down. The lights inside were so bright. They showed up the grass stains on my knees and the mud on my hoodie. They'd need a wash when I got home. Why did I ever think coming to the house was a good idea?

'You're lucky Frank didn't shoot you, skulking around the garden like that. Whatever were you thinking?'

Had he tried to shoot me? He said he'd fired deliberately over my head, but that didn't account for the fact I'd stumbled and fallen. Is that why he'd missed? I sipped the tepid water, wilting under the intensity of Esme's gaze. 'Sorry,' I said again.

'What are you doing here?'

I shrugged. I still hadn't worked out an explanation, so I figured silence was my best bet.

Esme folded her arms as Frank joined us. I was glad to see he'd put the gun away. 'If you wanted to speak to me again, you should have booked another appointment,' Esme said. 'You can't just turn up here. It's not professional.'

I hung my head in shame. 'I didn't mean to cause any trouble,' I said. 'I'm really — ' A swell of nausea bloomed in my stomach. 'I'm going to be sick.' I jumped up, clutching my hand to my mouth, afraid I was going to vomit all over their floor.

'This way. Quickly.' Esme showed me to a small bathroom under the stairs.

I locked the door and stumbled to the toilet just in time, emptying my guts of the little liquid still left in my stomach until I was dry retching. I knelt by the bowl with spittle dribbling from my mouth, wishing I could click my fingers and be transported home. Coming here had been a huge mistake.

I pulled the flush and slumped against the wall, wiping a hand over my face. I was still shaking even though it was warm in the house. Shock, I guessed. I'd never seen a gun before, let alone been shot at. And now I was trapped in the house, with no idea how the hell I was going to talk my way out of it. Perhaps I could claim I'd been so drunk that I didn't know what I was doing.

Or I could sneak out. Would they even notice if I crept silently down the hall and let myself out of the front door? I wasn't sure I could face them again. I hugged my knees to my chest and as the cistern finished filling up, I heard them talking. Did they realise I could hear them, their voices carrying from the kitchen? Were they talking about me? God, what were they saying? I shuffled across the floor and put my ear to the door.

'How was I to know?' Frank sounded defensive.

'You could have killed her.'

'Don't be melodramatic. It was a warning shot. Anyway, what's she even doing her?'

'I don't know, Frank,' Esme said, sounding exasperated. 'She's drunk.'

'I should have put cameras up.'

'You're overreacting.'

'Am I?' Frank raised his voice. 'You want to be safe here or not?'

'You promised this was going to be a better life for us.'

'And it will be.'

Esme muttered something incomprehensible. I pushed my ear more firmly against the door.

'It won't be forever,' Frank said, his tone softening. 'We just need to keep our heads down for a little longer. It'll all be worth it in the end. Trust me.'

'Trust you? How the hell can I trust you, Frank, after the mess you've made?'

'That's not fair.'

Why was he talking about putting cameras up? It was almost as if he'd been expecting someone to be prowling around outside. Maybe Frank hadn't threatened me with the gun because he was angry, but because he was scared. But of what?

'I don't like you having a gun in the house,' Esme said, her voice becoming fainter as if she'd walked away from her husband.

'And I don't like you questioning my decisions all the time.' Now Frank sounded angry.

'Don't raise your voice at me like that,' Esme said.

'And get rid of that girl. I don't like her here. Do we even know she is who she says she is?'

'You're being paranoid,' Esme said.

I'd heard enough. I thought I knew what was going on between Frank and Esme, but now I wasn't so sure. For the first time since I'd bumped into Esme on the beach, I had the sense I'd stumbled into something over my head. I didn't know what I'd got myself caught up in. Although I knew was that I wanted to go home. I needed some space to think things through. I washed my hands noisily, hoping they'd hear I was done.

When I walked back into the kitchen, they were standing in stony silence. 'I ought to get going,' I said, noticing the red stain on the wall had been washed off. No evidence left of what had gone on between them.

'Look, if you need to talk, we can sort something out,' Esme said. She put a friendly hand on my arm. 'But you mustn't come here again. Do you understand? It's not appropriate.'

I nodded, lowering my gaze to the floor.

'Why don't you call me in the morning and book another appointment?' she added. 'We can talk properly about what's really troubling you. How does that sound?' She'd adopted the same soothing tone she'd taken with me at Shurland Hall. Her counsellor's voice.

'Thank you for the water,' I said, remembering my manners.

'Where do you live?' Frank asked. He'd calmed down a little.

'Leysdown,' I said. 'I share a caravan with a friend.'

'Let me give you a lift home,' he said. 'I'll make sure you get back safely.' He pushed himself off a worktop.

'Really, there's no need,' I said. The thought of being alone with Frank in a car gave me the chills.

'I insist. It's no trouble.'

'I like to walk,' I said, firmly. 'It helps clear my head. And it's not far.' I didn't feel drunk anymore. Fear and adrenaline had burned off most of the alcohol.

'You can't walk home on that ankle,' Esme said. 'Let Frank drive you.'

'And besides, you're in no fit state to be wandering around on your own.' Frank marched into the hall.

I heard him pick up a bunch of keys and unlock the front door like it was settled and there was no point arguing. At least it wasn't far. And Esme was right, my ankle was still tender.

'I mean it, Sky,' Esme said. 'I think another session to pick up where we left off about your mother would be a good idea. Call me tomorrow? Promise?'

'Sure,' I said, although I didn't need, and couldn't afford, another appointment. Couldn't she see this wasn't about me? It was about the way Frank treated her. I'd seen a different side to their relationship tonight, heard things I wasn't supposed to hear, but I was still scared for her. Something wasn't right between them. I'd come to the house to help Esme, to find some evidence of Frank's abuse. Instead, he'd nearly shot me. I kicked myself. I'd failed again.

Esme leaned in to kiss me on the cheek like we were old friends. 'Goodnight, Sky.'

'I saw what he did,' I whispered in her ear as she came close.

'What?'

'I saw him throw a plate at your head.' At least I think I saw it.

A glimmer of a confused smile passed Esme's lips. 'No, you didn't.'

'I did,' I said. Why couldn't she just admit she needed help?

'Come on, let's get you home. It's late. We'll pick this up at our next session and we can work out why you're having these fantasies — '

'They're not fantasies.' I gripped her arm tightly. I had to make her understand. 'Don't you get it? I read your diary, Esme. I know what Frank does to you. I want to help you.'

'Are you coming?' Frank's voice bellowed from the hall.

'Sky, stop! It's all in your imagination. And you're drunk. Go home. Sleep it off. You'll feel better in the morning.' Her soothing tone had given way to some-thing harder edged. She was angry with me. I wasn't getting through to her.

'But Esme — '

'Goodnight, Sky.'

CHAPTER TWENTY-SEVEN

I flinched as Frank slammed his door shut, cowering in my seat with my heart racing. At least he didn't speak to me as we pulled away, up the drive and through the gates that magically swung open as we approached them. The silence hung heavy between us, but I kept my eyes fixed ahead. We crawled along the potted dirt track and only finally hit smooth tarmac when we reached the main road.

When Frank did eventually speak, his tone wasn't exactly friendly. 'Let me make one thing absolutely clear,' he said. 'I never want to see you at the house again. And if I do, I won't miss next time.'

I swallowed hard but didn't give him the satisfaction of responding.

'Whatever problems you're going through, you stay away from my wife. Got it?'

I bit my lip. His presence was suffocating. I couldn't believe I'd agreed to get into the car with him. I willed him to stop and let me out but couldn't find the strength to speak.

'Esme's going through a tough time right now and doesn't need a wacko like you stalking her.' He glanced at me, taking his eyes briefly off the road. I nodded. Anything to make him stop talking. 'We have an understanding, then? Stay away or I'll make your life a living hell.'

Why was he being so unpleasant? He'd made his point, and I'd apologised. It wasn't like I was stalking Esme. But at least he was proving my suspicions correct. He had a nasty streak and now he was showing his true colours. No wonder Esme was terrified of him.

'I mean it, Sky. You don't want to make an enemy of me.'

I thought about all the times he'd probably hit her. Shut her down when she dared speak out of turn. Cut her off from her friends. Her family. He was evil dressed up like a regular guy, someone you wouldn't look at twice if you passed him in the street. Grey hair. Sensible shoes. Lamb's wool sweaters. But it was a con. I knew what he was like inside. And it made my skin crawl. And who the hell was he calling me a wacko? I couldn't sit there and say nothing. 'I know what you are,' I breathed, the words slipping from my lips before I could stop them.

He glanced at me again. In the corner of my eye, I saw him frowning. 'What's that supposed to mean?'

'You know,' I said.

'Esme's right, you are a fantasist. I don't know what

you think's going on, but it's all in your head.'

'You're an abuser.'

'A what?' He almost choked.

'I know men like you. I know what you've been doing to Esme. That's why I was at the house if you really want to know. I'm going to get her away from you and take her somewhere you can never hurt her again.'

Frank hit the brakes so hard my seatbelt locked, and my head snapped back, hitting the head restraint with a dizzying thud.

'What did you say?'

'You'll never be able to hurt her again,' I said, rubbing the back of my neck.

He pulled off the road and swivelled to face me, the knuckles of his right hand turning white on the steering wheel. 'You think I've been mistreating Esme? Where the hell did you get that idea?'

'It's all in her diary. And that was before what I saw tonight,' I said, growing in confidence. I had him rattled, and it felt good.

Frank's eyes narrowed as he studied my face. 'What did you see tonight exactly?'

'I saw you throw that plate at her.'

'*Me*?' To his credit, he sounded incredulous. Not a bad bit of acting, but it didn't fool me. 'You saw *me* throw a plate at Esme?'

I nodded.

'Really? That's priceless.' He laughed. 'When Esme said you were fucked up, I didn't believe it, but that's some imagination.'

'Don't waste your breath denying it,' I said. 'I have pictures,' I added as an afterthought.

'Show me.'

'Alright.' I scrolled through the photos on my phone and found the clearest one of the plate smashed on the floor and the blurry red mark on the wall. I shoved my phone under his nose. 'There. See?'

He glared at the image. 'I didn't throw that plate,' he said, lowering his voice. 'Esme threw it at me.'

'Yeah, whatever, Frank. I'm not an idiot.' I snatched my phone back, my anger simmering. How dare he try to deny it and blame it on her. The least he could do was man up and admit I'd caught him out.

'I've never hit Esme. I could never do anything like that to her,' he said. 'Did she ever tell you I hit her? Or do anything other than worship the ground she walks on?'

I thought about the words in Esme's diary, the words that had been spiralling around my brain ever since I'd made the mistake of reading them.

I see I should have left him months ago. Is it so awful that sometimes I want to kill him?

'She's scared of you. She knows how you'd react if she told anyone,' I said.

Frank shook his head. 'It's not true. Yes, we argue. Sometimes things get thrown. It's complicated,' he said, scratching his head. He almost sounded convincing. 'The fact is, Esme has a spiteful temper and when she doesn't get her own way, she lashes out. Usually at me.'

'*You?*' I sneered. It was pathetic. Trying to make out that he was the victim. It made me sick.

'It's not something any man wants to admit,' he said. 'But it's true. I know deep down she loves me, but you're wrong if you think I'd ever do anything to hurt her. I love her too much.'

'You're lying,' I said, as I replayed the events of the evening through my head. The raised voices. Esme fleeing upstairs in tears. The broken plate. The smear on the wall.

He sighed. 'To be honest, Sky, I don't care what you think. But I was serious when I said I want you to keep away from us.'

Frank composed himself, pulled his shoulders back and put the car in gear. As we pulled away, I watched him, as if by staring hard enough I could peer through his skin and read the truthful essence of his soul. It didn't seem like he was lying and he certainly sounded plausible, but he would say that, wouldn't he? It was a classic deflection, but I wasn't stupid. I could see through his lies.

We drove on for the next few minutes in silence, but several questions still rattled around my head.

'Why do you keep a gun in the house?' I asked.

He shrugged. 'Can't be too careful.'

'You're scared of something, aren't you? What is it?'

He laughed like I was being stupid, but there was no hiding the nervousness in his eyes. 'I don't know what you're talking about. We're in a remote spot. An easy target for intruders,' he said. 'I keep the gun for security.'

'I heard you and Esme talking,' I said. 'While I was in the bathroom.'

Frank's grip tightened on the steering wheel, but he said nothing.

'Is someone looking for you?' I asked.

'Don't be daft. Now where's this caravan park?' he said, turning onto the promenade, past the Golden Sands Amusement Arcade.

'You can drop me off on the roundabout,' I said, as we approached the entrance to the holiday park I called home.

He pulled up, mounting the kerb. I jumped out as the car came to a halt, relieved the journey was over.

'Remember,' he said, winding down the window. 'Keep away from the house and from my wife. I never want to see you again.'

I watched his Range Rover roar off with my heart still pumping hard. As it disappeared into the distance, I took a deep breath to calm my nerves. The implicit threat in his warning to keep away should have made me run a mile. I never wanted to face Frank Winters and his shotgun again, and yet after everything that had happened over the last few hours, I knew I wouldn't be able to resist. Frank scared me, but there was definitely something going on between him and Esme. I was determined to find out what it was. There was no way I could simply walk away and forget about them. Absolutely no way.

CHAPTER TWENTY-EIGHT

It was gone two in the morning when Hanlon slipped out of his van and limped across the road with his head down. He crept up the path to Huxley's front door, past his BMW on the drive, and knelt on the doorstep with a small torch and a length of bamboo he'd bought earlier from a DIY store. He'd screwed a brass hook into the end of it and fastened it in place with a tight wrapping of tape.

He listened at the door, checking the house was in silence. Nobody up fetching a glass of water or watching TV because they couldn't sleep. Satisfied, he poked open the letterbox and shone the torch into the darkness, lighting up the bottom of the stairs and a messy pile of shoes in the hall. Several pairs of trainers, a pair of women's court shoes and a single black brogue, kicked off and left scattered messily across the floor. To the left of the stairs, wedged up against the wall, was a small, wooden table cluttered with a stack of unopened mail, three framed family photos and a vase of wilting flowers. Next to the vase was the prize he'd come looking for; Huxley's bunch of keys, casually tossed on the side.

With the care and dexterity of a surgeon, he threaded the bamboo cane through the letterbox and inched it towards the table with his heart racing, aware that one careless move could knock the keys flying onto the floor with a noise loud enough to wake a sleeping house.

Inch by painful inch he edged the hook closer until it appeared to be hovering directly above the keys. But in the darkness and with an obscured view, distance was difficult to judge accurately. It was like being a kid in an amusement arcade trying to hook out a soft toy with a mechanically controlled claw, trying to work out the angles and the distances by peering around the tank, stretching to keep your fingers on the control buttons. Except the stakes were much higher with his deadline to locate Duncan Whittaker looming.

Hanlon steadied himself. He wet his lips and held his breath. He lowered the cane. The hook brushed across the keys, nudging them perilously close to the edge of the table. He swore silently and reset himself, feeding the cane in another half an inch.

He lowered it again, angling it to line up with the looping metal ring the keys were bunched on, sweating with the concentration and effort, his t-shirt damp and perspiration beading on his forehead. Every tiny adjustment he made seemed to produce a much bigger movement at the other end of his homemade snare. His shoulder and upper arm ached, and his knee on the hard doorstep was screaming at him. But he put his discomfort aside to focus.

Closing one eye, he edged the hook delicately to the left. It slipped through the keyring. He rolled his wrist. Swivelled the cane to snag it. The keys rattled as they lifted off the table. Hanlon let out the breath he'd been holding and blinked away the stinging sweat that had rolled into his eyes. Almost there.

A floorboard squeaked in a room above. Hanlon froze, his muscles stiff with tension. Someone was out of bed. He killed the torch, thumbing it off with one hand, and waited. Footsteps crossed the landing. A door opened. The creak of a hinge. If they came downstairs, they'd spot the cane immediately. It put him in a dilemma. Hold his nerve and hope whoever it was stayed upstairs? Or drop the keys, withdraw his hook and risk making a noise?

A door opened. Closed again. A lock snapped into place. Hanlon breathed fast and shallow, a hard knot in his throat. The tinkle of water. Stop. Start. Someone clearing their throat. A man? Huxley? A flush being pulled, filling the house with noise. The lock snapping back. A door opening. Footsteps. The creak of the floorboard. And then...

Silence.

Hanlon counted to ten, forcing himself not to rush. He flicked his torch back on and noticed he'd inadvertently lowered the keys close to the tabletop. He lifted them. Retracted the hook, slowly, carefully, wincing with every jangle, until the keys were at the letterbox. He reached in and pulled them out, wrapping his hand around them tightly. Success.

The low rumble of tyres on asphalt warned him a vehicle was approaching. He ducked behind Huxley's BMW and watched a taxi roll into view. It halted a short distance up the road. A young couple spilled out, hanging on to each other, unsteady on their feet. She tottered on high heels, clutching a sparkly bag while he paid the driver. Hanlon kept low, hidden behind Huxley's car, and waited until the couple had let themselves into a house, giggling. The door slammed shut, and the taxi drove off. Hanlon scuttled across the street, back to his van, glad to reach its sanctuary.

He drove cautiously back into town, watching his speed. The last thing he needed was to be pulled up by a bored cop demanding to know why he was out so late.

He parked a short distance from the rental agency and covered the rest of the journey on foot with a baseball cap pulled down over his brow, hiding his face and doing his best to mask his limp. God knows where the CCTV cameras were positioned. They were all over these days, tracking your every move. He had to assume there were cameras on him now. Nothing he could do about it other than make it difficult for them to identify him.

He slipped on a pair of surgical gloves and pulled Huxley's keys from his pocket. He quickly found the two that unlocked the office door and let himself in. The security panel glowing green on the wall started beeping frantically, a countdown to a full-on alarm, a frantic reminder he only had seconds to act. He pushed the door closed and guessed at the code. Most people went for something memorable or didn't bother resetting the factory default.

He tried 0-0-0-0.

Nothing.

Something else, then.

1-2-3-4.

The pre-alarm continued to beep. Just his luck that Huxley was the one in ten who actually bothered setting the alarm with a unique code.

He jabbed the keypad with his finger for a third time.

9-9-9-9.

The beeping was getting louder and faster.

Hanlon dropped the bunch of keys in his panic. Swept them up in a hurry. If he couldn't disable the alarm, he'd have to make a run for it. How long did he have? Five seconds? Ten? He was about to put the keys back in his pocket, when he noticed a flat disc of plastic in the middle of the bunch. An electronic fob. Idiot. He should have noticed before. He swiped it across the keypad and a moment later it stopped beeping.

It had been close. Too close. He took a breath and exhaled slowly. Gave himself a moment to let his heart settle and slow.

With the light from his torch, he saw everything in

the office had been left exactly as he remembered. A charity collection box on the front counter. Two desks behind it pushed together. A monitor left on in Huxley's office glowing in the dark. And at the back of the main office, the rows of filing cabinets. Somewhere inside one of them was Duncan Whittaker's new identity and address. The problem was how to find it. Not quite a needle in a haystack, but not far off it.

Hanlon closed his eyes and visualised his encounter with the woman with the fake eyelashes who'd nearly given up the information to him. Which cabinet had she plucked Duncan's file from? The third from the right? No. The second. He was sure of it. Someone had even helpfully labelled it 'rentals'.

He moved cautiously, keeping his torch pointed low, the beam lighting his way across the floor. The top drawer of the cabinet opened smoothly. It was filled with cardboard suspension files and what looked like years of paperwork. Maybe a needle in a haystack after all. He studied them for a moment, looking for any sign that one had been recently pulled out and not put back properly. But it wasn't going to be that easy. All the files looked identical apart from that each had its own label slotted into a plastic tab, handwritten with a street name and filed in alphabetical order. Where the hell did he start?

His only clue was what the woman had let slip. Duncan was renting a house in Warden Bay, although it didn't narrow it down much. He started at the front, pulled out the first file and flipped it open. Details of a house in Leysdown. He put it back and tried the next. Same story. Again and again. It seemed hopeless.

He'd made it halfway through the files when he had another thought. He pushed the drawer shut and moved back across the office to the desk behind the counter where the woman had been sitting. Maybe she'd not put the file back.

Everything on her desk was neat. Pens bunched in a pot, computer keyboard lined up in front of her monitor, her phone at a slight angle, a red light blinking in the darkness. Hanlon shone his torch over a two-tier plastic in-tray and checked the three drawers in her desk. Nothing.

He slammed his hand against the back of her chair in frustration. Perhaps the better option might have been to have intercepted the woman after work. Put on a bit of charm. Flashed his warrant card again. She'd been so close to giving him the information. Too late now. He was here, and he had to find the file. No way was he going to admit to the Romanians that he'd failed.

He looked up and around. Maybe he'd missed something. If Huxley knew the file was important, had he put it somewhere for safekeeping? His gaze fell on Huxley's glowing computer screen. Maybe he'd put it aside until he'd found out why someone claiming to be a police officer had been asking about it.

Hanlon hurried into the pokey little side office, shouldering open the door. Huxley's desk was set up in the middle of the room with his chair positioned so he could see out of a window in the wall overlooking the front counter. A dusty pot plant in the corner. Framed certificates on the walls. A scruffy sofa under the window facing the desk.

The desk itself was uncluttered. A computer screen and keyboard. A mouse. Some pens, a stapler and some fluorescent-coloured sticky notes. But laying on top of the keyboard was a file. Hanlon allowed himself a satisfied smile as he picked it up, flipped it open and scanned the first page.

Rental details for a house in Warden Bay.

And at last, a name.

CHAPTER TWENTY-NINE

H anlon woke with a start a little after six, with his back stiff and his head woolly. He'd slept in the front seat of his van with his baseball cap pulled over his eyes, glad now he'd not bothered to pull out the bed in the back.

After returning Huxley's keys, threading them back through the letterbox and dropping them on the table where he'd found them, Hanlon had driven straight to Duncan's address. The house was in an isolated spot near the top of the cliffs at the end of a long dirt track. Nothing special. In fact, quite plain and anonymous compared to the big property in Essex. Scruffy garden. Weather-beaten window frames. A section of guttering hanging loose. He wasn't quite slumming it, but he wasn't exactly living the life of luxury either. A Range Rover with the personalised number plate, DW1 JWL, was parked up close to the front of the building, next to a sporty little Mercedes, both illuminated under the glare of a security light.

Hanlon had smiled to himself. The arrogance of the man to keep that number plate when he was supposed to be in hiding. What was he thinking?

He'd parked close to the house at the end of a dirt track. The advantages of travelling by campervan meant he could hide in plain sight. Just another tourist who'd found a quiet spot close to the beach. Although he couldn't see the house from the van, he had an excellent view of the top of the drive. His plan had been to grab a couple of hours' sleep and make a positive identification of Duncan first thing in the morning. All within his five-day deadline. Then he'd have to wait for further instructions. The fun bit.

Now, as he pushed the baseball cap off his face and rubbed his eyes, he realised the noise that had woken him was the clank of gates opening. The nose of Duncan's Range Rover appeared at the top of the drive, edging out onto the lane. Shit. Duncan was up and on the move already.

Hanlon snatched at the keys in the ignition, his heart racing. Where the hell was he going at this time in the morning? The Range Rover bumped and rocked down the potted lane as Hanlon pulled himself together. He yanked on his seatbelt and watched the car turn left onto the main road. When it had disappeared, Hanlon followed, gritting his teeth as the rough track threw him around inside the van.

Early mornings were always the worst time to tail

vehicles because of the lack of traffic. It didn't help that it was a Saturday. Quieter than normal. It meant Hanlon had to keep his distance with the Range Rover only just within sight. He'd lost the car once before and didn't want to repeat the mistake, but couldn't afford to let Duncan know he was being followed. And of course, the guy was going to be extra cautious, on the lookout for tails. At least in a tourist spot like the Isle of Sheppey, Hanlon's van stood out less than it might in the city.

At the junction with the fast road that ran the length of the island, Duncan turned right, towards Sheerness. Was he heading for the mainland? He didn't seem in any rush, so Hanlon doubted he'd been spooked. Maybe off to grab some milk or a newspaper. A supermarket run, perhaps? All he needed was to see Duncan's face, to make a positive identification before he called it in. Only one thing worse than failing to find his target, and that was identifying the wrong man.

Hanlon pulled out thirty seconds behind Duncan's car, as the Range Rover took a left down a meandering single-track lane. It wasn't the route Hanlon had expected him to take at all. He checked the sat nav. The road was a dead end, cutting through farmland and fields that didn't seem to lead anywhere. Curious, Hanlon followed, hanging back as far as he dared.

Duncan drove cautiously, his speed low, along a hedge-lined lane, cutting through fields and marshland as the southern tip of the island opened up in front of them.

After a couple of miles, the Range Rover finally pulled off into a deserted dirt car park, signposted as a viewing point for birdwatching. Funny, Hanlon hadn't put Duncan down as a twitcher. Hanlon pulled up at the side of the road, as the Range Rover parked and its lights went out. The man who climbed out of the 4x4 looked a lot like the guy in the photos of Duncan. Same grey hair. Fat nose. Ruddy cheeks. He was wearing a checked twill shirt, brown canvas trousers and dark coloured walking boots. He grabbed a Barbour jacket and a set of powerful binoculars from the back of the car, threw the jacket on and strung the binoculars around his neck. Hanlon double checked the picture he'd taken from Duncan's mother. Definitely the same guy.

'Gotcha,' Hanlon muttered to himself as he grabbed his phone from the passenger seat.

Duncan pressed his legs against a low wooden fence and put the binoculars to his eyes, scanning the wild, flat landscape fanning out before him as Hanlon dialled the pre-programmed number for the Romanian woman. She answered on the third ring.

'Da?'

'I've found Duncan Whittaker,' Hanlon said.

'Are you sure?'

'One hundred percent. What now?'

The woman hesitated as if she was gathering her thoughts. Had he woken her? It was still early, but she didn't sound at all sleepy. 'Deliver a message to him.'

'No problem.'

'Tell him he has twenty-four hours to return the money,' the woman said. 'Or you'll start taking his fingers.'

Pretty standard stuff. A threat with menaces. Nice. 'I can do that,' Hanlon said.

'And keep him under surveillance. Don't let him out of your sight now you've found him.'

'Goes without saying. And if he tries to run?' Hanlon asked.

'Stop him. Do whatever it takes.'

'You want me to collect the money?' Hanlon instinctively reached under his seat to check his knife. Fingers would be no problem.

'I'll give you further instructions tomorrow,' she said, hanging up.

Hanlon tossed the phone onto the dashboard and while Duncan was still pre-occupied with looking for whatever it was he'd come to see, he drove into the car park and pulled up alongside the Range Rover. Duncan lowered his binoculars and looked up, frowning.

Hanlon stepped out of the van with a smile, trying to look friendly. It wasn't a look that came easily.

'Lovely morning,' he said, as he slammed his door shut.

Duncan regarded him suspiciously. No wonder as he was still dressed in the dark clothing he'd put on to break into the estate agents' offices a few hours earlier. More cat burglar than birdwatcher. 'What are you hoping to see?'

'Marsh harrier,' Duncan said, pointing to a vague

shape drifting over a field, its wings beating languorously.

'Right,' Hanlon said with disinterest. It could have been the African savannah with herds of roaming elephants and lions hunting antelope under a majestic setting sun for all he cared. 'And what's that over there?' He pointed away to the right and as Duncan's head swivelled to follow his finger, Hanlon snatched the binoculars from his hand. Twisted the strap twice, so it tightened on Duncan's neck and left him gasping for air.

Duncan's eyes nearly popped out of their sockets with fear and surprise. His fingers grasped at the strap. Trying to loosen it. To catch his breath. His face turning berry red.

It was a genuine thrill to see the panic in his eyes. The sort of drug money couldn't buy. Hanlon wished sometimes he could bottle it. It was intoxicating. Electrifying. He took a deep breath, savouring the moment. Watching death approach. Finally, he released the pressure a little. Enough for Duncan to wheeze in a gasp of oxygen.

'You know who I am?' Hanlon asked.

'No,' Duncan said, coughing.

'You took some money that didn't belong to you,' Hanlon said. 'The people you stole from want it back.'

'I don't have it,' Duncan panted. 'Please, believe me.'

'You have twenty-four hours.' Hanlon checked his watch. 'Let's say by seven o'clock tomorrow morning. Repayment in full. No excuses.'

'I don't have it,' Duncan repeated, his body twisting and bucking.

Hanlon reapplied the pressure around his neck, bringing Duncan to his knees as a strangulated gurgling sound came from his throat. 'And if you can't find the money, I'll start taking your fingers. Understand?'

Duncan nodded vigorously. 'Okay, okay,' he choked.

'Good. Don't let me down now.'

Hanlon released his grip on the strap and Duncan crumpled to the floor, sucking in big lungfuls of air as he clutched at his throat.

'Remember, seven o'clock tomorrow morning.' Hanlon turned back to his van and had the door half open when he added, 'And don't try anything stupid. I'll be watching you like a hawk.'

CHAPTER THIRTY

I slept fitfully, my mind churning over the events at Frank and Esme's house; laying on the grass, staring down the barrels of a gun and the horrible car journey home trapped with Frank as he tried to make out Esme was the violent one. But I knew what I'd seen. He'd forgotten that. And I had the photos on my phone. He'd tried to put me off the scent and frighten me into keeping away. But it had only made me more determined to help Esme. I just needed a plan.

The insistent buzzing of my phone and the strains of an Ed Sheeran ringtone Amber had persuaded me to download roused me from sleep.

'We need you in for nine-thirty this morning.' I sat up and rubbed my eyes, Michelle's nasally drawl like fingernails across a chalkboard. 'Jimmy's coming in early for your disciplinary. Don't be late.'

I groaned, wide awake now. 'Are you sacking me?'

'Nine-thirty,' Michelle repeated and hung up.

It didn't sound good. I needed the job and I could have done without the hassle today. Esme's safety was all I cared about. I couldn't be distracted from that, no matter what was going on in my life. I kept thinking about the way Frank spoke to me. The fear as he stood over me with the shotgun. The threats. The contempt in his eyes as he drove me home.

It was rare to have such clear memories after a night out drinking. For once I'd not drunk that much that I'd blacked out, probably because I'd not had anything more after those two beers in the kitchen with Cam.

Cam. Oh, God.

With all the drama with Frank and Esme, I'd forgotten what an idiot I'd been, throwing myself at him like I was desperate.

I ran a hand over my face and checked the time on my phone. Already gone eight. Early for me but my hair needed a wash, so I ignored the temptation to snatch another thirty minutes' shut eye and threw off the covers. I needed to make myself look presentable if I was going to make a good impression on Jimmy.

I stretched and yawned, swinging my legs out of bed. As I stood, I felt a sharp twinge in my ankle. When I looked, it was swollen, but at least I could put weight on it. I hobbled out of my room, expecting to find Amber pottering around. She was usually an early riser, but there was no sign of her. Had she even come home last night? After the fight between Marc and Aaron, I should have stayed, been the friend she would have been to me, instead of abandoning her at the party. I checked my phone for missed calls, but as there weren't any, I assumed things had worked themselves out and Amber had stayed over.

I knocked on her door and stuck my head into her room. Her bed hadn't been slept in, confirming my suspicions. I'd call her later to check everything was alright. I was sure she'd have a good story to tell, but for now I needed to concentrate on not being late for work for once.

As I showered and dressed, pulling on clean clothes, I felt more optimistic than I'd been yesterday. I'd done the right thing when I'd left the booth to help that kid being bullied. What kind of monster would I have been if I'd stood by and watched as those other kids attacked him? It wasn't my fault someone saw an opportunity to snatch the cash. And it was only money. I'm sure Jimmy Steele could afford it.

When I arrived at the arcade, the shutters were down, and the only sign of life was the seagulls padding up and down the pavement outside. I approached slowly, still hobbling a little on my weak ankle. I repeated a mantra over and over in my head: everything was going to be alright. So why didn't I feel it?

I went to the side door, knocked and waited for what felt like an eternity with my palms damp and my nerves jangling. Eventually Michelle answered, her face stony. I tried to read her expression to work out if they'd already made a decision. Had they summoned me to be fired? Or were they interested in hearing my side of the story?

'Goes to show you can be on time when you put your mind to it,' Michelle sneered.

I gave her a wan smile. Bloody cow.

'Jimmy's in his office. Follow me.'

I traipsed up the back stairs with heavy legs, my heart in my mouth. I flicked my fringe out of my eyes and focused on being positive. I desperately wanted to make a good impression and to make them understand I had no choice but to leave the booth. And it really had only been for a minute or two.

Michelle knocked on the door to Jimmy's office, waited for a second, then pushed it open.

'Sky's here,' she said, ushering me in.

Jimmy was at his desk, wiry grey chest hair poking out from an open-necked shirt, his paunch hanging over the top of his trousers. I'd always thought something was a bit off about him with his perma-tan and his unhealthy interest in the girls in the arcade. I don't think he'd ever crossed the line with any of us, but he was overly familiar. A bit too touchy feely. I smiled, hiding how much I disliked him.

The guy was crazy rich. Supposedly he'd made his money in property. According to Michelle, he owned half the town. It was no wonder he lived in a place like Shurland Hall. Michelle reckoned he had holiday homes in Spain too and owned his own helicopter. And a yacht. I don't think he was married though. I'd certainly heard no mention of a wife, at least.

Jimmy looked up and smiled grimly, like a police officer about to deliver bad news. It didn't fill me with much hope. 'Sit down.' He waved me to a chair against a wall.

Michelle stood by the door, guarding the entrance, hands behind her back, the shadow of a faint, smug smile creeping across her face. She was loving this.

'I have to say we take a very dim view of your behaviour yesterday,' he said, lacing his fingers across his corpulent stomach.

'I can explain — ' I said.

But he held up a hand to stop me. 'While your back was turned, several trays of coins were taken. Is that correct?'

'Yes, but it was — '

'That's a dereliction of duty. To leave your booth was unforgivable, and the fact a substantial sum of money was taken means we've no option but to consider disciplinary action,' Jimmy said.

My heart sunk into my boots. They were going to sack me after all. 'I'm sorry about the money, Mr Steele, but I only left it for a moment because there was a kid being bullied outside.' I hadn't intended to beg for my job. It was pathetic and demeaning, but I couldn't help myself. 'Please don't sack me.'

'Kid?' Jimmy raised an eyebrow.

'I don't know who he was, but when I saw him being picked on by these bigger kids, I thought they were going to hurt him. I only stepped out for a second.

And when I got back, the money was gone. I reported it straightaway.'

Jimmy leaned back in his chair. The intensity of his gaze making me feel like I'd been shrunk to half my normal size. I glanced down at my hands in my lap and picked at my fingers.

'You understand this is such a serious offence the termination of your contract is something we need to consider?' he said.

Come on, really? I don't even remember signing a contract. I'd found the job advertised in the back of a local paper and had a brief chat with Michelle when I popped in to enquire about the position. She'd offered it to me on the spot and I'd started the following day. After a couple of hours' training, she left me to get on with it. I'm sure I never signed anything. At least not that I could remember.

'Why didn't you ask one of the others to cover for you?' Jimmy asked.

'I looked but I couldn't see anyone.'

'In which case, you shouldn't have left the booth.'

'It all happened so quickly, I wasn't thinking,' I said, hoping Jimmy would take pity on me.

'And your lack of thought has cost the arcade the best part of a hundred pounds,' he said.

'I'll pay it back,' I said, even though I didn't have that kind of money.

'It's not that simple. This is a serious offence,' Jimmy said, his brow knotted.

'I'll do better in future. I promise,' I said. 'It'll never happen again.'

Jimmy sucked in air through his teeth like he was wrestling with his decision. Maybe all hope wasn't lost. He was wavering. I could see it. 'Please, Mr Steele,' I pleaded.

'Michelle, what do you think we should do?'

Before Michelle could answer, a loud knock on the office door made us all jump. The door swung open, almost knocking Michelle off her feet.

'Jimmy, I need to talk to you.' Esme bowled into the room, a little out of breath and her face pale. 'Oh, I'm sorry. I didn't realise you were in a meeting. The back door was open.' She glanced at me and Michelle and back to Jimmy again.

He sprang out of his chair. 'That's okay. What is it?'

'Can I speak to you alone?'

I glanced down at my feet. Esme had stormed in, but it felt like *I* was intruding on something private between them.

'Can you give me five minutes? I'm just finishing up something here,' Jimmy said.

Esme looked at me again and narrowed her eyes as if she'd not recognised me at first. 'Yes, of course. I shouldn't have barged in like that. I'll wait downstairs.'

I smiled weakly at her, but she ignored me, turning on her heel and pulling the door shut behind her as she left.

'Sorry about that,' Jimmy said, retaking his seat. He

chewed his lip and glanced out of the window, distracted momentarily by his own thoughts.

What the hell was that all about? Something to do with the room rental at Shurland Hall? And then a chill ran through me, a flush warming my neck. What if she'd come to complain about me turning up at the house last night? If she told Jimmy that Frank had caught me sneaking around their garden drunk, he would surely sack me, never mind about the stolen money. But then, what did it have to do with Jimmy? What I did in my own time was my business. It had to be something else then. Frank? Was Esme here to confide in him he was abusing her? She'd point-blank denied it to me, so why would she choose to confess to Jimmy?

'Where were we?' Jimmy asked, clearing his throat.

'You were asking for my opinion,' Michelle chipped in.

'Hmmm?' Jimmy said, like he'd forgotten she was even in the room.

'I think Sky's had plenty of chances in the past, but this is the last straw — ' Michelle continued.

But Jimmy cut across her. 'I'll tell you what we're going to do,' he said. He slapped his hands on his knees. 'We all make mistakes. I'm prepared to give you another chance.'

'Mr Steele!' Michelle blurted out.

'Thank you, Michelle.' He raised a hand to silence her. 'Given this is your first disciplinary offence, I think it would be harsh to let you go. I'm going to issue you with a formal caution in the form of a written warning. It will go down on your records, of course, and will be taken into consideration should there be any further disciplinary issues in the future. Do you understand?'

They kept records? That was news to me, but at least he wasn't firing me. 'I can keep my job?' I asked, hardly able to believe it.

'Yes,' he smiled. 'But don't do anything like that again.'

'I won't,' I gasped. In the corner of my eye, I saw Michelle's face turn sour, like she'd been sucking on a lemon.

'And given the mitigating circumstances, I think it would be unfair to dock your wages,' Jimmy added. 'Michelle, can you sort out the paperwork?'

Michelle's mouth dropped open.

'And send Mrs Winters up on your way down,' he added.

The look on Michelle's face was priceless. 'Yeah, sure,' she said, trying to sound casual but you could see how much it pissed her off to be spoken to like she was his skivvy.

Esme was waiting at the bottom of the stairs, pacing up and down, her arms folded. She glanced up when she heard us coming down.

'Hey, Esme,' I said brightly, still buzzing from my reprieve.

She gave me a tight smile. 'Sky,' she said with a subtle nod. Her gaze drifted up the stairs towards Jimmy's office as she fingered her beautiful necklace.

'You can go up now,' Michelle said, deadpan.

Esme shot past us, rushing up the stairs and straight into the office, the door closing behind her.

'What the hell was that about?' Michelle said.

I wasn't sure if she'd aimed the question at me or if she was thinking out loud. But I was wondering the same thing. Something was clearly on Esme's mind, but I had absolutely no idea why she needed to speak to Jimmy so urgently.

CHAPTER THIRTY-ONE

I didn't care about the written warning. I'd kept my job. The bonus was watching the way Jimmy had treated Michelle and completely undermined her authority. It brought a smile to my face as I hauled up the heavy steel shutters, switched on the lights and powered up all the machines. In no time at all, I'd brought the arcade to life with sound and light.

But as I settled into my booth, sorting my float into the plastic trays, I thought about Esme again. She'd been in my thoughts so much recently, but now I had a new puzzle to ponder. Why had she come to see Jimmy? Surely, she wasn't telling him what I'd done last night? I pushed the thought away. It had nothing to do with him. Jimmy Steele couldn't tell me what I could and couldn't do in my own time.

All I could do was get on with my job, and as I waited for the first customers of the day, I hummed a tune that had wormed its way into my head from the party. Oh God, the party. With everything else that had happened, I'd almost forgotten about Amber. That fight between Marc and Aaron had been sickening to watch. I wondered how the rest of the evening had played out. I thought about calling her, but I didn't want to be caught on my phone at work, not after I'd been given a second chance. It wasn't worth the risk.

And yet I couldn't shake the niggling feeling that something wasn't right. It wasn't like Amber to go to ground, but she hadn't called or texted and the last time I'd seen her she'd been in tears trying to pull Aaron and Marc apart, when I'd walked away and left her to deal with the fallout on her own. If it had been the other way around, there would have been no way Amber would have left me.

'Sky, I'm glad I caught you.' Esme's voice startled me from my thoughts. She approached my booth from the direction of the back office, with a broad, friendly smile. It was like she was a totally different woman to the tense and shifty one I'd seen in Jimmy's office earlier. 'I wanted to talk to you about last night.'

My heart skipped a beat. I was right. She had been complaining to Jimmy about me. 'I'm really sorry,' I mumbled. 'I shouldn't have gone to your house. I'd had too much to drink and… It won't happen again.'

'No, you don't understand,' she said, still smiling. 'It's me who should be apologising.' She pressed a palm to her chest. 'I'm afraid Frank is a little on edge at the moment. And when he saw you in the garden in the dark, he over-reacted.'

My mouth opened and closed like a goldfish, but no words came out. Where the hell was this coming from? The change in her attitude was nothing short of miraculous.

'You're going through a tough time, especially with everything that happened with your mum. I've no idea what Frank was doing, threatening you like that. I've told him he's got to get rid of that gun,' Esme continued.

'It's fine,' I muttered, totally thrown by the change that had come over her. Her last words to me at the house were to accuse me of being a fantasist. Did this mean she was finally ready to admit Frank was abusing her?

'No, it's not,' she said. 'It's unacceptable. Can you imagine if he'd actually shot you?' She laughed, but I didn't see the funny side. 'Anyway, the point is we'd like to make it up to you.'

What the hell? Make it up to me. Was I dreaming? 'There's no need,' I mumbled. 'Honestly.'

'I insist. We'd like you to come to dinner. Our treat, to say sorry.'

Dinner? Was she kidding? Frank had made it blatantly clear that if he ever saw me at the house again, he'd kill me. Was it a test? A joke? I didn't know how to react.

'Are you free tonight? Please, say yes.'

'I don't know,' I said, my mind whirling. What was the rush? Something felt off.

'I wasn't going to do anything fancy. Just a casserole. Shall we say be at ours for seven?'

My head was spinning so fast, but I couldn't think of a polite excuse, and I found myself agreeing to go, even though there wasn't anything I'd rather do less.

'Wonderful. Frank will be delighted. He feels awful. We'll see you at seven then.'

Before I had the chance to protest, she trotted off in a waft of expensive-smelling perfume. I watched her leave, stunned. It was so weird. Dinner with Frank and Esme? After my last experience with them at their house, it sounded like hell on earth. And yet I was intrigued.

What were they playing at?

CHAPTER THIRTY-TWO

B y midday, I'd still not heard from Amber. No missed calls. No texts. No messages. And when I tried calling during my lunch hour, her phone went straight to voicemail.

'Amber, it's Sky,' I said. 'I'm worried about you. Call when you pick this up, okay?'

I hung up with a dark sense of foreboding. It was so uncharacteristic of her. My mind went into overdrive, imagining the worst, picturing her cold, dead body washed up on the beach.

I was over-reacting. It had only been a few hours. I was sure there was a perfectly reasonable explanation. I just couldn't understand what it might be.

I fired off a text message for good measure.

Hey hun, what's going on? Are u ok? Call me when you get this.

I watched the message send and waited in vain for confirmation it'd been delivered. Only one greyed out tick. Her phone was either switched off or dead. An image of her pale, limp fingers wrapped around the phone as her body lay undiscovered, her eyes wide and staring, flashed through my mind. I screwed my eyes shut and willed the image away. She'd be fine. Probably hanging out somewhere quiet, licking her wounds. Or making up with Marc. No reason at this stage to think anything worse than that. And yet the needles of worry pricked at my insides. Was it too soon to raise the alarm? Would the police even take it seriously if it was less than twenty-four hours since I'd seen her? Probably not.

After lunch, I left my phone out, half-hidden behind a box of tissues on the counter. If Amber called or texted, I wanted to know straightaway. Michelle had hardly shown her face in the arcade all day, no doubt embarrassed by the way Jimmy had spoken to her in front of me, so the risk of her catching me with my phone was slim.

When my relief cover arrived at five, I couldn't get away fast enough. I grabbed my bag and phone and rushed to the staff room to collect my coat. I decided that if Amber wasn't at home, I'd call the police. It would have been almost twenty-four hours since I'd last seen her, and as I didn't have Marc's number, it was the only thing I could think to do.

Michelle caught me as I was leaving. 'Don't be late tomorrow,' she said. 'Remember, I have my eye on you.'

Yeah, yeah, whatever. 'I'll do my best,' I said.

'I mean it, Sky. You were lucky to get away with a warning this morning.'

I wanted to scream at her to get off my back. I had far bigger concerns on my mind than worrying about being a couple of minutes late for work. My best friend was missing, and I was supposed to be going to dinner with a man who'd threatened to kill me. So I said nothing, brushing past Michelle on my way out with a roll of my eyes that I hope she didn't catch. In my haste to leave, I almost didn't notice the forlorn figure standing on the steps outside, her hair a lank mess and her face streaked with make-up.

'Amber!'

She looked dreadful, like she'd been sleeping rough, if she'd slept at all. She was still wearing the clothes she'd had on at the party; a short skirt and high heels that looked completely inappropriate for a late afternoon in the middle of Leysdown's tourist strip. She was hugging herself tightly, tears streaming down her cheeks.

'What the hell's happened? Are you okay?' I asked, relieved that at least she wasn't dead. 'I was worried sick about you. I've been calling and texting.'

I wrapped her in my arms. She was so thin. All bone and sinew. Sobs racked her body.

'I needed some time to think,' she said. 'I had my phone switched off.'

'Where have you been?'

'A friend let me crash on their floor last night,' she said. 'I've spent most of the day walking around, trying to make sense of everything.' She burst into another torrent of tears.

'Hey, what's wrong?' I held her at arm's length, trying to read her face. I'd never seen her so upset.

'Everything's turned to shit. My life's over,' she bawled.

'Why? What's happened?'

'Marc found out I'd slept with Aaron and now they both hate me.'

'Slow down,' I said. 'You slept with Aaron?'

'It was a stupid one-night thing but Marc found out and now he's done something really bad,' Amber continued without drawing breath.

'What do you mean? What's he done?'

'Ruined my life. What am I going to do?'

I brushed the hair away from her face. 'Look, whatever it is, whatever he's done, I'm sure we can fix it.'

Amber shook her head. 'You can't fix this.'

'It can't be that bad, surely?'

'It's my fault. I should never have let him film us, but he said everyone did it. Now he's posted the footage online and everyone's going to know.'

My heart plummeted. 'Intimate videos of the two of you?'

'I'm such an idiot.'

How could anyone think of doing something so despicable to someone like Amber? She was the sweetest, most caring person I'd ever known. Marc must have known it would destroy her. And he did it anyway. I don't care how angry he was with her or how betrayed he'd felt. It was unforgivable. If I ever saw him again, I'd kill him.

'Can't you talk to him? Get him to take them down?' I said.

'It's too late. They'll be everywhere by now. Oh God, what if my parents find out?'

People walking past had noticed Amber's distress and had started to stare. I needed to get her home. 'Come on, let's get you cleaned up. We'll work this out together. Don't worry.'

'You can't work this out, Sky,' Amber wailed. 'Don't you understand?'

'Don't say that. I promise, we'll make this better. It seems bad now, but there must be something we can do.'

'No, there isn't. My life is finished,' Amber sobbed. 'I'll never be able to show my face anywhere again.'

We walked back to the caravan and while Amber was cleaning herself up, I ran to the off-licence for supplies of wine and vodka. It was going to be a long night.

When I returned, Amber was sitting staring into space on the U-shaped couch that formed a lounge at one end of the van. She'd washed the make-up off, tied her hair back and dressed in a comfortable pair of jogging bottoms and Barbie pink hooded top. She looked deathly pale, her spirit broken. Men could be such bastards.

'I trusted him,' Amber said, as I poured two large glasses of white wine.

'Men are all the same. They all end up screwing you over in the end. Have you thought about reporting it to the police?' I asked.

'No! I couldn't.'

'You have to tell someone.' I pulled out my phone and opened up the internet, hoping to find some advice. She wasn't the first girl with a scumbag for a boyfriend who'd done the same thing.

'What are you doing?' Amber asked, her voice going up an octave. 'You're not looking for them, are you? I don't want you to see them.'

'Of course not. I'm trying to find out what your options are,' I said, feeling like the tables had been turned. Normally Amber was the sensible one who looked out for me. It was good to do something positive for her after I'd abandoned her at the party.

I found a useful BBC article about revenge porn. 'Look, it says here that by posting those videos Marc's actually committed a criminal offence,' I said, showing her my phone. 'And there's a helpline you can call. Do you know where he's posted them, because it says you can apply to have them taken down and there's a right to be forgotten, too. It all looks pretty straightforward,' I said, doing my best to sound optimistic, even though I had my doubts it would be anything but easy.

Amber started crying again. She buried her head in her hands, despair seeping from every pore in her body.

'I know it doesn't feel like it right now, but this isn't the end of the world,' I said.

'That's easy for you to say. It's not your naked body plastered all over the internet.'

'No, but I'll help you. We'll do this together. We're not going to let a shit like Marc get away with this.'

'But everyone's going to know. How can I ever show my face in the town again?'

'You're stronger than that. You'll get through it. It seems bad at the moment, but we'll get it sorted. I promise.'

Amber shook her head. 'I just wish it would all go away.'

'And it will. Now have some more wine.' I fetched the bottle and topped up Amber's glass.

'At least you're on my side.'

It was the least I could do after walking away when Marc and Aaron were squaring up to each other. I'd been too caught up in my own drama. I could be so self-centred sometimes. 'Sorry I left you at the party,' I said. I couldn't look Amber in the eye, so I busied myself rummaging through the kitchen cupboards for two shot glasses. I cracked open the vodka and poured two shots.

'I shouldn't have dragged you along.'

'You thought you were doing the right thing, and anyway I'm big enough to make my own choices.'

'Why did you leave so early?'

I threw back a shot of vodka and winced as the alcohol hit my throat. 'Long story.'

'I've got all night.'

'Cam and I… ended up upstairs.'

Amber's eyes widened. 'You and Cam?'

'Don't get your hopes up. It's not what you think. I made a fool of myself. I'm sorry I didn't stay.'

'It's alright.'

'It's not though, is it? You've always been there for me and when you needed me, I wasn't around.'

'There's not much you could have done,' Amber said, sipping her shot. 'Forget it.'

But I had to explain to Amber why I'd left when she needed me most. It wasn't only about Cam. My head had been all over the place ever since I'd found Esme's diary. It had totally taken over my life. I didn't have the head space for anyone else's problems. 'Ever since I found out what Esme's been going through, it's brought back some bad memories,' I said.

Amber sat up straight, helping herself to more wine. 'What do you mean?' She looked horrified.

'My mum,' I said. I took a deep breath. It was time to tell Amber the truth. I should have told her before. 'Her partner killed her.'

'Jeez, seriously?'

'I found her in the kitchen.' I poured another vodka and drank it straight down. 'He'd beaten her to death, and I did nothing to stop him.'

Amber stared at me, open-mouthed. 'I don't know what to say.'

'You don't have to say anything, but I wanted you to know that's why the diary upset me so much. I should have said before. When I left the party, I went back to Esme's house. I was drunk, and I'd got it into my head that I could find some evidence her husband was abusing her. I thought if I had proof of what was going on, Esme would stop denying it to me.'

'And?'

'I overheard them having a huge row.' I poured another shot. 'Her husband caught me sneaking around the back garden and tried to shoot me.'

'Sky! Are you serious?'

'He said it was a warning shot,' I said. 'But the weird thing is Esme came to find me in the arcade earlier to apologise.' Shit. It had completely slipped my mind that I was supposed to be going there for dinner tonight.

'What's wrong?' Amber asked.

I shook my head, frowning. 'Esme wanted me to go around there tonight, for dinner, to apologise. But it's okay, I'm not going. I'm not leaving you on your own.'

'You have to go,' Amber said.

'No, I'm staying with you. You need me.' I couldn't abandon her for a second time.

'I'll be fine. I've got wine,' Amber said, holding up what was left of the bottle. 'And it sounds like Esme needs your help more than me.'

'It's not important.'

'Of course it is. Go.'

I was torn. Amber was the perfect excuse to back out of going, but the dinner would also be an opportunity to find out what was really going on between Esme and Frank. And her attitude towards me had changed so radically, I wondered if it was her way of reaching out to me to finally admit she needed help. 'Are you sure?'

'Of course I'm sure. Get ready or you're going to be late.'

CHAPTER THIRTY-THREE

The gates at the top of the drive were open this time; a welcoming invitation in, but as I approached the house a squeeze of apprehension gripped me. I couldn't imagine how the evening was going to go, me, Frank and Esme sitting awkwardly around a table making small talk about what exactly? The only thing we had in common was the one thing I couldn't persuade Esme to talk about.

Esme answered the door, pulling off a blue striped apron. Underneath it, she was wearing a pretty figure-hugging dress and, as always, her hair and make-up were perfect. I probably should have made more of an effort, but I was comfortable in jeans and she'd said it wouldn't be anything fancy. Should I have brought some flowers or chocolates, though? In my haste to make it on time, and dealing with Amber's crisis, the thought hadn't even crossed my mind.

'There you are,' Esme said, beaming. She leaned

over the threshold and kissed me on both cheeks before guiding me inside by my arm. 'Make yourself at home. Dinner's almost ready.'

As I followed her into the kitchen, I caught the aroma of something delicious cooking; onion, bacon and herbs. 'Smells good,' I said.

'It's nothing special. Only a chicken casserole. Drink?'

She was already pouring two large glasses of white wine before I could answer. I took a large mouthful to steady my nerves. It was refreshingly chilled and tasted expensive. Not like the cheap crap Amber and I usually drank. I took another sip, not sure where to stand so I wouldn't be in the way, desperately trying to think of something to say while Esme buzzed around, chopping vegetables and setting pans to boil on the hob. They'd set the long table in the conservatory with three places around a centrepiece of flickering church candles. Above it, fairy lights strung from the beams twinkled prettily. Each place had been laid with silver cutlery, glasses and stripy napkins. Esme had clearly gone to a lot of trouble for a meal she'd said was nothing special.

'Is Frank joining us?' I asked, hoping he might have been called out unexpectedly, leaving the two of us alone to chat woman-to-woman. Maybe over a meal and a drink I could finally persuade her to open up to me.

'He's upstairs getting ready. In fact, where the hell is he? I could do with his help.' Esme put her head around the door and bellowed up the stairs. 'Frank!

What are you doing up there? Our guest is here. I need you down here now.'

I stood up straight, shocked by how aggressively she'd called to him. When she came back, I took another large sip of wine, unable to look her in the eye, unsettled by her tone.

Footsteps thudded on the stairs. I forced myself to smile as Frank swept into the room dressed in jeans and a grey waistcoat over a garish floral-patterned shirt. But he didn't even make eye contact with me, let alone smile. Esme, busy at the stove, didn't seem to notice. I wondered if he'd been as keen as Esme had suggested to have me as a dinner guest.

He went straight to the huge American-style double-doored fridge and poured himself a glass of wine from the bottle Esme had opened.

'Where've you been?' Esme snapped. 'I could have used your help half an hour ago but as usual I've been left to do everything myself.'

There it was again. That sharp, aggressive tone that made my toes curl. Had they been fighting already?

'Don't start.'

I swallowed more wine.

'At least make yourself useful and finish the table. There's bread on the side that needs putting out, and put some butter on a dish,' Esme said. 'Think you can manage that?' she added, with a large dollop of sarcasm.

'Don't take that tone with me,' Frank hissed back at her.

I slunk away from the kitchen, embarrassed to witness their petty bickering, and drifted into the conservatory to drink in the view over the estuary. 'It's an amazing spot,' I said, hoping light conversation might diffuse the dark mood. 'So beautiful on an evening like this.'

Although it was already getting dark, the brooding sea, roughed up with choppy peaks and troughs by a slight breeze, contrasted against a moody sky.

'Yes, it's lovely, isn't it? I especially love it in the morning,' Esme said, 'when the sun rises.'

I wasn't normally up in time to see the sun rise, unless I'd pulled an all-nighter, but I imagined it must be stunning to watch from the house. I pictured a hazy, shimmering orb emerging from the horizon on a still summer's morning. 'I love living by the sea. It's so calming,' I said.

I could tell Esme wasn't listening. She was still fussing around the kitchen, making sure everything was just right.

'Have you lived here long?' I asked.

'No, we're newbies on the island.' She smiled weakly.

'Oh, where were you before?'

'Essex,' she said.

I'm sure I saw Frank stiffen and shoot her a barbed look. I couldn't understand what she'd said that he didn't like. Whatever it was, it went over my head, but the tension between them was palpable. I wondered if I should have come.

'What about you? How long have you lived here?' Esme asked.

'A couple of years now. I originally came with a friend for work,' I said. 'We lived together in London and she heard about some jobs going at one of the caravan parks, you know, seasonal work. So we packed up our stuff and moved down. I loved it and stayed. But she's gone back to London now. It was too quiet for her down here.'

After Esme had chopped up a pile of carrots into batons with a long knife, and scraped them into a pan, she handed Frank three plates which had been warming in the oven and ordered him to put them on the table.

'Is there anything I can do to help?' I asked.

'No, no, you're our guest tonight. You relax.'

As Frank leaned across the table, he knocked one of the empty wine glasses. It toppled over and smashed with a loud crack.

'For Christ's sake, Frank! Can't you do anything right?' Esme ranted like a woman possessed. 'Get out of the way. Let me clear it up.' As she physically shoved him away from the table, I noticed his fists clench, his knuckles turning white. He stared daggers at her but said nothing as she began picking up the jagged pieces of glass with her bare fingers, collecting them in her palm, the palm that was still bandaged from when she said she'd injured herself on a wine glass before.

'You'll cut yourself,' Frank said, his lips barely moving, his jaw clenched.

'Honestly, you're like a bull in a china shop. So

clumsy. It would have been easier to do it myself. There's glass everywhere now.' Her icy tone chilled me to the bone.

Frank threw his hands up in submission. 'Fine. Sort it out yourself then.' He stomped off into the kitchen to wash his hands, fury seeping out of every pore.

I stood like a statue, watching, unsure what to say or do. At least I was getting a picture of what he was really like.

'Careless, that's what you are,' Esme continued to rave.

The way she went on, it was like she was trying to provoke him into reacting. I had a feeling that if she'd pushed it much further, he would have gone off like a firecracker. She must have known she was goading him to the point where he might lose control and literally hit back. Did she get a thrill out of getting under his skin and riling him to raise his hand to her? Was that what it was like with my mother? Like Esme, she always spoke what was on her mind. She wasn't one to kowtow to anyone, even if it was a man who liked to settle arguments with his fists.

Esme threw the broken fragments of glass into the bin while Frank topped up my glass, and with the mess cleared up, she invited me to sit, her face flushed and beads of perspiration forming on her top lip. She brought a bright orange Le Creuset pot to the table and lifted the lid to reveal chicken quarters in a rich sauce.

'Dig in,' she ordered, returning to the kitchen to fetch enormous bowls of steaming rice and vegetables.

'It smells delicious,' I said, peering into the casserole pot and savouring the aroma, but I didn't like to help myself. After seeing the mood she was in and how she'd spoken to Frank, I was afraid she might start shouting at me. So I sat on my hands and waited.

Esme served me a healthy portion, far more than I thought I could manage, but I didn't want to cause offence, so said nothing.

'Frank, where's the red wine?'

Frank shot her another filthy look before scraping his chair back and grabbing a bottle open on the side.

'Red?' he asked, grumpily, showing me the label.

I didn't know the first thing about wine but nodded. What the hell. I'd have drunk anything to get through the torture of the evening.

He poured it into a fresh glass at my place, but as I reached for it, Esme started screaming again.

'Frank! That glass is dirty! You can't give that to her,' she said, snatching it away.

'It's fine,' I tried to say, as I sensed Esme's stress levels skyrocketing. It looked perfectly alright to me.

'Don't be silly, I'll fetch you another one.' She hurried back into the kitchen with it. She'd been up and down like a jack-in-the-box. Not exactly a relaxing meal so far.

As Esme ferreted through the cupboards looking for a clean glass, Frank started eating, shovelling meaty forkfuls of rice and chicken into his big mouth while I picked at my food, wishing the ground would open up underneath me.

'So, did you grow up in London?' Frank asked, surprising me with his attempt at conversation.

'Yes, I'd always lived in London before I came to the island,' I said. I tried to keep my life before coming to Kent as private as possible. Esme knew about my mum, but there was so much of my life that I wasn't proud of. I certainly didn't want to be quizzed on it. Least of all by Frank.

Esme handed me a fresh glass, which she'd filled with wine. She must have squeezed the best part of the bottle into it. 'Thank you,' I said, gratefully taking a big mouthful.

'Couldn't have you drinking from a dirty glass, could we?' Esme said, scowling at Frank. She sat down, puffed out her cheeks and flapped her napkin onto her lap. 'What do you think of it?'

I looked at her blankly, not sure what she was talking about.

'The wine,' she said. 'Do you like it?'

I lifted the glass to my lips and took another sip. I rarely drank red, but this one was delicious, although it had a slightly bitter aftertaste. 'It's good,' I said.

Frank looked up from his plate as I drank. 'Yes, but what do you taste?' he asked, like I'd said the wrong thing.

He was obviously one of those wine snobs. Just my luck. 'I–I don't know,' I stammered. 'I don't know much about wine.'

'You don't need to know about it,' Frank said. 'You just need to know what you like.'

239

'Drink some more,' Esme urged. 'Take a mouthful and let it sit on your tongue while you breathe through your nose. That's the best way to appreciate the flavours.'

I squirmed in my seat, wishing they'd leave me alone. It was wine. It was nice. But that was it. What more did they want from me?

'Come on. A big mouthful,' said Frank, tipping the glass up higher to my lips. 'Now don't swallow just yet. Let it sit in your mouth and describe what you taste.'

'Think about the flavours,' Esme said, her gaze so intense I couldn't look her in the eye.

It was really hard. All I could taste was red wine. 'Umm, blackberries?' I suggested, grasping for something to say.

'Good,' Frank said, nodding. 'What else?'

For God's sake, give me a break. 'Cinnamon?'

'Excellent!' Esme clapped her hands with glee. 'You have a talent for this.'

I did?

'You're getting the hang of it now,' Frank said. He smiled, but there was no humour behind it.

I didn't like their sudden attention, but I suppose it meant they weren't squabbling anymore, and the chill atmosphere had thawed a little. I took another mouthful, uncertain what they expected of me. Was it some kind of cruel game?

My cheeks and jaw were numb now from the alcohol. The backs of my thighs were hot and sweaty, and my head was swimming. Maybe hitting the vodka with

Amber before I'd come out had been a bad idea. The room swayed, and I flushed with a hot sweat. I wasn't feeling so good.

I wiped my forehead with my napkin and dropped it in my lap, my lips feeling as if they were swollen. What was wrong with me? I'd not drunk *that* much. I guess the wine was stronger than I was used to. Esme was watching me intently. Staring at me. Did I have something between my teeth? I glanced down at my plate, the rice and chicken fading in and out of focus. I scooped up a forkful and swallowed, thinking it might help soak up the alcohol.

'Try some more wine.' Esme's voice sounded faraway, like she was talking to me from another room. 'Really try to taste the subtle notes.'

I didn't want to upset her or risk her anger, so I reached for my glass again. Sipped it.

'You swallowed it without tasting it,' Frank said, slapping his hand noisily on the table, sounding disappointed. 'Try again.'

I really didn't want to. I wasn't feeling so great. My head was light and spinning and I was struggling to focus on anything in the room.

'I just need to — ' I said, my voice sounding detached from my body. 'Bathroom,' I slurred. ' … some fresh air.'

I pushed my chair back to stand, but my legs buckled. I grabbed the table. Tried to stop myself from falling. Knocked my plate flying. Rice and chicken sprayed across the floor. My head was thick. Heavy. Full of clay.

I opened my mouth to speak. But my jaw wouldn't work. The floor rushed up to meet me. My chair crashed backwards.

And then -

Blackness.

CHAPTER THIRTY-FOUR

The sound of my phone ringing interrupted a weird and rambling dream. I reached an arm out of bed, my fingers brushing soft carpet. But there was no carpet in my room. And the sheets smelt different.

Odd.

I peeled open my eyes and blinked at the strange surroundings; fussy wallpaper behind a white chest of drawers, pink flowers blooming on spindly, leafy stems and pretty blue birds with yellow chests.

My heart thumped hard and fast. My head was pounding and my lips were dry. I tried to remember how the evening had ended. There had been dinner, of course. An odd evening with tensions running high. Red wine. Blackberries and cinnamon. My knees buckling and a plate flying. I remembered hitting the ground. And then – nothing at all.

Drunk to the point of oblivion again. Frank and Esme must have put me to bed in a spare room because

I was incapable of making it home. I sank deeper into the soft mattress, pulling the duvet up to my chin. How was I going to face them after that performance? If only the bed could swallow me up and make me disappear. I was so embarrassed. At least I was in a warm bed with clean sheets and a thick duvet, even if I was brewing the hangover from hell.

When my phone rang again, it made me start. It felt early. Way too early for anyone to be calling. Although the first glimmer of daylight was teasing its way through the curtains, it was still dark. It was probably Amber worried that I'd not made it home last night. I hung off the mattress and fished around under the bed until my fingers located the phone, jammed up against a cardboard box where I guess I must have dropped it.

'Hello?' I said, my voice husky and raw.

'It's me,' whispered the voice on the other end of the line.

'Esme?' I propped myself up on my elbow, surprised she was phoning. Couldn't she have just knocked on the door?

'Are you okay?' she asked.

'A bit of a sore head and worried I made a fool of myself last night,' I said. 'What time is it?'

'Just gone five. I've not slept a wink, have you?'

As I rubbed my eyes with the ball of my hand, I saw it was caked in a brown crust. It was under my nails and in the folds of skin between my fingers and flaked off easily when I made a fist. 'Where are you? What's going on?'

'Don't you remember? You told me to leave.'

'Why would I tell you to leave your own house?'

'You don't remember anything, do you?' Esme said.

'No.' I couldn't even recall how I'd ended up in bed, still wearing my jeans and t-shirt which were sticking to my skin with what I assumed must be sweat.

I kicked off the bedclothes and gasped at the dark red marks that had soaked into my clothes and the white sheets. Ugly, scarlet streaks of blood. I was covered in it from head to toe.

I clamped a hand over my mouth to silence a scream.

'Sky? Are you there?'

My entire body trembled, and my hands shook so badly I could barely hold the phone to my ear.

'Wh - what the..?' I stammered.

'Calm down, Sky.'

I scrambled out of bed. 'There's so much blood. Where's it come from?'

'Deep breaths,' Esme said in my ear.

'What happened? Please, just tell me.' My breath was ragged. Too fast. Too shallow.

'Listen to me. You need to stop freaking out.'

'Where are you?' A dizzying nausea swelled in my stomach as I felt the walls closing in. I had to get some air before I was sick, but as I rushed for the door, I spotted a knife on the floor. Just like the one Esme had been using to prep the carrots last night. Black handle. A thin, curved blade. On the carpet. Between the bed and the door. Dropped casually. And like my clothes, it was smeared with blood.

I jumped backwards with a scream.

'Listen to me carefully, Sky,' Esme said. 'You're in shock. But I need you to do exactly what I say.'

What the hell had I done? I stepped around the knife and onto the landing, my mind whirling. Why couldn't I remember? After that moment I collapsed at the table, there was nothing except a big black hole of emptiness. Hours of time that had vanished from my life as if they'd never existed.

'Sky? Are you there?'

'Yes,' I gasped. Where the hell was she?

I tried each of the doors to the other bedrooms, peering inside. But they were all empty, and none of the beds had been slept in. I'd thought maybe I'd been caught up in a sick joke and that Esme was going to pounce out from her hiding place at any moment with a big grin on her face, laughing at how I'd fallen for her silly prank.

But the house was silent. Empty.

The only sound was Esme's soft breath in my ear and the creak of floorboards under my feet.

'You need to go downstairs,' Esme said, her voice barely louder than a whisper.

'Why, what's down there?' I asked, my imagination rioting. I had a bad feeling the answers to all my questions were in the rooms below.

'Take a deep a breath and do it now.'

'I don't want to,' I said.

'You have to.'

She was wrong. I could run away. Throw myself through the front door, up the drive, down the lane and onto the beach. Whatever was downstairs, I didn't want to see it or think about it. 'Please come home,' I begged.

'You have to understand what you've done.'

She was right. I didn't have a choice. I had to face up to whatever had happened last night. And at least Esme was going to help me through this, whatever it was.

I placed a tentative foot on the first step and gradually made my way downstairs, the blood rushing in my ears, my body shaking.

A loud screech made me jump. An unearthly sound. Splitting the deathly silence in the house. I caught my breath and swallowed my fear. A seagull. Outside, circling the house, sounding like it was taunting me, laughing at my cruel predicament. A rectangle of weak daylight spilled through the kitchen door.

'I'm in the hall,' I whispered into my phone.

'Keep going. I'm right here with you,' Esme replied. I was glad. I don't think I would have had the strength on my own.

I detected the hint of something unpleasant, a sweet, metallic odour, mingled with the morning-after stale cooking smells. I placed the back of my hand to my nose and tiptoed across the hall, stopping at the door to the kitchen, steeling myself.

The first glow of the early morning sun about to rise in a cloudless sky cast a dull light into the room through the conservatory windows. Someone had cleared the long table of dishes and the kitchen work-tops had been wiped down and cleaned. Nothing looked out of place. Everything was as it should be.

'I'm in the kitchen,' I said, hovering in the doorway.

I edged another step forwards and saw the feet first. A pair of shoes. Expensive brown leather. And then legs. Frank's legs, the rest of his body concealed under a dark red sheet. No, not a sheet. A tablecloth.

I slapped a hand over my mouth and gagged.

A viscous pool of blood congealing in a big puddle was seeping into the cracks between the floor tiles under Frank's body.

The phone fell from my hand. I couldn't breathe.

Surely, it wasn't possible.

Had I done this?

Had I killed Frank?

CHAPTER THIRTY-FIVE

I staggered back into the hall, my lungs constricting, my world collapsing. I thought I was going to suffocate as I dropped to my knees and wailed, the weight of what I'd done pressing down on me.

I'd killed Frank.

There was no other explanation for it. Either in a fit of anger or to save Esme. I'd grabbed a knife from the kitchen, stabbed him and left him to die in a pool of his own blood.

I stared at my trembling, blood-caked hands as if they were no longer a part of me, wondering how they'd been capable of such violence. I'd lost control. And now Frank was dead.

Dead.

Oh my God.

The enormity of what I'd done washed over me. My entire body spasmed, shaking uncontrollably, the image of Frank's body lying on the kitchen floor haunting me.

What kind of monster had I become? The worst thing was that I couldn't remember a single second of it. It was like my brain had erased all the bad memories. A coping mechanism to make me believe it had never happened. But it had. The blood and the body were testament to my violence.

I staggered to the toilet just in time, emptying the contents of my stomach and clutching the bowl with both hands as I turned myself inside out. And when there was nothing left, I shrunk to the floor with my head in my hands. What the hell was I going to do?

I couldn't think straight, my thoughts fleeting and erratic. I had to pull myself together. I had to get a grip.

My phone rang again. Could that Ed Sheeran ringtone have been any more inappropriate? I crawled back into the kitchen with tears and snot running down my face and snatched the phone off the floor where I'd dropped it, trying hard not to look at the body.

'What have I done, Esme?' I said as I answered, scurrying back to the relative safety of the hall and slumping against the front door.

A long pause. Esme sighed. 'I guess you were only trying to do the right thing.' Her voice was mouse like.

'The right thing?' I screamed. 'But I've… ' I couldn't bring myself to say it out loud. It would make it too real.

I remembered the evening was bad tempered. Frank and Esme had been arguing from the moment I'd arrived. But something must have happened for things to escalate. Had he hit her? Or worse, launched into a sustained attack? Maybe it had triggered memories of what happened to Mum and something deep in my subconscious had snapped. It didn't matter. The fact was, Frank was dead, and I was responsible. I'd taken a man's life in the most brutal way, and I'd have to live with that for the rest of my life. It was fucked up beyond belief.

'Esme, I'm scared,' I said. I pulled my knees up to my chest and hunched my shoulders, curling into a tight ball. 'Where are you? I need you.'

She took another long pause as I imagined she was gathering herself. 'After you... ' Even Esme couldn't bring herself to say what I'd done. 'I had to get out of the house. To clear my head. Don't you remember? You were screaming at me to leave, anyway. You didn't want me implicated, which was sweet of you.'

Sweet? I felt anything but sweet right now. 'Please come back.'

'I will. I promise. But not right now. Not while Frank's... ' Her words drifted off. 'I can't be in the house with him. We need to work out our story and what we're going to do.'

Our story? I'd killed Frank. That was the story. Plain and simple.

'I don't remember doing it,' I said, the words sticking in my throat. 'I don't remember killing him.'

'Nothing at all? Are you sure?'

'Nothing,' I said, shaking my head. 'The last thing I remember is collapsing at the table. Tell me what happened after that.'

There was another long pause, and I wondered if Esme was still on the line. When she eventually spoke, her voice was weak with emotion. 'I don't even remember why Frank lost his temper. Something I'd said, as usual. I thought he'd be better because you were there, but it didn't seem to make any difference to him. He just, I don't know, blew his stack and started… ' It was as if the words were too painful to say out loud. 'You don't know what he's like when he gets in a rage like that. You tried to stop him, but he pushed you away. I remember you were screaming at him to stop, but he knocked me to the ground and started kicking me.'

I closed my eyes, trying to shut the image out of my mind. It was a painfully familiar scene. Just like Stefan and Mum. 'What happened then?' I asked, desperate to know but not really wanting to hear it.

'That's when you picked up the knife,' Esme said.

'I'm sorry,' I croaked. 'I didn't mean to — ' The problem was I had no idea what I'd meant or not. I'd been off my head. Out of control.

'I can't believe he's gone. It's been going around and around my head all night. For all his faults, I loved him,' Esme said.

'But I was right. He was abusing you, wasn't he? Why didn't you admit it when I asked you about it?'

'What could you have done?' she snapped. The sudden change in her tone caught me by surprise. 'You're not much more than a child.'

'I could have helped you get away from him.'

'Well, it's too late for that now, isn't it?' There was a bitterness in her voice I didn't care for. 'And anyway, I think you knew exactly what you were doing.'

'What do you mean? I never planned to hurt him.'

'Really? Don't you remember our first counselling session?' Esme said. 'I admit, even I thought little about it at the time.'

My mind was racing. What had I said? I remembered telling her all about Stefan and my mum. She'd dragged it out of me before I could stop myself. But there must have been something else.

'I thought they were empty words,' Esme continued. 'I never imagined you'd actually do it. People say all sorts of things when they're going through therapy. Don't you remember, you told me you'd kill any man you saw abusing a woman.'

'I didn't mean it literally,' I spluttered. Oh my God, was she suggesting that I'd planned Frank's murder? That was insane. I'd never even wanted to go back to the house, but Esme had been insistent. It was all her idea.

She let the silence hang between us. It was a meaningless denial, and we both knew it. Whether I'd meant to kill him, Frank was dead. I'd stabbed him with a kitchen knife, and I'd have to face the consequences.

'When you attacked him, you had such a wild look in your eye,' Esme said eventually. 'It was like you would never stop. You just kept stabbing and stabbing — '

'Stop! Please!'

253

'It was horrible. I suppose I should be grateful you stopped him, but I just feel numb. I can't believe he's gone.'

I wanted to tell her she was better off without him. But it didn't seem like the right thing to say. 'If I could turn back the clock, you know I would.'

'Would you? Really?' she sneered. One minute she was acting like my best friend and the next she was behaving like a wronged wife. It was so unsettling. At first, she sounded like she was on my side, but now I wasn't sure if I could trust her entirely. 'You wanted him dead all along, didn't you?'

'No! Of course I didn't, but he didn't love you, Esme. If he did, he would never have treated you like that.'

'He was my husband,' Esme sobbed, her voice cracking with her tears. 'For better and for worse. And now he's dead. What am I going to do?'

'I should call the police,' I offered. I had to face the consequences of my actions, even if I couldn't remember them. But the thought of making the call filled me with dread. In a heartbeat, everything had changed. My life as I knew it was over. I was going to jail for a long, long time.

'Let's not do anything hasty,' Esme said. 'It would be so easy for the police to draw the wrong conclusion. We need to get our stories straight.'

'What do you mean, the wrong conclusion?'

And then she said something that took my breath away.

'It was an accident, wasn't it? I'm sure you never intended to hurt Frank. But he came at you and you had to defend yourself.'

Self-defence? Now I really was confused. One minute she was accusing me of plotting Frank's death and the next she was suggesting it was an accident. But either way, it looked bad for me. I'd killed Frank and then taken myself calmly to bed. That wouldn't look good to anyone.

'We should meet up,' Esme said. 'I can't face going back to the house though. Can you meet me on the beach? I'll wait by the pillboxes. Make sure no one sees you.'

'Yes,' I gasped, relieved to have an excuse to get out of the house. Esme would know what to do. And she was right. We needed to agree on what we were going to tell the police. 'What should I do with the body?'

'Leave it,' she said, sharply. 'Come now. I'll see you in five minutes.'

She hung up, and I pulled myself unsteadily to my feet, my legs still shaking. I started hunting for my boots before I remembered my clothes were covered in blood. I couldn't go out like that. What if someone saw me?

I ran upstairs, into the bathroom and ran the shower, peeling off my t-shirt, jeans and underwear as the water heated up and the room filled with steam. I dumped them in a heap and stepped under the scalding jets of water. They hit my skin like needles. I let the water soak my hair and watched it run pink around my feet as it drained away, the warmth comforting. Once the police had arrested me, I wasn't sure when I'd next be able to enjoy a hot shower like this.

I concentrated on my hands, scrubbing them with a bar of soap until my skin was red raw, making sure every trace of blood under my nails and between my fingers was washed off.

But no matter how hard I scrubbed, I knew I would never erase the horror of what I'd done.

CHAPTER THIRTY-SIX

After showering, I found some of Esme's clothes; a garish pink t-shirt that looked about my size and a pair of jeans folded up in a drawer. I'd only ever seen Esme in dresses and never imagined her wearing jeans. I pulled my hair into a ponytail and checked my appearance in a mirror. I was pale and gaunt, and in Esme's clothes I looked like I was dressed in hand-me-downs. But who was going to see me at this time in the morning? And anyway, I had bigger things on my mind than what I looked like.

I left the house avoiding the kitchen and hurried towards the beach, looking forward to seeing Esme. She would know what to do, and at least now I knew she was no longer in any danger from Frank. His days of terrorising her were over. Not that I ever imagined things would end like this. I hated what he did to her, but I never wished him dead. Not really.

With my head down, I strode purposefully along the

dirt track at the top of the drive and staggered onto the beach. Normally I enjoyed walking along the shore, but I was in a hurry and it was hard to move quickly with my feet sinking into the soft sand. Ahead, the pillboxes were silhouetted against the rising sun. As I walked, I shaded my eyes against the bright glow, but there was no sign of Esme.

I thought she might be sheltering inside one of the pillboxes, but I checked all around and she wasn't there. Surely she hadn't stood me up? I found her number in my phone and in my panic made a video call.

She answered almost immediately. She looked pale and haggard. Her eyes were rimmed red and her hair was unusually messy.

'Where are you?' I asked. 'I'm at the pillboxes like you said, but I had to take a shower first. Sorry, I had to borrow some of your clothes. Hope you don't mind.' I pasted a fake smile on my face. 'Is everything okay?'

'No, Sky, not really.' Her face bobbed around the screen in between snatches of sky as though she was walking with her phone in her hand.

'Are you still coming?' I asked.

'Why did you have to kill him?' Her face crumpled as she sobbed.

'You said yourself, it was an accident,' I said. 'I never meant to hurt him, but I had to stop him, otherwise it could have been you.'

'I've been thinking things over and I've changed my

mind. I can't see you right now. I'm sorry,' she said. 'I'm not ready.'

'What? Esme, please. I need you. I can't deal with this on my own. What am I supposed to do?'

'Go home, Sky,' she said.

'Home?'

'Back to your caravan and wait there. Does anyone know you came to dinner last night?'

'Only my flatmate, Amber.'

'Don't tell her anything.'

'But — '

'Sky, do as I say. Please, don't make this any worse for yourself.'

'Okay,' I said. I guess she knew best. 'I'll go back if you think that's the right thing to do. I can call the police from the caravan. I'll tell them everything.'

'No,' she said, her eyes opening wide. 'I said do nothing. Go back, keep your head down and wait for my call.'

'Why?' I didn't understand. I trusted her, but why did she want me out of the way? Not that I wanted to be anywhere near Frank's dead body, but surely it would be better if I stayed at the house. And what about the police? The longer it took to call them, the worse it was going to look for both of us. Like we had something to hide. There was no getting away from the fact that I'd killed Frank, and the sooner I confessed to it the better.

'Go back to the caravan and stay there until I can figure things out, okay?' she snapped. 'Do nothing.

Don't speak to anyone. Don't go anywhere. Is that clear?'

'Yes,' I said. 'I understand. But what are you going to do?'

The picture broke up for a second and when it stabilised, Esme was staring at me with dead, emotionless eyes. 'I'm going back to the house.'

'The house? Why? Let me meet you there and we can sort things out together.'

'I'll deal with it,' she said.

'What do you mean, deal with it? Esme, what's going on?'

'What do you think? You killed Frank, but what if the police think I was involved? What if they don't believe your story and think it was me?'

'I'll tell them everything, exactly as it happened.'

'But you can't remember what happened, can you?'

She had a point. Everything I knew about Frank's death was what she'd told me.

'Frank and I had a tempestuous relationship,' Esme continued. 'You know that. You saw how his temper got the better of him. And if you can't remember attacking him with that knife, they're going to think that either I did it or that I put you up to it. I can't take that risk. Leave this to me. I'm going to make it go away.'

She hung up, cutting me off abruptly. I was left standing shivering, even though it wasn't cold. Had I understood correctly? Was she suggesting she was going back to the house to remove evidence that I'd killed Frank? But what about his body? I couldn't let her do that. It was insane.

I rubbed my eyes, feeling small and alone. Esme clearly wasn't thinking straight. If she tampered with a crime scene and the police caught her, that was going to make her look as guilty as hell. I had to stop her before she made a terrible mistake. Frank had controlled her life when he was alive. I couldn't let him rule it after he'd died.

With my mind made up, I turned and trudged back to the house, determined to make Esme see sense. I'd call the police and confess everything, making sure they knew exactly how Frank used to treat her and that she had nothing at all to do with his death.

I crept down the drive and pushed open the front door I'd left on the latch.

'Esme?' I shouted. 'Are you here?'

No answer. The house was silent.

Good, I'd made it back first. No harm done. Still time to talk her out of doing something she might regret. We could call the police together and there was no reason she should be implicated.

I sat on the stairs and waited, my foot tapping impatiently on the floor as I chewed a fingernail. All my plans and dreams were over. I was never realistically going to go back to college but at least I'd had the option before. Maybe even get a place at one of those fancy universities. That would never happen now. All I had to look forward to was the inside of prison. Tears of self-pity bubbled up from a deep well inside me, and

I sobbed my heart out. Perhaps I could plead self-defence after all. Or maybe a sympathetic jury would take pity on me. They had to consider the circumstances, surely?

I was startled by the sound of my phone ringing again. Another video call from Esme.

'What are you doing back at the house?' she asked. She looked angry. 'I told you to go home. You're going to ruin everything.'

'You can't touch the scene, Esme. I won't let you,' I said. 'Come home. Let's call the police together and we can explain that I acted in self-defence.'

'You stupid girl,' she hissed. 'Why can't you follow a simple instruction?'

'But — '

'I'm not going to jail, Sky. Not for you. Not for Frank. Not for anyone.' She'd worked herself up into near hysterics.

'You're not going to jail. There's no reason the police won't believe I did it. They don't need to know I can't remember anything. And my fingerprints will be all over the knife, anyway. I'll tell them Frank was attacking you and that I thought he was going to kill you. I'll tell them it was the only way I could stop him.'

Esme was crying again, shaking her head. 'He didn't deserve to die. Not like this,' she said. 'I can't forgive what you did.'

'I'm so, so sorry, Esme. I don't know what to say.'

'How am I supposed to go on without him? He loved me, I know he did,' she said.

I had to stop myself from telling her he had a funny way of showing it. 'I know,' I said. 'But remember how he treated you.'

She'd started walking again, her head swinging in and out of shot, but it was hard to tell whether she was on the beach or somewhere else.

'He's gone,' she said. 'And I can't get the image of him lying there out of my head, his eyes staring at the ceiling, and his skin pale and cold.'

My plan had always been to save Esme. It broke my heart that I was now responsible for so much heartache. I deserved to go to jail for that. 'I'm going to call the police,' I said.

'Do what you like. I can't go on without him.'

My heart thundered under my ribs. 'Esme,' I shouted. 'Don't do anything stupid.' She wouldn't, would she?

'What's the point of going on without Frank? He was my life.'

'Please, Esme... ' But I had no other words of comfort. What could I possibly say to make it better?

She stopped and put the phone down, propping it up at an angle so I could see the upper half of her body, slightly tilted to one side, revealing she was on the beach somewhere, muddy cliffs and scrubby clumps of vegetation in the background. She sat and leaned towards the camera, placing something across her lap. It was long and thin and metallic. Oh God. Frank's shotgun.

'Esme, what are you doing?' I jumped up, my breath

catching in my throat. 'Whatever's going through your head right now, we can work it out.'

'Frank was everything to me,' she said with a startling calmness. She'd stopped crying and her face was devoid of any emotion.

'You're frightening me.'

'Goodbye, Sky.'

'No, no, no,' I screamed down the phone. 'You don't have to do this. We can fix it. Tell me where you are. I'll come and find you.' I was frantic.

'It's too late, Sky. I can't live without Frank and I can't take the risk that the police think I killed him,' Esme said, staring off into the distance. She lifted the gun, dropped one end into the sand and aimed its barrels at her head.

'Esme! Don't!' I yelled.

As she adjusted her position, angling the gun under her chin, her foot kicked the phone, knocking it over, leaving me with a close-up view of the sand and a snatch of the sea rolling onto the shore.

'Esme! Talk to me!'

I heard the gunshot twice.

First through the speaker of the phone and a fraction of a second later, echoing from the beach, dulled by the thick walls of the house.

CHAPTER THIRTY-SEVEN

There was no mistaking the sound. A gunshot, echoing off the cliffs and carrying on the still morning air. Hanlon, in the back of his van, looked up and cocked an ear. It sounded as if it had come from the beach. But who the hell was shooting at this time of the morning, especially on a Sunday? None of his business. He couldn't afford to be distracted. He had a job to do. He checked his watch. Less than an hour until Duncan's deadline was up.

He'd followed the Range Rover back to the house and parked up in the same spot at the end of the dirt track where he could observe the house. If Duncan had any sense, he would have spent the last twenty-four hours doing everything in his power to lay his hands on the money he owed the Romanians. Unless the guy was an idiot or so arrogant he thought he could somehow get away with it.

Hanlon removed the Glock from its case, checked

the magazine and chambered a round. Then he grabbed the hunting knife from under the driver's seat and ran a thumb over the blade to check its sharpness. He was about to look for a leather belt or a strap, something to hold Duncan's arm down as he tackled his fingers, when his phone rang.

'Hanlon,' he said, clamping the phone to his ear.

'It seems your message wasn't clear enough.' He loved that Romanian accent. Exotic and so full of promise. 'We've had no word from Duncan Whittaker.'

Hanlon wasn't surprised. The last time he'd seen him, Duncan was letting himself back into the house, looking pale and shaken. But he hadn't left the property since, although there had been a few other comings and goings. First a woman, who Hanlon assumed was Duncan's wife, had driven off in a hurry in the sporty little Mercedes. She returned a couple of hours later, glancing only briefly at Hanlon's van.

And then there was the girl who'd arrived at the house as it was getting dark. He wasn't sure what to make of her. She looked familiar but couldn't place where he'd seen her. Long black hair. T-shirt and jeans. A canvas bag slung over her shoulder. She'd approached the house cautiously, almost with trepidation, but had been eagerly welcomed inside. He thought she'd maybe brought the money. But maybe not. Their daughter, possibly? Curiously, she seemed to have stayed the night.

She'd emerged from the house a short while ago, wearing different clothes; a bright pink t-shirt and baggy jeans. She looked drawn and upset, like she'd been crying. She'd hurried past Hanlon's van without noticing him, heading for the beach, and had returned less than ten minutes later, looking no happier.

'He tried to tell me he didn't have the money,' Hanlon said. 'Maybe he's struggling to lay his hands on it.'

'They always say that.' It was the first time he'd heard the woman laugh. It rattled in her lungs like she was a smoker.

'You want me to put the squeeze on him again?'

'You warned him of the consequences of not delivering?' she asked.

'The money or his fingers. Yes.'

'Good. Start with his left hand. Two fingers. And give him another twenty-four hours. Show him we're serious. But that's it.'

'Of course,' Hanlon said. 'Not a problem.'

'People like Duncan Whittaker are bad for business, you understand?' she said. 'They think they can take us for a ride. That we're soft. I want you to make an example of him. Send a clear message that we don't tolerate being messed around.'

'I can do that.' Hanlon licked his lips, relishing the challenge. Gangs like hers operated their businesses around fear. You had to believe that if you crossed them, it would end badly. Without fear, the business proposition collapsed. He understood that. 'Anything in particular?' he asked.

'I'll leave it to your imagination,' she said.

CHAPTER THIRTY-EIGHT

The phone fell to the floor as it slipped from my hand and I sat back on the bottom stair, numb with shock. I could hardly believe what I'd witnessed. In the space of a few hours, two people had died because of me. Why hadn't I kept my nose out of Esme's business? She'd never asked for my help and I shouldn't have interfered.

I felt more alone than I'd ever felt in my life. More alone even than when I'd discovered my mother beaten to death by her so-called boyfriend. More alone than that first night, sleeping rough on the streets, huddled in a shop doorway, cold and shivering with fear, terrified that every shadow was a looming threat. My world had imploded like a collapsing star. Frank and Esme were dead, and it was all my fault. Why couldn't I have left them alone?

Tears rolled down my cheeks and dripped onto my jeans, soaking into the denim in dark spots. The deafening silence of the empty house echoed in my ears and wrapped its cold arms around me, a reminder of the terrible thing I'd done. How could I ever get over that or forgive myself? I doubted that I ever would.

I had to call the police. I'd already left it too long, made everything look too suspicious. But now Esme was dead, there was no point delaying. I stared at my phone lying at an angle between my feet. What would I say to them? Where to begin? The truth. That's all I could say. Starting with the diary and what I'd read. My suspicions that Frank had been abusing Esme, and that maybe it had been going on for years. I willed my arms to move, to pick up the phone, to dial the number, but they wouldn't respond. Shock paralysed my entire body.

Inside, I was hollow, as if all my hopes and dreams had been scooped out, incinerated and thrown to the wind. All the things I'd dreamed I'd do one day were now nothing more than wrecks at the bottom of the ocean of my mind. I'd never go travelling or see the world. I'd probably never get married or have kids. I didn't even know how long you got for murder. And what about Esme's death? Would they hold me responsible for that as well?

How had I let it happen? First my mother and now Esme. I'd let them both down. What was I, some kind of angel of death? If it hadn't been for me, both of them would still be alive. Did I even deserve to live? Maybe it would be better for everyone if I was dead. It would be so easy to run a bath, slip into the water, slit open my wrists and let my life flow away. And the saddest thing was, no one would miss me. Nobody cared.

I took a deep breath. Could it be that easy? I was trying to stand, shaking on weak legs, when my phone rang. Jeez, that bloody Ed Sheeran ringtone. I almost didn't answer it until I saw it was Amber calling. No doubt worried about me. Being the friend I should have been for her. Someone else I'd let down.

'Hey, did I wake you?' she asked. Her voice was faint against a background rumble. It sounded like she was in a car.

'No, it's okay. I was already awake.'

'I thought you were coming home last night. Is everything okay?'

I was wrong. Amber cared. A lump swelled so large in my throat, it almost hurt to swallow. I'd been stupid and selfish to think about taking my own life. 'I stayed over at Esme's,' I said. 'Sorry I didn't text. I had a bit too much to drink.'

'You sound a bit… odd. Are you sure you're okay?'

'I'm fine,' I lied.

'Okay, well look, I wanted to let you know I'm going home. I called Dad last night after you went out and told him everything. He drove straight down to help me pack. We're leaving the island now. We thought we'd make an early start. No point hanging around.'

Her words struck me like a body blow. What was she trying to tell me? That she was abandoning me? I knew she was upset about Marc and the videos, but it was a bit extreme. 'Home? What do you mean?' I asked, my hand tightening around the phone.

'I'm going back to Berkshire.'

'But why?' I couldn't disguise the panic in my voice.

'Dad agreed it would be best for me to get off Sheppey for a while. He knows this lawyer who can help to get those videos taken down, and he's already reported Marc to the police.'

'Amber, you can't — '

'I'm sorry, Sky. I have to. You understand, don't you?'

'You can't leave me,' I gasped.

'Come and visit when things have settled down, yeah? I didn't want to leave you in the lurch with the rent, so Dad's left some money on the side to cover the next couple of months. That should give you time to find a new flatmate. I can't stay though, not after what he did. It's for the best,' Amber said.

'The best for who? I need you, Amber. I've done something terrible.'

'I'm really sorry, hun. I'll call you later, yeah?'

'I mean it, Amber. I've seriously fucked up. I don't know what to do.'

'Look, I'll call — later — home,' she said, the line breaking up.

'What? I can't hear you. Amber?'

'I have to — '

'Amber?' I stared at the screen of my phone as Amber's voice faded out.

'Don't go,' I pleaded, but the line went dead. I tried calling her back, but it went straight to voicemail. I screamed in frustration. Even my best friend had deserted me.

I dropped my head in my hands with my heart racing like a sports car, the enormity of everything crashing down on me. I had to call the police, but I didn't want to face them on my own. I couldn't. I needed someone on my side. But who else could I turn to? I didn't have any family and my best friend was leaving. There was Michelle, but the thought of turning to her for help made me want to puke. She'd be next to useless, anyway.

Karma? No. I was hardly going to turn to the local drug dealer. And besides, she was only interested in herself. Not someone you could rely on.

The only other person I could think of was Cam. Oh God, the thought of calling him after he'd blown me out at the party made me cringe. But he was exactly the sort of person I needed right now. Someone I could rely on.

He answered my call on the second ring. The sound of his voice alone made me want to weep again. 'Hey, Cam, it's Sky,' I said, sheepishly, unsure how he'd react to hearing from me. I'd not spoken to him since the party.

'Sky, what's up? It's a bit early. Is everything okay?'

'Not really,' I said, twirling a length of my hair around my fingers. 'I've done something terrible, and I didn't have anyone else I could call. I'm sorry, I know I shouldn't have phoned. I'm sure you're busy.'

'Slow down,' he said. 'It's fine. What's happened?'

'Can I see you?' I asked.

'I'm in the shop. What's going on?'

'I can't talk over the phone,' I said. 'I'm at Esme's house. I stayed here last night, but... ' My words dried up. How could I explain?

'Sky?' When I heard the concern in Cam's voice, I knew I'd done the right thing calling him. He was the only person I could trust.

'It's Esme's husband, Frank,' I said. 'Something awful's happened. Please, just come.'

CHAPTER THIRTY-NINE

I was still sitting on the bottom stair drowning in my
thoughts when a loud knock echoed through the
silent house.

'You came,' I said, throwing open the front door to
find Cam standing there with a worried look on his
face. The urge to put my arms around his neck and hug
him, to collapse into his chest, was overwhelming. But
it didn't seem right. Nothing could undo what I'd said
to him at the party.

'Of course I came,' he said. 'I grabbed a taxi as soon
as you called. Dad's looking after the shop. So what's
going on? You sounded upset on the phone.'

I dragged him into the house by his arm and
slammed the door closed, shutting out the outside
world.

'Sky? Talk to me.'

I bit my lip and looked at my feet, the intensity of

his gaze scorching my soul. 'I'm sorry, I didn't know who else to call.'

'Is Esme here?'

I shook my head. One thing at a time. He needed to know about Frank first.

'After the party,' I said, cringing as I mentioned it, remembering the awkwardness between us, 'I came here.'

'Why?'

'I don't know,' I said. 'But the point is, Esme's husband, Frank, caught me sneaking around the garden and shot at me.'

'He did what?'

'It's okay, he missed. It's not important.' I wished he would just listen. 'And then yesterday, Esme invited me to dinner to apologise. But I had too much to drink and passed out at the table.' Cam's eyes opened wide. 'When I woke up this morning, I was in a bed upstairs.' I hesitated, choosing my words carefully. 'I was covered in Frank's blood.'

His mouth dropped open in shock. 'Sky? What have you done?'

I drew in a breath and let it out slowly. 'I killed him, Cam. I stabbed Frank to death in the kitchen. I found his body this morning.'

'I don't understand,' Cam stuttered. 'You *killed* him?'

'Yes.'

His eyes flicked towards the kitchen, his pupils large and black. 'Is he still…?'

I nodded, picking at the fabric of my borrowed t-shirt. It was a hideous shade of pink I'd not normally have worn in a million years.

'But how? Why?' He shook his head as if he couldn't believe what I was telling him, pacing up and down the hall, chewing his finger.

It wasn't the reaction I'd been hoping for. 'I don't remember.'

'You killed him, Sky. You must remember something.'

'I blacked out. Esme said I stabbed him when he started attacking her.'

'Where is she? Is she here?'

'No,' I said.

'Have you called the police?'

'No.'

'What have you been doing?'

'I don't know, Cam!' I yelled at him, all my anger and frustration pouring out in a torrent. 'I've been sitting here trying to make sense of it all. I was going to call them, but I needed someone with me. I'm sorry I phoned you.' Now I wondered if it had been a good idea after all. Cam was usually so calm and collected. I hadn't expected him to get into a flap like this.

He stopped pacing and looked me in the eye. 'Do you want me to do it?'

'No. I should do it myself.' I glanced at the phone in my hand and my stomach cramped.

Cam took a tentative step towards the kitchen, his breathing slow and heavy. He wet his lips with his tongue and ran a hand across his mouth. 'And you've not touched him?'

'Of course not.'

'So how do you know he was dead?'

'He was lying in a pool of his own blood and Esme had pulled a sheet over his body,' I said.

He took another step and stopped, glancing back at me. 'If Esme knew, why didn't she raise the alarm last night?'

'I guess she was trying to protect me.'

'But you'd killed her husband.'

I swallowed hard. 'Only to save her.'

'This is so crazy.' Cam reached the kitchen door and grabbed the frame to steady himself, the knuckles of his hands turning white.

I followed, hiding behind his body with no desire to see Frank's corpse again. It was an image I'd never get out of my head. It didn't need reinforcing.

Cam froze as he peered into the room, every muscle tense. I waited for him to react, not sure what he was going to do.

'I don't understand,' he said.

'What do you mean?'

'You said the body was in the kitchen?'

'Yes.'

'Well, it's not there now.'

What was he talking about? I pushed past him and looked for myself. Sure enough, Frank's body was gone. The only evidence of what I'd done was a pool of congealing, dark red blood, now smeared across the floor like someone had dragged a rubbish sack through it.

'But he was right there,' I said.

'Are you sure?'

'Yes, of course I'm sure,' I snapped.

'Maybe he wasn't dead after all,' Cam suggested. 'Perhaps you only injured him.'

I blinked rapidly, clearing my eyes as if they were deceiving me. 'No, Cam, he was dead. I'm sure of it.'

The conversation I'd had with Esme on the phone came back to me, how she told me she was going to return to the house to clean up, worried she'd be implicated. But how could she have possibly made it back before me and removed Frank's body on her own? He wasn't a big man but moving him wouldn't have been easy. It made little sense, but there was no other logical explanation.

'What is it?' Cam asked, reading the frown on my face.

'Esme was so scared the police would think she'd put me up to killing him. She told me she was going to make it all go away.'

'Meaning what, exactly?'

'Getting rid of Frank's body, I guess,' I said.

Cam puffed out his cheeks and blew out a stream of air. 'So where is she now?'

I tugged at my bottom lip, toying with how to explain. 'She wasn't here when I woke up, but she called to tell me what I'd done. I arranged to meet her on the beach to talk, but she didn't turn up. When I called her again, she said she was going to deal with things.'

'Where is she?' Cam repeated.

I might as well tell him. He was going to find out, anyway. 'Dead.'

Cam went pale. 'Dead? You said you spoke to her this morning.'

'She took Frank's shotgun and shot herself. I watched it happen on a video call, down on the beach somewhere.' I lowered my gaze. 'She said she couldn't go on without him.'

'Jeez. When?'

'Half an hour ago? I don't know.' Time had lost all meaning. 'She was upset. Understandably.'

'Are you sure?'

I nodded. Cam started pacing again, rubbing his chin, his gaze darting around the room. I regretted getting him involved. This wasn't his problem, but I'd had no one else to turn to. 'It's okay,' he said. He grabbed my shoulders and looked me earnestly in the eye. 'We'll sort this, okay?'

'How?' I shrugged off his hands. My head was light, and I was breathing fast. How the hell was he going to sort it out? All sorts of random thoughts were firing off in my head, how the house would soon be crawling with police and a vision of being handcuffed roughly and shoved into the back of a patrol car.

'I don't know.' He scratched his head. 'It's a mess.'

'I think I should call the police now.' I couldn't keep putting it off.

'Hang on a minute. Let me think.' Cam guided me out of the kitchen and back into the hall, away from all the blood. 'Tell me everything that happened since you came to the house last night.'

'Why?'

'Because something doesn't add up,' he said.

'Like what?'

'Like Frank's body going missing for a start.'

'What's the point?' I threw my hands up in despair. Frank and Esme were dead, and I was responsible. Just like I'd been responsible when I'd let Stefan murder my mother.

'Humour me,' Cam said.

'Fine,' I said with a huff. 'I turned up at about seven and they were already arguing.'

'Arguing? About what?'

'I don't know. Maybe not arguing but bickering because Frank hadn't helped Esme with dinner.'

'Okay. So not a full-blown argument?'

'No.'

'What next?'

'Frank broke a glass and Esme nearly had a melt-down. I really thought he was going to lose his shit with her.'

'Did he?' Cam asked.

'Not at that point. Something must have happened later that I don't remember.'

'Go on.'

'Then we sat and ate and they were going on and on about this stupid wine, getting me to tell them what flavours I could taste. I didn't feel so good. Too much vodka, probably. I'd been drinking with Amber before I came out,' I said. 'And the next thing I passed out at the table. That's all I remember until I woke up this morning.'

Cam frowned. 'How much wine did you drink?'

I tried to recall. 'A couple of glasses of white. Maybe a glass of red.'

'Doesn't sound that much.'

Come to think of it, it didn't. Amber and I could normally polish off a couple of bottles of wine between us of an evening without too much of a problem. 'I guess I was tired,' I said. I racked my mind, trying to think of anything else that might be relevant. 'That's it, really. I mean, Frank's temper was simmering all night until he'd had enough, and he pinned Esme up against the wall,' I said. Or had I made that bit up? I was struggling to distinguish my memories from what Esme had told me afterwards.

'But you have no recollection at all of actually picking up the knife and stabbing him?'

I shook my head and closed my eyes trying to dredge up a memory but there was nothing. 'I don't think so.'

'Think, Sky.'

'I have been thinking! I can't remember anything!' I shouted at him.

'It's just that I can't believe you wouldn't remember doing something like that, no matter how drunk you were.'

'I promise, I can't.' Why didn't he believe me?

'In which case, the only evidence that you killed him is Esme's word. And she's dead.'

I opened my mouth and closed it again. 'But my clothes were covered in his blood and there was a knife in my room.'

'That proves nothing.'

'I'm calling the police,' I said, unlocking my phone.

'Are you sure? Do you want me to do it?'

'No, I'll do it. What number do you think I should ring?' Was it an emergency or was there another number you were supposed to call for things like this? I didn't have the first clue.

'I think 999 should do it,' Cam said.

My finger was poised over the keypad but before I could dial, a loud hammering on the front door startled us both. Three sharp knocks. Officious. Serious. Someone outside who meant business. Cam and I stared at each other with eyes wide and mouths open.

'Who's that?' I hissed under my breath.

'I've no idea.'

CHAPTER FORTY

Duncan Whittaker had missed his deadline, and now it was time to make him pay. Hanlon rolled open the rear door of his van and climbed out onto the dirt track, slipping the Glock into the waistband of his trousers and concealing the knife up the sleeve of his jacket. He grabbed his baseball cap from the front seat and was pulling it on when he noticed a car approaching.

It was travelling slowly along the pitted track, pitching and rolling as it navigated the potholes. Hanlon narrowed his eyes as it came closer. A white saloon with a green taxi sign mounted on the roof. He ducked out of sight behind the van, pretending to busy himself, as the vehicle pulled up outside Duncan's house.

A young guy climbed out, looking lost, like he wasn't sure if he was in the right place. The taxi turned around and drove off. The guy was left standing there, looking the house up and down.

Who the hell was this? One of Duncan's associates? Whoever it was, it had just added another layer of complication to the job.

The guy glanced around, looking straight past the van, and strode down the drive. He knocked on the front door. Someone answered almost immediately. The guy slipped inside and was gone.

There were at least four people now in the house that Hanlon was aware of. Three more than he would have ideally liked. He'd seen the girl leave and come back again, but there had been no sign of Duncan since he'd returned from his birdwatching trip the day before. And then there was the wife.

Barging in with all guns blazing could be problematic. If they were scattered throughout the house in different rooms, it would be too easy for one of them to raise the alarm. And that's the last thing he needed.

He checked his watch again. It was past seven. He'd have to ride his luck. He zipped up his jacket, marched down the drive, up to the front door and knocked.

CHAPTER FORTY-ONE

'You'd better answer it,' Cam whispered as we stood like statues in the hall.

'Maybe they'll go away if we keep quiet and ignore them,' I said, horrified.

'Open up! Police!' a voice yelled as the banging started again.

I stared at Cam open-mouthed. How had the police found out? Maybe they were responding to the gunshot on the beach. Or had they found Esme's body?

'Just answer the bloody door,' Cam hissed.

'And what am I supposed to say?' I threw up my hands, despairing. It wasn't supposed to be like this. I wanted to tell the police in my own time, on my terms, not have them batter down the door and drag it out of me.

'Tell them the truth.'

The truth? I didn't even know what that was anymore. My hands were shaking and my legs threatened to buckle as I tiptoed towards the door, my racing heart in my mouth. This was it, then. The moment I was supposed to confess everything. The moment that life as I knew it changed forever. The end of my freedom. The end of my dreams. My throat was as dry and as coarse as sandpaper as I reached for the latch.

I cracked the door open an inch and saw a lone figure outside. He had dark foreboding eyes partially hidden under a baseball cap, and a crooked mouth which gave me the creeps. He didn't look much like a cop and there was something instantly disagreeable about him, but I forced a smile.

'DC Barraclough, Met Police,' he said, flashing a badge in a wallet in my face too quickly to read. 'I need to speak to Duncan Whittaker.'

Duncan Whittaker? Oh my God, I could have burst out laughing if things weren't so serious. The guy had got the wrong house. I tried not to let the relief show on my face. 'I'm sorry,' I said, shaking my head. 'There's no one here with that name.'

'That's odd because his car's parked on the drive,' the officer said, pushing the door open wider. I glanced at the Range Rover with its funny number plate, parked up next to Esme's little silver sports car. 'You might know him as Frank Winters.'

My mouth fell open as the guy barged inside, knocking me backwards. Cam caught me as I stumbled, held me upright and placed a hand on my shoulder, giving the hint we were together. A united front. The blood chilled in my veins. What was going on? As if the day wasn't weird enough. Who the hell was Duncan Whittaker?

'What's this about, Officer?' Cam asked.

'Detective,' the man corrected him. 'Sorry to call so early. I need to speak to Frank urgently.'

'Why, what's he done?' I asked.

'I can't divulge that, I'm afraid. Where is he?' He craned his neck to see into the kitchen and I took a step to my left to block his view.

Something in the back of my mind clicked; something I'd overheard Frank and Esme talking about the first time I'd been in the house, when I was in the bathroom under the stairs.

'You promised this was going to be a better life for us.'

'And it will be. We just need to keep our heads down for a little longer. It'll all be worth it in the end.'

I'd not understood at the time, but now their words made sense. Frank was on the run from the police. But why? What had he done?

'You need to get him for me. It's urgent,' Barraclough said, his eyes narrowing. 'I know he's in here, so don't mess me around.'

Clearly the guy had no idea what had happened. Nor that Esme was dead. Cam and I stood in terrified silence, staring at the strange man in the hall, unsure what to say or how to say it.

Cam took a deep breath, his expression grim. 'Look, I think you'd better come and sit down, Detective,' he said. 'There's something we need to tell you.'

'I don't want to sit down,' the man growled. 'I need

to see Duncan. Or Frank. Or whatever he's calling himself these days.'

'It's not that simple,' Cam said.

'I've been watching the house for the last twenty-four hours. So I know he's in here,' he said. 'Duncan! Time's up. Come out and let's get this sorted,' he yelled.

'He's not here,' Cam said, softly.

'Who are you two anyway?' he asked.

'Cameron Searle. I'm a friend of Sky's,' Cam said.

'Sky?' Barraclough asked, looking at me, his stare drilling through my skin.

I cleared my throat. 'Sky Warehorn. I'm a friend of Frank and Esme's.'

'Right.' Barraclough raised a disbelieving eyebrow. 'I'll ask you one more time. Where is he?'

I tugged at the hem of my borrowed t-shirt as I played around with the words in my head. How could I explain? To soften the blow? How on earth was I going to confess to murder when the guy didn't even know Frank was dead?

'The thing is, Detective… ' Cam began.

'He's dead. They're both dead. Frank and Esme.' The words exploded from my mouth like I'd shot them from a cannon. And now they were free. I'd said it. And actually it was a relief. A weight lifted. 'I killed Frank with a knife and Esme shot herself on the beach this morning. We assumed that's why you were here.'

The detective went quiet, staring at us like he didn't believe a word of it. 'Dead?' he said, eventually. 'How?'

'I was drunk,' I explained. 'I grabbed a knife when he

started attacking Esme. It was the only way I could stop him.' Cam took my hand and squeezed it tight. 'I found out he'd been abusing her a few days ago and when he started hitting her after dinner, right in front of me, I snapped.'

Still Barraclough remained silent, confusion and something else written all over his face. Disappointment?

'You can see for yourself,' Cam said, pointing to the kitchen.

I stepped out of the way, willing my legs to work even though they felt like jelly.

Barraclough brushed past us and stopped at the kitchen door, studying the room before he entered, taking it all in. I guess he was making a mental note of how everything looked. When he spotted the blood on the floor, he dropped to one knee to examine it more closely.

I didn't know what to say, so I said nothing, expecting him to jump on his phone and call for back-up. Soon the house would be overrun with police and forensics people. Would he arrest me first?

'The guy was attacking his wife. He would have killed her if Sky hadn't stopped him,' Cam said. 'That's got to be a mitigating factor, right?'

'Where's the body?' Barraclough glanced up at us, his face stony cold.

'I think Esme may have come back to the house and moved it before she shot herself,' I said, my voice sounding timid.

Barraclough stood slowly, watching us. He shoved his hands in his pockets. 'Esme came back and moved his body? On her own?'

'Yes,' I said. 'It's the only explanation.'

'And why do you think she'd want to do that?' Barraclough asked.

'Because she was afraid it would look like she had something to do with Frank's death,' I said.

'Did she?'

'No.' I shook my head vigorously. I had to make him understand it was me. Sure, I could have blamed her, or at least pretended she'd put me up to it. It might even have spared me jail time. But it wasn't the truth. It was me, and I deserved to be punished for it. 'Are you going to arrest me?'

'Tell me what happened from the beginning,' he said, leaning against a worktop and folding his arms.

I took a breath, steadying myself. It was important to get the facts straight. I'd heard how the police could twist your words and pick up on inconsistencies in your story. I didn't want any suspicion falling on Esme. She'd had it bad enough in life. At least I could spare her in death. I told him about finding Esme's diary and how I'd been determined to uncover evidence against Frank. How he'd fired his shotgun at me when I'd come to the house and about Esme inviting me to dinner to apologise. I explained how the evening had descended from petty bickering into a full-blown fight between them and how I'd had too much to drink, blacked out and only discovered what I'd done that morning.

Barraclough listened intently, his eyes growing wider as I told my story. 'Are you in the habit of blacking out when you've been drinking?' he asked.

'Sometimes, yes.' It was embarrassing to admit it, but it happened, and I'd always known one day it was going to land me in trouble.

'How much did you drink over the course of the evening?'

I told him about drinking vodka with Amber before I'd left the caravan. 'When I arrived, I had a couple of glasses of white wine and maybe a glass of red,' I said.

'Does that seem like an excessive amount for you?'

'Not really,' I said. 'But I was tired. It's been a stressful few days.'

'And it came as no surprise when you passed out?' The way Barraclough said it made it sound like he thought I was lying. 'Is it possible your drink could have been spiked?'

'What, by Esme?'

'Or by Frank.'

'No! Why would they do that?' I said, shocked by the idea.

'I'm not asking whether you think they did it, I'm asking whether it was possible,' Barraclough said.

This was what I was afraid of. He was twisting it. Making it sound like something it wasn't. But then I remembered Esme's insistence that she change my dirty glass, even though I had seen nothing wrong with it. I'd not watched her fill the clean glass, so it was theoretically possible she could have slipped something into it. But for what conceivable reason? It was a crazy idea.

'Is it possible?' Barraclough repeated.

'Yes,' I said, unable to stop myself sounding exasperated. 'It's possible. But there's no reason they would. I killed Frank. There's a pile of my clothes in the bathroom covered in his blood and a knife in the bedroom upstairs. You'll find my prints all over it. I did it. I confess everything. Just arrest me and do what you have to do.'

'Sky, stop,' Cam said, grabbing my shoulders. 'Don't say any more.'

'I want this over with.'

'But you can't confess to something you don't even remember doing.'

'I know what I did.' I was guilty, and I deserved to go to jail for it.

'He's right.' Barraclough pushed himself off the counter. 'You should listen to your boyfriend.'

Boyfriend? Oh God, he'd assumed we were together. 'But I'm guilty. Why won't you listen to me?'

'I assume you have Esme's number?' Barraclough said, pulling his phone out of his pocket.

'Yes, but I told you, she's dead!'

'Just give me the number.'

'Fine, but she's not going to answer, is she?' I said, as I scrolled through my phone.

Barraclough typed the number into his phone as I read it out. Then he dialled and put the phone to his ear. We all waited with bated breath. I heard it ring and then the tinny sound of Esme's voice.

'Straight to voicemail,' Barraclough said.

He dialled another number, which was answered almost immediately. He spoke to someone called Neil, who seemed to be a colleague. He gave him Esme's number and asked for a trace on it, plus a list of outgoing and incoming calls over the last twenty-four hours.

'Right,' he said, hanging up. 'I'm going to look upstairs. Wait here and don't move. Understand?'

We both nodded enthusiastically as we watched him disappear out of the room and heard his footsteps on the stairs. I hardly dared to breathe, grateful I'd finally got my confession off my chest, but worried Barraclough hadn't taken me seriously.

'Do you trust him?' Cam whispered.

'What? Of course. Don't you?'

'It's all a bit strange, don't you think?'

'What do you mean?' I asked.

'Well, what are the odds of him turning up here just hours after you supposedly killed the man he's been looking for? It's a bit of a coincidence,' Cam said.

'I did kill him.'

Cam shook his head. 'You only have Esme's word for that and she's dead. And did you notice how he didn't seem at all shocked or surprised when he saw the blood?'

'I guess he's seen a lot of murder scenes.'

'Maybe.'

'I wonder what Frank had done,' I said. 'It sounded serious.'

'And what's with the change of name too? Is it Duncan or Frank?' Cam said.

'I reckon he changed his name to escape from the police.' The conversation I'd overheard in the bathroom under the stairs echoed through my mind. Frank was definitely in hiding from someone. I'd just never imagined it would be the police.

'A fugitive?' Cam said. 'Whatever he did, it must have been serious.' He tugged his lip as he stared blankly across the room. 'Why hasn't Barraclough called for back-up? You'd have thought he'd have called it in the second he realised he'd walked into a crime scene. The house should be crawling with forensics by now. Instead, he's upstairs rummaging around on his own while we've been left down here alone. It doesn't seem right, does it?'

'I don't know.'

'Something's off with all of this. I just wish I could put my finger on it.' Cam had resumed pacing up and down, agitated.

I pulled out a chair at the table in the conservatory and slumped down, my body as weary as my mind. 'I wish I'd walked away when I first saw Esme on the beach,' I said. 'I wish I'd never stopped to talk to her or found her diary.'

My life wasn't perfect. I hated working at the arcade. I was living in a caravan, drinking too much, taking too many drugs. But I'd have given anything at that moment to return to my old, uncomplicated life. My life before Esme and Frank.

'What do you think we should do?' Cam asked.

'Wait here for the detective.' What else could we do?

Cam ran his fingers through his hair and let it flop back down in a mess that kind of suited him. 'Don't you feel like we should do something? Waiting here doing nothing is driving me crazy.'

He was right. What I really wanted to do was run away, just like I'd run away when they'd tried to put me into foster care; like I'd run away from my shit life in London at the first chance of a job on the island. Running away was what I did best. I could almost feel the cool sand between my toes as I let the fantasy play out in my head. I could hear the soft hush of the surf washing over the shore and taste the salt crusting on my lips. But I couldn't run. Not this time. That would only make things worse.

'He's coming back,' Cam said, stiffening as footsteps padded down the stairs. Adrenaline threaded through my veins like amphetamine.

We both looked at the detective expectantly, like we thought he was going to deliver some kind of revelation, some damning proof he'd found.

'What?' he growled.

'Find anything?' Cam asked.

But before he could answer, his phone rang. He turned his back on us as he answered, pulling out a notepad and pen from his jacket. He scribbled down some notes as he listened, and when he hung up, he had the shadow of a smile on his lips.

'That was the station,' he said. 'They've run a trace on Esme's number. Unfortunately, the phone's switched off so we can't locate it, but we have been able to access the call history. It looks like several calls were made late last night to a number registered to someone called James Steele. Mean anything to either of you?'

Why the hell was Esme calling Jimmy Steele in the middle of the night? 'That's my boss,' I said.

'Know where I can find him?'

'Doesn't he live — ' Cam began, but I spoke across him to shut him up.

'He has an office at the Golden Sands Amusement Arcade. You'll probably find him there.'

'On a Sunday?'

'He likes to catch up on paperwork while it's quiet. It's on the promenade by the beach,' I said.

Barraclough flipped his notebook shut and slid it back into his jacket as he headed for the front door.

'Hang on,' Cam said. 'You're leaving?'

'Looks that way,' he said.

'But what about us?' I'd prepared myself to be arrested and whisked off to the nearest police station for questioning. But here he was, about to abandon us. 'Should we stay here or what?'

Barraclough shrugged. 'Do whatever you like,' he said. 'I don't care, although personally I wouldn't hang around if I were you.'

'You're not arresting her?' Cam said. 'She's free to go?'

'I guess so.'

'Don't you at least want to take a statement and our contact details?' Cam glanced at me, his face clouded with bewilderment.

'Not really.' Barraclough was already out of the door and about to pull it shut when he hesitated. 'But I would suggest you find some bleach and give that kitchen floor a good scrub before you leave.'

CHAPTER FORTY-TWO

Hanlon pulled the door closed, his anger simmering. Whatever had happened in the house overnight, Duncan Whittaker and his wife had run rings around him. They'd both vanished under his nose and with it the chances of getting back the money they owed the Romanians. But he wouldn't give up that easily. Failure wasn't in his vocabulary. Besides, he had a reputation to protect. So far, the only evidence that Duncan was dead was the blood on the kitchen floor and that girl's word for it. But even she couldn't remember exactly what had happened. The fact she'd apparently blacked out after drinking too much seemed all a bit too convenient. There was definitely more going on here.

Apart from Duncan's missing body, there was something else bugging him. How had his wife slipped out of the house without him noticing? He'd deliberately parked up with a good view of the property. She must have left in the middle of the night when he'd thought it was safe to grab a few hours' kip. He wasn't a machine. He needed to sleep sometimes. That's when it paid to work in pairs, to have a second set of eyes. But in this line of work, he preferred to operate on his own.

The only lead he had was this guy, James Steele. What was his connection to Duncan and his wife? And why had she called him in the middle of the night? Was he a lover? A shoulder to cry on? Or something else?

As for those two kids in the house, he was confident they were just victims used by Duncan to his own ends. The fear in that girl's eyes was real. She'd become caught up in something way out of her league. He almost felt sorry for her.

He marched up the drive, determined Duncan Whittaker wouldn't get the better of him. He'd dealt with far worse scumbags than him, and by the end of the day, he would have the money one way or another. He tossed his gun and knife on the front seat of the van and covered them over with his jacket.

Traffic was light at that time on a Sunday morning as he headed back into Leysdown and he was able to park directly outside the Golden Sands Amusement Arcade, on double yellow lines. Heavy steel shutters were pulled down over its frontage but after a quick inspection, he discovered a locked side door. He hammered on it loudly with his fists and waited, listening. When no one answered, he banged on the door again, loud enough to wake the dead.

Eventually, he heard the lock turn, and the door

creaked open. A rat-faced woman with long hair tied in a ponytail peeked out, frowning.

'We don't open until ten,' she said.

Hanlon flashed his fake identification in her face. 'DC Barraclough. Met Police. I'm looking for James Steele. I understand he has an office here.'

The woman looked confused. 'Yes, but it's Sunday. He won't be in today.'

The girl had lied to him. 'Are you sure?'

'Of course I'm sure.'

'What's your name?' he asked.

'Michelle. I'm the manager. What's this about? I could take a message for him if you like.'

'I need to look around,' Hanlon said. He'd learned from bitter experience not to take people at their word. 'Can I come in?'

The woman hesitated, unsure.

'It's a serious crime I'm investigating. Mr Steele may have some vital information,' he said, fixing her with a determined stare.

The woman huffed. 'Okay,' she said, opening the door for him.

'Where's his office?'

She pointed to a back staircase and followed him up. He threw open the door and stuck his head inside. No lights. No computers on. It was deserted. It looked like she at least had been telling the truth.

'If you want to speak to him, you're best going to his house,' the woman said.

'Do you have an address?'

'Yeah, he lives in that big place in Eastchurch. Shurland Hall. You can't miss it.'

'Thank you,' Hanlon said, rushing out of the door and running back to his van.

CHAPTER FORTY-THREE

Cam was the first to break the silence.

'Did you hear that?' he said, looking incredulous. 'He just told you to clean the kitchen with bleach. Who the hell was that guy?'

I shook my head, my mind struggling to process what was going on. Things were getting weirder by the second. Nothing made any sense beyond the fact that I'd killed Frank and Esme was dead. I couldn't understand why I'd not been arrested. Barraclough hadn't even called for back-up. I needed answers. And Jimmy seemed to be the only man who might have them.

'Do you think he was even a real cop?' Cam asked.

'No,' I said, mulling over the hushed conversation I'd overheard between Frank and Esme when I'd first been in the house. If they hadn't been on the run from the police, then from who?

'We have to get to Jimmy before he does,' I said, snapping into action. 'Something odd's going on.'

Cam nodded. 'I agree. You should call him.'

'I don't have his number,' I said, snatching Frank's keys from the side. 'Come on. We don't have much time. I'll drive.'

It didn't take me long to get the feel for the Range Rover, even though it had been a while since I'd last driven. Not that I'd ever officially passed a test or held a licence, but I knew the basics. That was the education a misspent childhood in East London got you.

It was only a short drive to Shurland Hall and with Cam directing from a map on his phone, we were soon racing down a narrow high street, past a row of terraced houses and bouncing over speed humps before we reached a turning onto an unmade road that led to Jimmy's mansion. I jumped on the brakes a bit too aggressively and skidded onto the gravel drive. I pulled up behind Jimmy's Aston Martin and ratcheted on the handbrake.

'Can you stay here and keep an eye out for Barraclough?' I said to Cam as he threw open his door and climbed out.

'What? No, I'm coming with you,' he said. 'I'm not letting you out of my sight.'

I didn't have the time to argue with him. 'That's sweet,' I said, touching his arm. 'But I need a pair of eyes out here. Barraclough's going to be here any minute. Call me when he turns up.'

'But Sky — ' Cam tried to protest.

'For me,' I said, firmly. 'Please, Cam.'

He looked wounded but eventually nodded. 'Alright. I'll be here. But any trouble, let me know.'

'Thank you.' I leaned across and pecked him on the cheek. 'I'm glad you're here.'

'Be careful, alright?'

I hopped out of the car, tossed the keys to Cam and strode up to the over-sized wooden door, trying to compose my thoughts. The last time I'd been to the house was to see Esme, and that hadn't turned out too well. If only I'd been able to convince her to confide in mc about Frank at that point, things might have turned out so differently. I could have helped her escape, taken her somewhere safe where he'd never hurt her again. But it was too late to worry about that now.

I heard footsteps from inside. The door creaked open and Jimmy appeared, his smile evaporating when he saw it was me.

'Sky? What are you doing here?' he asked, frowning.

'I'm sorry, I didn't know what else to do. Can I talk to you for a minute?'

'Umm,' he glanced over his shoulder, looking shifty. 'It's not a good time.'

'It's urgent,' I said, my voice trembling. 'It's about Esme's husband, Frank.' I hesitated for a beat, not sure how he'd take it. 'I killed him.'

Jimmy's eyes opened wide. 'Killed him?'

Saying it out loud didn't make it any easier to accept. 'He was… ' I took a breath, made myself slow down. 'He was attacking Esme. I was worried he was going to really hurt her.' I could almost picture it happening now. Almost a memory. But not quite. 'And I grabbed a knife and I... ' I reached for the door frame to steady myself, my stomach churning.

'What are you talking about, Sky?' Jimmy looked at me like I was insane.

'I found his body in the kitchen this morning. But then, and I know this is going to sound weird, it was gone. I think Esme might have moved him.' I could see from Jimmy's expression that I wasn't explaining it particularly well, but I carried on regardless. 'Then there was this man who came to the house claiming he was a detective, but I'm pretty certain he was lying. Anyway, he traced the calls made from Esme's phone last night.'

The colour drained from Jimmy's face and his Adam's apple bobbed up and down as he swallowed.

'He said she called you several times, so I wondered if you might know what the hell's going on? Did you speak to her? Why did she call you?'

Jimmy shuffled from one foot to the other and stared over my shoulder, back up the drive. 'I think you'd better come in,' he said.

I stepped inside the cavernous hall, the smell of dusty antiques and furniture polish reminding me with sadness of my first visit to see Esme.

'If you know anything, please tell me because I'm going out of my mind,' I begged him. I glanced down at my boots. 'And I'm afraid there's some bad news about Esme.'

When I looked up, Jimmy's eyes had narrowed, his face twisted in confusion. It would be best if I just came right out and told him. 'I'm sorry, Mr Steele. I know you were close to her, but Esme's dead too. She took her own life this morning.'

I don't know how I expected him to react, but he just stood staring at me. If he was shocked, he certainly didn't show it. In fact, he remained remarkably composed.

'Did you hear me?' I said. 'Esme's dead. She shot herself with Frank's gun. I'm so, so sorry.'

'The man who was at the house this morning,' Jimmy said, 'what did he look like? Did he give you a name?'

'Mr Steele, did you hear what I said?'

'Oh God, Sky. You shouldn't be here. You need to go home.' He reached for the door as if he'd made a mistake inviting me in and wanted to usher me out again. But I refused to move, my arms crossed.

'You want to know about the man who came to the house? I'd give it about ten minutes and you can find out for yourself. He's looking for you. I sent him to the arcade, but it won't take him long to realise you're not there. And everybody knows where you live,' I said.

He blinked rapidly, chewing his bottom lip as he stared at me, wide-eyed and a bead of sweat pearling on his brow.

'You know who he is,' I said with a dawning realisation. 'And you knew he was going to turn up at the house, didn't you? What's going on?' My raised voice echoed around the hall.

'It's not safe for you here,' he said. 'Please, go home.'

'Not until you start talking. I want to know what's going on. I have a right to know.'

A loud thud like a cupboard door being forcefully closed punctuated the tense silence between us. Jimmy's eyes darted towards a passageway running behind a wide staircase. When he looked back at me, guilt was written all across his face. He was hiding something. Or someone.

'Is there someone here?'

'No,' Jimmy said too quickly.

He tried to grab my arm as I pushed past and marched down the passageway towards the noise I'd heard, but I shrugged off his hand.

'Sky! Stop!'

I had no idea where I was going or what I expected to find, but I didn't give it a second thought. My entire life was spiralling out of control. I didn't know who I was or what was happening to me. Was I cold-blooded killer or just a pawn in a bigger game? All I knew for sure was that the answers lay somewhere in this house.

The corridor opened up into the largest kitchen I'd ever seen. It had enormous picture windows on three sides with views over sweeping lawns and formal gardens. Cupboards and worktops stretched along the length of one wall, and a huge pine table and chairs dominated the centre of the room.

But my eyes were drawn to only one thing - the

figure leaning against a counter, frozen with surprise when he saw me. My heart pounded in my chest like I'd seen a ghost.

I *had* seen a ghost.

'Sky,' Frank said, swallowing. 'I can explain.'

CHAPTER FORTY-FOUR

F or a man I thought I'd stabbed to death, Frank Winters looked in remarkably ruddy health. 'I don't understand,' I said. 'I thought you were dead. You were on the floor - the kitchen - your blood was everywhere.'

'Sky — ' He held up his hands.

I was slowly beginning to understand. 'You wanted me to *think* you were dead,' I said. I didn't know whether I was more furious or relieved. 'This whole thing was… faked.'

It was definitely Frank's body I'd seen lying on their kitchen floor, but in my shock I never even thought to check for injuries or whether he was breathing. The tablecloth over his body had helped conceal the truth, and I'd allowed myself to fill in the blanks, believing what I thought I was seeing. 'But why? Why would you do that to me?'

'It's complicated,' Frank said, edging closer to me.

'Did you hate me that much? I was only ever trying to help Esme,' I screamed at him.

'Is that what you think this is about?'

'Isn't it? You were trying to frame me because I'd found out what you were doing to her. Did you think you'd get away with it?'

'You have a wild imagination,' Frank said.

'Don't patronise me. Come on, what was the plan? To frighten me off? And I guess the guy you sent around this morning was supposed to add some realism, was he?'

'Guy?'

'Your detective friend.' I made speech tags in the air with my fingers. 'Did you know about this?' I turned on Jimmy, who'd followed me in and was standing in the doorway.

'Know about what?' he said, his brow puckering.

'That Frank faked his own death to scare me away when I found out he was abusing Esme?'

'Frank?' he said, glancing at him. 'What's she talking about?'

'She's out of her mind,' Frank said. At least he had the decency to look worried. He was wringing his hands and shuffling on the spot. It was small comfort to have him on the ropes.

'But what puzzles me is how you persuaded Esme to play along with it. Did you threaten her? Promise her another beating? You make me sick!'

'You don't know what you're talking about,' Frank said.

'She's not dead either, is she?' I said. 'Let me guess, you made her take your shotgun and fake her suicide.' It occurred to me now that I'd never actually seen her die. At the moment she'd pulled the trigger, she'd kicked the phone away. It looked like an accident but I could see now it had been deliberate. What had Frank expected? For me to blame myself for their deaths? To run away and forget about them? That's exactly what the old me would have done; run a mile at the first sign of trouble. Perhaps he knew me better than I thought.

'Why were you at the house?' Jimmy asked, looking at me and back to Frank again.

'I was invited to dinner, supposedly as an apology for the way Frank had behaved, but I'm guessing now you'd planned this all along?' I said. 'And you drugged me. That's why I blacked out, isn't it? Not because of how much I drank.'

'Don't be ridiculous,' Frank said.

I studied his face, trying to read his expression. 'Stop lying to me. It's pathetic.'

Frank looked at Jimmy, like he was having to deal with a petulant child. 'She doesn't know what she's saying,' he said. 'She's been seeing Esme for counselling for some psychological issues. Childhood trauma, you know?'

Was he serious? 'Jimmy, he's lying to you.'

Jimmy pinched the bridge of his nose. 'I'm sorry, Sky, I'm not following this at all. How do you know Frank and Esme?'

'It's a long story,' I said. 'I found Esme's diary. That's

how I worked out Frank has been abusing her. And yes, it's true I booked a consultation with Esme, but it was the only way I could see her without Frank being around. I was trying to rescue her from him.'

'You see?' Frank said. 'Totally delusional.'

'I'm not making this up,' I yelled.

'Maybe I should run you home, Sky.' Jimmy pulled a wan smile.

'You don't believe me, do you? Frank tried to set me up. What kind of man does that? And why would I make something like that up?'

I was shaking with anger. What Frank had done was bad enough, but that Jimmy thought I was deranged made it ten times worse. What could I say to make him believe me? As my brain tried to deconstruct everything that had happened over the last few days, sifting the truth from the lies, another thought unfurled in my mind. 'What are you doing here anyway, Frank?' I asked.

'What?'

'Well, if Jimmy didn't know what you'd done, why are you here?'

Jimmy stiffened. 'We were discussing the terms of the rent for Esme's consulting room,' he said, clearly grabbing the first thing that came to mind.

'On a Sunday morning? Liar,' I said. 'Try again.'

'Look,' Jimmy hung his head, 'I was just helping them out with something, that's all.'

'Helping them out with what, exactly?' I put my hands on my hips and narrowed my eyes. As Frank seemed incapable of telling anything but lies, I focused on Jimmy instead.

'You don't want to know,' he said.

I was so caught up in my anger and frustration, I didn't hear the footsteps in the corridor.

'Sky? What are you doing here?'

I spun around to encounter my second ghost of the day, although I was less surprised to see Esme than I had been to find Frank alive and well. 'So I was right. You're not dead either.'

She ran her tongue over her teeth as she looked me up and down. 'So it would seem. Surprised?'

Her cutting tone caught me off guard. Why was she being like that? Was she putting it on because Frank was there? 'It's okay, Esme, you can stop pretending with me. I know what's been going on.'

'Do you?'

'And you don't have to put up with this anymore. We can leave right now. He's not going to stop you,' I said, although I wasn't confident Frank wouldn't put up a fight. If he'd gone to the lengths of faking his own death to protect his marriage, he was capable of anything.

Esme rubbed her forehead with the ball of her hand like she was easing away the pain of a tension headache. 'You really don't get it, do you?' she hissed.

'Esme?'

'Oh, for God's sake. How many times do I have to tell you? Frank has never laid a finger on me. It's always been in your head,' she said.

It stunned me into momentary silence. I couldn't understand why, after everything, she was still denying it. 'But when you phoned me first thing this morning and told me Frank was dead, you said it was because he was hitting you and wouldn't stop. That's when I — '

'God, you're so naïve, Sky. Will you stop and think about it for a second.'

'Please, Esme. All I ever wanted was to help you,' I said.

'You had your chance to help me this morning when I told you to go home. Instead, you went back to the house and now you've ruined everything, you stupid, stupid girl.'

Her spiteful words stung me into silence like a hard slap across the face.

Frank chipped in with worry etched on his face. 'She said she spoke to a man posing as a detective at the house this morning.'

'What did you tell him?' Esme snapped at me, her face flushing.

'Nothing,' I said. 'Why, who is he?'

'He traced your phone and knows you called Jimmy last night,' Frank said, scowling. 'Sky sent him to the arcade but the chances are he's on his way here now. We don't have long.'

'Jesus.' Esme's eyes grew wide and black. 'Any news on that chopper, Jimmy?'

Jimmy checked his watch. 'Should be here any minute,' he said.

'Call them. Tell them to get a move on. We can't be here when he arrives,' she said.

'I'm sorry, Esme, I can't do anything about the fog. As soon as it clears, they'll be able to take off,' Jimmy said.

Just when I thought I'd untangled everything, the mists in my mind surfaced again. 'Who was that guy at the house?' I asked. 'He's not really a detective, is he?'

Esme laughed sarcastically. 'No,' she said. 'He's most definitely not a detective.'

'So who is he?'

'You don't want to know, trust me,' she said.

'I think I have a right to know.' I pulled my phone from my pocket and held it up as if it was the detonator to a bomb. 'I think this has gone on long enough. I want the truth or I'll call the cops and they can sort this mess out.'

'Don't be stupid,' Esme said. 'Put the phone away.'

'Start talking,' I demanded. 'What chopper? Where are you going?' I pressed two nines on the numerical keypad and held up the phone so they could see I was serious.

'Come on, don't do anything silly,' Frank said, raising his hands in submission. 'Look, we need to disappear.'

'What do you mean disappear?' I asked.

'I did something foolish,' he said with a sigh. 'And now there are some bad people looking for us. If they find us, they'll most likely kill us. We came to the island to hide, but they won't leave us alone until they get what they want.'

'Frank! Shut up!' Esme barked.

'I think she has a right to know,' he said, 'after everything we've put her through. Jimmy kindly offered us the use of his helicopter to take us abroad. It's better you know no more than that.' Suddenly his tone had softened. He was being almost conciliatory. It was Esme who was being the aggressive one. Maybe I'd misjudged them both.

Slowly, the pieces of the giant jigsaw I thought I'd nearly completed rearranged themselves in my head. While it was true Frank and Esme had staged their deaths, I'd been completely wide of the mark about the reasons. 'You needed me to confess to your murder,' I said as I worked it out, 'because without a body, you needed someone to confirm the death.' I was stunned. Even as I said it, it sounded ludicrous. How could they have been so callous when all I'd ever wanted was to help Esme? They'd used me and tossed me to the wolves to save their own skins. Fury burned in my chest.

'It wasn't anything personal,' Frank said. 'We were desperate. We didn't know what else to do.'

'Let me get this straight,' I said, battling to keep my emotions in check. 'Esme convinced me I'd killed you, so that I would confess to the police?'

'We had to come up with a plan in a hurry,' Frank explained. 'The guy who told you he was a detective works for the people we're running from. He found me yesterday morning and gave me until this morning to repay some money I took. The only way we could think to get him off our backs for good, was to convince him we were dead.'

'Hang on a minute,' I said. 'What money?'

'Criminal money. It was stupid but seemed like a good idea at the time.'

'Jimmy, if that chopper isn't here in the next two minutes, we have a serious problem,' Esme said, getting agitated.

'Shut up,' I said. 'You're not going anywhere until I've sorted this out.' I waved my phone in her face. 'Keep talking.'

'Well, we knew you'd become obsessed with Esme and had it in your head I was mistreating her,' Frank said. 'We thought it would be easy to convince you you'd stabbed me when you saw me attacking her. And it would have worked, if you'd followed Esme's instructions and gone home when she told you.'

'And Esme's suicide? How were you going to explain that away?'

'Her body taken by an incoming tide,' Frank said with a shrug. 'It was the best we could manage at short notice.'

'But your diary?' I turned to Esme. 'It was full of details about how Frank was abusing you.'

She shook her head and laughed cruelly. 'Of course it wasn't. You thought I was a victim, and you took the words you'd read and fitted them to suit your own truth. Yes, I was in turmoil when I wrote the diary, but not about Frank abusing me. It was the situation he'd put us in that upset me. He'd robbed us of our lives as we knew them and for a while I hated him for that, knowing we'd always be looking over our shoulders, always wondering if they were about to catch up with us.'

'Everything I did was for you,' I said. 'And this is what I get?'

'You made it too easy, Sky,' Esme said with a smirk that fuelled my anger. 'Especially after I found out what happened to your mother. It wasn't difficult to make you think history was repeating itself, except this time we convinced you you'd stepped up and done the right thing.'

Bitch. I could have killed her myself.

Jimmy was standing open-mouthed, listening without saying a word. I don't think he knew any of this. He was just another pawn in their game.

But I was still struggling with their story. So much of it made no sense. 'But the blood?' I said. 'I didn't imagine it. It was all over the kitchen floor. On my clothes. Even in the bed.' I shook my head, reliving the last few hours when I'd been ready to believe I was capable of murder.

'Pig's blood,' she said, still with that smirk on her face like she'd been so clever. 'Easy to get hold of. After you passed out, we splattered some of it on your clothes and put you to bed. The knife in the room was a nice touch, don't you think?'

'No, that doesn't make sense,' I said, shaking my

head. 'The police wouldn't have believed my confession on its own. They'd have needed some evidence. Pig's blood wouldn't have fooled them.'

'Why do you think I needed you out of the house? I was planning to go back and clean it up. We were going to leave a few spots of Frank's blood in the kitchen. Just enough to convince them you were telling the truth.'

'And Frank's body?'

'I don't know. They'd think you'd got rid of it somehow.'

Jesus. They'd thought of almost everything. They'd been so cold, so calculating. My entire body trembled. 'Jimmy, please tell me you weren't a part of this.'

He shook his head. 'No,' he said, glowering at Esme. 'I didn't know that's what they were planning. The first I even knew they were in trouble was yesterday when Esme came to see me. She told me they needed to get off the island quickly. I'm sorry. I had no idea they were going to involve you.'

I looked him in the eye and trusted he was telling me the truth. It made sense. To them, he was just a guy with a helicopter. Someone else to use for their own selfish ends.

'So that's it? You're going to fly off into the sunset and live happily ever after?' I said.

'It wasn't quite the plan we had in mind,' Esme said. The look she gave me could have soured milk. 'They know we're still alive, thanks to you, so they'll keep coming for us. We'll never be free.'

'You know I can't let you go, don't you?'

Esme laughed. 'And how are you going to stop us, Sky?'

I glanced at my phone and raised an eyebrow. 'For a start, let's see what the police have to say.'

'Don't you dare!' Esme screamed at me. 'Frank, get her phone. Take it from her.'

Frank hesitated for a second and then lunged at me. I screamed and turned my back to him, holding my phone high above my head, trying to put it out of his reach. But he was taller and stronger. He snatched my wrist and yanked my arm down roughly.

'Get off me!' I yelled at him as he grappled for the phone. But I was determined not to let it go. It was my lifeline to safety.

He'd bent two of my fingers back and almost had it prised out of my grasp when the phone rang, surprising both of us. We looked at each other and I caught a glance at the screen. Cam calling.

'I think that's my friend letting me know that our fake detective has just turned up,' I said. 'It looks like time's up for you.'

CHAPTER FORTY-FIVE

F rank released my wrist and backed away like I
was toxic. I answered the call and listened to
Cam breathlessly confirm what I'd already guessed.

'He's here,' he said. 'He's going to the door.'

'Did he see you?'

'I don't think so,' Cam said. 'Should I try to stop
him?'

'No, stay out of sight. He's dangerous,' I said. 'I don't
want you to get hurt.'

'Are you okay, Sky? What's going on in there?'

'I'm fine. Stay where you are.' I hung up and looked
around the room at the three expectant faces staring
at me.

I nodded. A second later a loud banging came from
the entrance hallway. 'Is that him?' Jimmy gasped,
twitching nervously. 'What do I do?'

'Let him in,' Esme said with a calmness I wasn't
expecting.

'Are you crazy?' Frank turned on her with a wild look in his eye. 'You remember why he's here, right?'

'Just do it. Don't question me,' she fired back with venom.

Jimmy puffed out his cheeks. 'Okay, fine,' he said. 'If you're absolutely sure.'

He trudged from the kitchen and as he disappeared down the corridor, Esme threw herself at the cupboards, flinging open doors and rummaging through their contents until she found a heavy, cast iron pan with a wooden handle.

I watched her suspiciously, wondering what the hell she was playing at now. A few days ago, I'd felt sorry for her. I genuinely believed she was a victim in need of my help to escape a violent partner. Now I knew I couldn't trust her. She wasn't the woman I thought she was.

She weighed up the pan in two hands and, apparently satisfied, marched to the window nearest the door to the corridor. 'When he gets here, keep him talking and do exactly as he says,' she instructed Frank. 'And if he asks where I am, tell him I'm upstairs using the bathroom.'

Frank nodded, but his eyes had glazed over like he was lost in some faraway place. Fear could have a funny effect on people.

'And what about me?' I asked. Was I supposed to stand there saying nothing? They'd dragged me into their mess and all I wanted to do was walk away. But I couldn't.

'Keep your mouth closed and say nothing,' Esme snarled as she slipped behind a heavy curtain and vanished from sight.

Footsteps heralded Jimmy's return, followed closely behind by the guy claiming to be a detective we'd met at Frank and Esme's house. He had a gun pointed casually at Jimmy's back, aiming low down at the base of his spine. Jimmy's face had lost its usual easy congeniality. He moved stiffly, his jaw tight. I couldn't take my eyes off the gun. Such an ugly, brutal lump of metal.

'Look who we have here,' Barraclough said with a chilling menace. He gave a lop-sided grin as he surveyed the room. 'The co-conspirators all together.' He shoved Jimmy in the back, pushing him into the middle of the kitchen. 'I don't like it when people lie to me.' He turned the gun on me, his aim steady. He pointed it at my chest and my bottom lip trembled. 'That was a silly thing to do.'

'I'm sorry — '

'Shut it,' he said.

He must have understood I was a victim here, that Frank and Esme had used me. I wasn't part of any conspiracy. Maybe if I got the chance, I could explain to him and persuade him to let me go.

'And Duncan,' he said, shifting his attention to Frank. 'I thought you would have known better than to run. I thought I'd made myself quite clear.'

Frank or Duncan, or whatever his name really was, backed away with his hands up. 'I was trying to get the money for you, that's all. Just doing like you asked.'

'Is that right? And the elaborate murder scene you left at the house? What was that all about?' Barraclough's gun arm straightened as he aimed for a spot in the middle of Frank's forehead.

'I - I can explain.' I thought Frank was going to crumple like a soggy paper bag. He looked scared witless. Served him right after the way he'd treated me.

'This should be good.'

'Alright, I'm sorry. It was a stupid thing to do, but I told you, I don't have the money. I didn't know what else to do,' Frank mumbled.

'And I told you, that's not my problem. The people who employ me want their money back. The money you stole.'

'I don't know what to say to you.' Frank was shaking his head, his skin deathly pallid.

'You know, if you're going to play with the big boys, you need to grow some big boys' balls, Duncan. You understand?' Barraclough chuckled to himself. 'So how can I persuade you I'm serious?' He glanced around the room again, at me and Jimmy, as if he was looking for something in particular.

'I know you're serious,' Frank said. 'You don't have to prove anything. You're the one with the gun.'

'That's right. I am. Where's your wife, Duncan? I assume she's here with you and that she didn't blow her brains out with your shotgun as you tried to make this poor young girl believe?'

'Leave my wife out of this. It has nothing to do with her,' Frank said.

'But she is involved, isn't she? Where is she?'

'Please.' Frank's head sagged. 'Let's keep this between the two of us. Man to man.'

'Like I wanted to do all along, but you couldn't play by the rules, could you? Where is she?' Barraclough asked again, with a sinister quietness.

'She's upstairs,' Frank said with a sigh. 'Using the bathroom. I'm sure she'll be down in a minute.'

'Fetch her,' Barraclough ordered Jimmy. 'And don't try anything stupid.' He lowered the gun and levelled it at Frank's legs. 'It would be a shame to make a mess in this nice kitchen.'

I resisted the urge to glance at the curtain where Esme was hiding, wondering when she was going to make her move. Jimmy hopped from one foot to the other, as if he was caught by indecision.

'It's okay, Jimmy. Do as he says. Tell Esme to come down and let her know he has a gun.' There was a tremor in Frank's voice.

Jimmy faltered.

'Hurry. Go,' Frank urged him.

Jimmy finally nodded and shuffled out of the room. A moment later, I heard the creak of his weight on the staircase.

'I don't know why you people always have to make it so difficult for yourselves,' Frank said. 'You can't win, so why try? And you know I'll need to punish you for that, right?'

'Look, can't we work something out?' Frank asked.

'Not my style, I'm afraid,' Barraclough said. 'I have a reputation to preserve.'

'I can pay you.'

Barraclough laughed. 'But you've already told me you can't pay back the money you stole. So how are you going to pay me off? Idiot.' For the first time, a flash of irritation danced across his face.

In the corner of my eye, I saw the curtain where Esme was hiding twitch. It took all my willpower not to look. I assumed she was readying herself to pounce, but she'd have to cross four or five metres of ground to reach Barraclough. And if he turned or caught sight of her movement, well, he was the one with the gun.

'But listen, while we wait for your lovely wife, I have a question for you,' Barraclough said. 'I was watching the house last night, as you well know. So how did you both sneak out? The only person I saw leave was the girl.'

Frank stood up straight and smiled liked he'd finally got one over on the other man. 'A gap in the hedge at the back of the garden,' he said. 'It takes you out onto fields on the top of the cliff and you can head either back into Warden Bay or follow a path down to the beach.'

'I missed that,' Barraclough said, nodding sagely. 'So you could come and go as you pleased, and I was none the wiser. A foolish oversight on my part.'

'And while you were watching the front of the house, we were moving bags out and down to the back of an abandoned pub where Jimmy picked us up and brought us here.'

Barraclough nodded again. 'Fair play to you. You nearly had me.'

I clenched every muscle in my body as Esme emerged from her hiding spot, gripping the pan with both hands like a baseball player stepping up to the plate, bat in hand, ready to take a swing. She tiptoed towards Barraclough with baby steps, moving in slow motion.

Frank's mouth opened and closed as he spotted his wife, his eyes growing wide. He looked down at his hands and mumbled something unintelligible. Oh God, he'd frozen. Right at the moment Esme needed him to keep Barraclough distracted. If he turned his head even a fraction right now, he was going to see her.

I bolted from the spot where I was standing, springing into action. 'Why don't I put the kettle on,' I said, fixing a smile on my face.

Barraclough stared at me like I was out of my mind, but at least he was watching me, his attention distracted as Esme continued to creep up behind him.

I snatched up the kettle from the side. 'Tea or coffee?' I asked as I filled it noisily from the tap.

'Get back where you were,' he shouted at me. 'And put that bloody kettle down.'

Esme was within an arm's reach of Barraclough. I held my breath, waiting for her to strike, but whether he glimpsed her reflection in a window or heard the creak of a floorboard, he turned suddenly, whipping his gun around as she gritted her teeth and swung the heavy pan at his head.

He raised an arm to defend himself but wasn't quick enough. She hit him flush across the temple. With a gut-wrenching crack of bone, he fell sprawling across the floor, dropping the gun, his eyes rolling back in his head.

Esme stood panting over him, the pan hanging at her side, a wisp of hair fallen out of place over her brow.

'You've killed him,' I gasped.

CHAPTER FORTY-SIX

Frank knelt at Barraclough's side, feeling for a pulse in his neck. 'Not quite,' he said. 'He's still alive.'

Jimmy raced back into the room, out of breath. 'Jesus, what happened?' he asked, skidding to a halt as he spotted Barraclough's still body on the floor.

Nobody replied. We all stood motionless, staring at the twisted figure. I let out a sigh of relief, the adrenaline still pounding around my body like a greyhound at a racetrack.

'Get rid of him,' Esme ordered.

'Where?' Frank looked up at her, his brow furrowed.

'I don't care. Just lose him,' she said.

Frank looked around the room and out of the windows. The grounds of the house seemed to stretch on for miles.

'No,' said Jimmy. 'You're not leaving him here. Oh, Esme, what have you done?'

'It was him or us. Don't go getting sentimental on me. How did he get here?' Esme said.

'There was a campervan out front when I answered the door. I guess that must be his,' Jimmy said.

Esme calmly walked to the sink, dropped the pan into a bowl and leaned back against a worktop, folding her arms across her stomach. 'This is what you're going to do,' she said. 'Put him back in his van and Jimmy, as soon as we've gone, stage a crash. Make it look realistic and burn the vehicle if you can.'

'What?' Jimmy said, like he couldn't believe what she was suggesting.

'It's that or we kill him here and bury him in the grounds. It's up to you. But it's better if it looks like an accident.' Esme pushed herself off the counter, picked up Barraclough's gun and began pacing up and down, her shoes clip-clapping across the stripped wooden floorboards.

I couldn't stand by and do nothing. As much as Barraclough was a crook, I couldn't let them get away with murdering him. Plus, I wasn't sure what Esme had planned for me. I wasn't convinced she was just going to let me go. As Frank slipped his hands under Barraclough's arms to lift him, I turned my back on them and unlocked my phone.

'Put that down right now.' Esme's voice was steely cold.

I heard a click which I presumed was something to do with her cocking the gun and when I turned around, she was aiming at my head, holding the weapon with both hands like she knew what she was doing. I raised my hands slowly as Frank started dragging Barraclough across the floor.

'Don't just stand there,' he said to Jimmy. 'Give me a hand.'

I watched as the two men manhandled the body out of the room and into the adjacent corridor. Esme didn't flinch or take her eyes off me.

'Throw me the phone,' she said.

I tried to keep my movements slow and deliberate, but the phone dropped short and clattered to the floor.

'What happens now?' I asked as she kicked the phone out of my reach. 'You know they'll hunt you down wherever you go. There's no escape from people like that.' I didn't know what I was saying. I only knew that I had to keep her engaged and talking.

Esme's grim smile sent a shiver of fear down my back. 'Nothing's changed,' she said. 'They'll still think we're dead. Nobody other than that idiot they sent to find Duncan knows the truth. No doubt it'll be all over the papers, along with your picture.'

'What are you talking about?' I said. 'It's over. I'm not going to confess to the police that I killed Frank.' Had she finally lost the plot?

'Imagine the scene,' she said, reaching for her hand-bag. 'The police are called to our house. No sign of me or Frank, but they find traces of his blood in the kitchen and the shotgun on the beach. Upstairs, in the bedroom, your dead body. A post-mortem will find you took an overdose, and they'll conclude that after killing

Frank and witnessing my suicide, you couldn't live with what you'd done and took your own life.'

My mouth fell open. Was she serious? 'Took my own life?' I said.

Esme pulled out a small plastic medicine bottle from her bag and prised off the cap. Then she tipped out a dozen white pills into her hand.

'No, you're crazy,' I screamed at her, backing away.

'Don't be melodramatic,' she soothed. 'There's no other way. It'll be quick and painless. You won't feel a thing.'

With the gun still pointing at my head, she edged towards the kitchen cupboards, found a glass and filled it with water. There was nothing I could do but watch with horror as she then grabbed a spoon from a drawer and began crushing the pills into a fine white powder.

'Please, don't do this,' I said. 'I won't tell anyone what's happened. It'll be our secret.'

'Come on, Sky, you know there's only one way for two people to keep a secret and that's for one of them to die.'

I glanced at the door to the corridor and contemplated making a run for it. Could I make it? Was she that good a shot? The trouble was, I had no idea.

But even before the idea was fully formed in my mind, I'd missed the opportunity as Frank and Jimmy returned looking hot and sweaty, blocking my way out.

'What's going on?' Frank asked as Esme scraped the ground powder into the glass of water and swilled it around with the spoon.

'You're back just in time.' She handed Frank the glass as the two men stepped across the kitchen to see what she was doing. 'Make her drink this.'

'Jimmy?' I said, appealing to the one person in the room who could help me. But he lowered his gaze and stared at the ground, ignoring me, too spineless to act. 'Please, stop them.'

'Stop whingeing,' Esme yelled at me. 'You're making a fuss.'

She was about to kill me. Of course I was making a fuss. Frank held the glass up to the light. Little specks of powder danced around the water like stars in the night sky. 'How am I supposed to make her drink it?' he asked.

For a second, Esme took her eyes off me, the gun wavering. I looked to the door again. I calculated it would take me at least seven or eight strides to reach the corridor. But if I kept low and fast, maybe I could make it. I was going to die, anyway. I might as well take my chances. It was now or never.

CHAPTER FORTY-SEVEN

I bolted for it, pumping my legs. I was quick, adrenaline fuelling my panic. But Frank was quicker. He shot after me, his feet pounding on the wooden floor. I almost made it. No gunshot. I reached the door and ducked into the corridor, banging my shoulder painfully against the frame. But then Frank's hand was around my arm, snatching my wrist, dragging me back. I kicked and screamed as if my life depended on it. 'Let me go!' I yelled in his face, my arm twisting against its socket in agony.

He slapped me hard across the face.

The shock of it instantly broke my spirit. I touched my cheek and stared at him, disbelieving.

'Sit down!' he ordered, pulling up a chair around the big pine table and pushing me down roughly.

'Jimmy, stop them,' I sobbed. 'Do something.'

He looked up at me briefly and I could see he wanted no part of this. A dark melancholy had stolen his smile. But still he didn't move. I couldn't believe it. He was going to let it happen. Too scared of Esme to stop her. He was my only hope, but he wouldn't act. I was on my own.

'Please... please - I don't want to die.' I wailed with thick, hot tears pouring down my cheeks.

'Frank!' Esme shouted, shoving the glass under his nose, but he'd frozen again, his eyes dull and glazed.

He wasn't going to do it. For a second, my spirits were revived. He'd seen sense and was standing up to her, refusing to be any part of it. But my hope was short-lived.

'Fine, I'll do it myself, you useless man,' Esme said, huffing like he was a feckless teenager, incapable of doing anything himself. I'd misjudged their relationship.

She took a step behind me, put the gun on the table and with no warning grabbed my nose, pinching it closed so I couldn't breathe, and yanked my head back so I was looking up at the ceiling. I screwed up my eyes and bunched my fists, but I was helpless to resist.

'Just a minute,' she said, letting me go, my head flopping onto my chest. 'You ought to leave a note. Jimmy, get some paper and a pen.'

'Do we really have time for this?' Frank asked. I was glad to see he was looking uncomfortable, arms crossed over his chest and his brow hooded. 'The chopper's going to be here any minute.'

Esme shot her husband a look of pure disdain. 'You want to leave this to chance after everything you've got us into? We do this right and we can concentrate on getting on with the rest of our lives. Jimmy, paper. Now!'

Jimmy finally looked up from the spot on the floor he'd been staring at. He looked like he'd aged several years in the space of a few minutes. Worry lines furrowed his forehead, and he was pale and gaunt. 'No, I'm sorry, I can't do it,' he murmured.

'What?' Esme scowled at him.

'It's not right,' he said. 'Sky's not done anything to deserve this.'

'Jimmy, come on, please,' Esme said, almost tenderly, her tone changing like someone had flicked a switch. 'Do it for me?' She even made puppy dog eyes at him.

'I'm sorry, I can't be part of this,' he said, shaking his head.

'You know we can't do this without you, Jimmy, and you've been so good to us,' she cooed. 'One more little thing. That's all I ask. Do it for me?'

Oh my God, was she flirting? It made my stomach churn. So that was the power she held over him and why Jimmy had been so happy to put himself out to help. He had a crush on her, and she was exploiting it for all it was worth. I glanced at Frank, but he was watching impassively, showing no emotion. Could he even see what was going on here?

Jimmy sighed and looked to the ceiling, clearly conflicted.

'Jimmy, they have to believe we're dead or they'll

never let us live in peace. They have to believe that Sky killed Frank, and she was so filled with regret that she took her own life. Don't you see, it's the only way,' Esme said.

'I'm sorry, Esme. I can't do it. You're asking me to be an accessory to murder,' he said.

'You can and you will!' Esme raised her voice, her tone switching again, showing her true colours. 'Anyway, we'll be doing her a favour. Her life was ruined the moment she let her mother die. What does she have to live for on this God forsaken island?'

Is that what she thought about me? Did my life mean so little to her? I wanted to scream and yell and tell her she was wrong, that I had so much to live for, but my words stuck in my throat.

'I'll help you get away. Of course I will. A promise is a promise,' Jimmy said, stepping towards her. 'But this is murder. It's wrong. I'm sorry.'

'Grow up, Jimmy. What do you think is going on here? This is serious.' She slammed the glass of water on the table and snatched up the gun, waving it in his face.

'Let her go,' Jimmy said, growing in confidence. He wasn't letting her get under his skin and he wouldn't let me die after all. I could have hugged him.

'Don't take the moral high ground with me,' she said.

'I won't be bullied into this. It's wrong.'

'Don't be a hypocrite. I know what you are, Jimmy.'

'What's that supposed to mean?' Jimmy cocked his head, his eyes narrowing.

'I've seen what was on your laptop. I know you have some… exotic tastes.'

'What are you talking about?'

'It's the sort of stuff that can get you put away for a long time. One anonymous call and you'd lose everything. The house. Your business. Your reputation.'

'What kind of stuff? I don't know what you're talking about.'

Esme batted her eyelashes. 'It won't be difficult for the police to find,' she said.

'What have you done?' Now he was looking seriously worried. 'I lent you that computer in good faith to help you start up the business. Have you downloaded something onto it? Are you trying to set me up?'

'I don't know what you mean,' Esme said with a nasty smile.

'After everything I've done to help you and now, you're threatening me.'

'Darling, of course I'm not threatening you. Nobody needs to know what a filthy pervert you are. It can be our little secret.' Esme said it with such glee, I thought Jimmy was going to slap her. 'Now, do you have something to write on?'

Jimmy shook his head, looking as if he couldn't believe the depths to which Esme would sink to save her own skin. He ought to count himself lucky. At least she'd not tried to frame him for murder.

They stood face-to-face for what felt like forever.

Eventually, Jimmy turned away and shuffled out of the room, broken. Esme might have been bluffing, but I could see now it was something she was quite capable of doing. When it came to saving her own skin, she was pure evil.

Jimmy came back, his face thunderous, clutching a ball-point pen and a scrap of paper which he slapped down on the table.

'Excellent,' Esme said. 'Now let's get this note done.'

I shook my head. She might have had a hold over Jimmy, but she couldn't force me to write my own suicide note. 'I'm not doing it,' I said.

'Of course you are.' Esme casually turned Barra-clough's gun on me, pressing the cold metal barrel against my forehead.

'Fine, shoot me,' I said. 'And how would you explain that away exactly?' I allowed myself a self-satisfied smile.

Esme's face clouded. 'Don't mess me around, Sky. Take the paper and pen and start writing.'

'No,' I said as calmly as I could manage.

'We don't have time for your little tantrums, young lady. You'll do as I tell you.'

'I won't and you can't make me,' I said, enjoying her seething anger.

'Frank, her fingers. Break one every time she tells me no again.'

'What?' Frank said, as if he couldn't believe what she was asking him to do.

'Take her hand for God's sake,' Esme said. 'Why do you always have to question everything?'

'Jeez, Esme. Really? Is this necessary?'

'Just do it!' she screeched, making us all jump.

Frank crossed the kitchen like a man on his way to his own execution and yanked my left arm free. He pinned my hand down on the table by my wrist and pulled my little finger up until the pressure in the joint made me scream in agony. It felt as if my entire hand was on fire. I couldn't breathe. I couldn't think. I'd never felt pain like it.

'Alright, I'll do it,' I gasped.

'Good. That's more like it,' Esme said, nodding at Frank to let me go.

I snatched my hand back and rubbed the feeling back into it, embarrassed that I'd capitulated so easily.

'Write something about not being able to live with the guilt after you killed Frank. That should do it. It doesn't need to be long,' Esme said, handing me the paper and pen.

I scribbled down a few sentences I thought captured what she wanted me to say, signed it and dropped the pen on the table. 'Satisfied?' I asked, handing her the paper.

'It'll have to do, I suppose,' she said, casting a disdainful eye over my words. 'Right, tie her up, Frank.'

Frank didn't even question her this time. He went up to a window and tore off a short length of scarlet rope with tasselled ends tying the curtains back. He bound my hands to the back of the chair. It was pointless struggling. I didn't fancy another slap around the face and besides, I couldn't escape. There was nowhere to run. I was trapped. What was the point of fighting anymore? It was hopeless. Even Jimmy couldn't or wouldn't help me.

If only I'd never gone to the beach on the night I first met Esme. If only I'd listened to my gut and walked on, left her alone, and not stuck my nose in. If only I'd not picked up her diary or been tempted to read it. Maybe it was my own stupid fault for reading into it what I wanted to believe. How had I got it so wrong? How had I so completely misunderstood Esme's character? She was no victim. It was Frank I felt sorry for. The way she belittled him and spoke down to him. Maybe this was a just punishment for my foolishness.

There wasn't much to live for anyway? My life had spiralled out of control the moment my mother died. I'd been homeless at fourteen, and I'd never really got back on my own two feet. The move to Leysdown was supposed to have been a new start, but I'd ended up in a crap job with a horrible boss. Few real friends. No money. No prospects. No boyfriend. No hope.

So when Esme handed Frank the glass of water and he grabbed my nose, jerking my head back, I didn't resist, resigned to my fate. He placed the glass against my lips, tipping water into my mouth. It was tepid and bitter, but I swallowed it without a fuss, wishing he'd get on with it.

He tipped the glass up again, but too quickly, and I

coughed and spluttered, spitting most of it out down my front.

'Sorry,' I gasped as Frank let go of my nose. 'I couldn't breathe. I wasn't trying to be difficult.'

'It's okay.' Esme was suddenly at my side, like a caring aunt, her demeanour completely altered from a few moments before. 'Drink it down nicely and this will soon be over.' She smoothed down my hair tenderly.

I didn't know how long it would take, but I imagined I'd soon slip into a peaceful, dreamless sleep and never wake up. That didn't seem so bad.

But after finishing half of the glass, I felt nothing other than a little nauseous.

Frank let me drink the rest without holding my nose closed, which made it easier to swallow, and I was thankful for that small kindness. The only unpleasantness was the bitterness of the pills that coated the inside of my mouth and left my tongue furry. I guessed from the taste that it was paracetamol, but I couldn't be certain. Not that it mattered. I only prayed death would be quick and painless.

When I'd finished the whole glass, Frank dabbed my chin with a tissue and I closed my eyes. I never expected to be so calm at the moment of my death, but all my worries and anxieties had evaporated. What did they matter now, anyway? I didn't believe in heaven or hell, not in the traditional sense at least, but I wondered if I'd soon be reunited with Mum.

I tuned into the chorus of birdsong outside. Blackbirds and robins and sparrows singing and chirruping without a care in the world. It made me sad to think I'd never hear that again, but as I concentrated on listening, another sound drowned out their calls. A low throbbing. A rhythmic pulse. Getting closer. Getting louder. Thrumming and shaking the fabric of the house. Was it in my head? Poisoned blood rushing through my veins? A manifestation of my heart hammering in its death throes?

'The helicopter,' Esme shouted. 'It's here. Frank, quickly, grab the bags.'

CHAPTER FORTY-EIGHT

With the sudden commotion in the room, my eyes sprang open, and I watched with curiosity as Frank and Esme busied themselves gathering up their belongings, while Jimmy stood in the corner, cowering, his head in his hands.

Esme kissed him on both cheeks. 'Jimmy, darling, you've been wonderful. Thank you for everything. We'll always be grateful to you, of course.'

How could she be so amiable while I was sitting only a few metres away, dying? She was obscene. I hated her with every cell in my body.

'Please take Sky back to the house when we've gone.' She pressed a key into his palm. 'She's going to be in a lot of pain soon.'

Wait. What? What happened to the slow, comfortable death? I didn't want to be in pain. That scared me a lot more than dying. You didn't know when you were dead, but you sure as hell knew if you were suffering. I struggled against the bonds around my wrists.

'Give her something to drink and try to make her as comfortable as possible in a room upstairs,' Esme continued, raising her voice over the noise of the helicopter.

She'd known all along that I was going to die horribly.

Jimmy nodded but looked like a defeated man. He, like me, had been ruined the moment he'd first let her into his life. While a sense of injustice had driven me, what had driven him? Lust and maybe the hope of something more with her? Whatever it was, she'd played us both, and we'd lost.

Esme floated across the room to where I was still tied to the chair. She knelt at my side and I cringed as she put a tender hand to my cheek.

'Goodbye, Sky. I'm sorry it had to end like this, but I hope you understand we had no choice. And it was never anything personal.' She kissed the top of my head and for a second I could almost believe her compassion was real and that she cared something for me.

But it wasn't real. There wasn't a compassionate bone in Esme Winters' body. There was only one person she cared about. She was cold, callous and calculating. A woman who would do anything to get her own way. Absolutely anything. And to think I'd spent so long feeling sorry for her.

'Screw you,' I said, a dagger of pain catching me by surprise as it seared through my abdomen.

Esme's face darkened and as she stood she slapped me hard across the cheek.

'Enjoy the next few hours, Sky. They'll probably be the worst of your pitiful life. When your kidneys and liver start to shut down, you'll be begging Jimmy to put you out of your misery.'

I could have punched her, ripped her eyes out with my bare fingers, anything to wipe that grin off her face. I screamed in frustration and she laughed.

On the other side of the room, Frank threw open a set of double doors that led out into the garden. The noise of the helicopter was deafening, even as the pilot shut down the engine and the rotor blades slowed with a high-pitched whine.

So that was it. They were going. Off to a new life, leaving the wreckage of their old lives behind. Esme trotted out of the house ahead of Frank, leaving him struggling with the cases.

'Jimmy,' I gasped, doubling up in pain. 'Help me… ' He was standing with his hands in his pockets, his chin on his chest. 'Untie me. Quickly.'

He glanced up and squinted. 'I wish I'd never met her,' he said.

'My hands - please -' Another stab in my side made me cry out as I strained against the bonds behind my back.

'I can't help you. Sorry,' Jimmy said. 'She'll destroy me.'

'No, she won't.' The pain eased a little, but I braced myself for the next wave I knew would inevitably come.

'If I die, the police will know it wasn't suicide. They'll find out you were involved, and they'll hold you responsible. Who knows, they might even think you killed Frank and Esme.'

'No, they won't,' he said, as if he was trying to convince himself.

'They might. Do you really want to go to jail?' I felt a sharp-edged lump like a fist growing in my stomach. 'To protect Esme? Help me. We can stop them.'

'It's too late.' Jimmy glanced out of the window towards the helicopter.

'It's not.' I screamed again, giving a vent to my suffering as another jagged dagger cut me up from inside.

'But my laptop… '

'I'll tell them she confessed to it. Oh God, please, Jimmy. Untie me.'

'You swallowed all those pills,' he said, sadly. 'You're going to die, anyway.'

'Not if — ' I gasped, catching my breath, ' — I can get to a hospital.'

He shook his head like a man in the depths of despair. I had no idea what he was going to do next.

'Jimmy… ' I begged.

He continued to stare at me with blank eyes, unmoving.

'Please do the right thing.'

'I'm not sure what I can do.'

And then his gaze fell on Barraclough's gun that Esme had left lying on the counter. He picked it up and

347

wrapped his fingers around it, turning it over and examining it with such a faraway sadness that it scared me. Please don't let him do anything stupid.

He stood up straight and looked me in the eye. 'Alright, I'll call an ambulance,' he said.

Thank God. 'And the police,' I said, wincing. 'But first, untie me, for God's sake.'

'Right, yes. Sorry.' He rushed over and with a few grunts released my wrists. I sprinted to the sink and forced my fingers down my throat, purging my stomach until my legs were weak and I collapsed on the floor clutching my stomach.

Jimmy was already on the phone talking to the emergency services, urging them to hurry. As he gave them the address and directions, I thought about Cam outside in the car, remembering how he'd directed me to the house. He must have been wondering what the hell was going on. If ever I needed him, it was right now. With my stomach still cramping, I scrabbled across the floor for my mobile.

Shit. Half a dozen missed calls from him. I'd forgotten I'd left it on silent. I called him straight back, and he picked up immediately.

'Sky, what's going on? Are you okay?'

'I'm fine,' I lied.

'I saw them bring out Barraclough's body.' He sounded breathless. 'I didn't know what to do and then you weren't answering your phone.'

'I don't have time to explain right now, but Frank and Esme are trying to leave,' I said.

'The helicopter?'

'Jimmy arranged it but we need to stop them.' I bit my lip to stop myself screaming as another wave of searing pain hit me. 'I'm not feeling so good. I need your help. I'll let you in the front.'

'Sky, what's wrong?'

'No time to explain. I'll see you in a minute.'

I staggered out of the kitchen, along the corridor and into the hall. Cam was already waiting on the doorstep, looking worried.

'Jeez, you look dreadful,' he said, as I opened the door.

I did my best to hide that I was in agony. No point worrying him. Nothing he could do.

'Come on, this way,' I said, leading him back to the kitchen.

Jimmy was just coming off the phone. 'An ambulance is on its way and the police are sending an armed unit,' he said.

I nodded but didn't stop as we headed for the double doors out onto a huge formal garden and a sweeping lawn beyond it where the helicopter had landed. Frank was loading luggage into a small compartment at the rear of the fuselage as casually as if they were off on a holiday in the sun. Fury fizzed in my veins.

I staggered into the garden with Cam at my side, and shielded my eyes against the sun, watching as a pilot in aviator glasses and a crisp white shirt lent Frank a hand with the cases. We walked slowly towards the aircraft, my mind racing. How the hell were we going to stop them?

'What now?' Cam asked.

'I don't know. But we can't let them leave. We need to delay them, at least until the police get here. Any ideas?'

'A diversion,' Cam said, looking around the grounds for inspiration as a figure darted out of the shadows, running through the garden from the front of the house.

When Frank saw him, he froze, his face screwed up in fear and surprise.

'What the hell?' Cam gasped.

'Barraclough,' I said. He had a knife in one hand and congealed blood smeared down one side of his face.

Right at that moment, Esme emerged from inside the chopper. Frank threw his body in front of her, shielding her as Barraclough ran towards them them, waving the knife menacingly.

Barraclough yelled something I couldn't hear and the pilot slowly lowered himself to the ground with his hands behind his head. Frank backed away with his hands up in surrender. Desperate to understand what was going on, we crept forwards, but I wasn't watching my step and slipped on a rise in the lawn, still damp from a morning dew, yelping as I fell.

Barraclough's head snapped around at the sound and Frank snatched the opportunity, launching himself, grabbing Barraclough's wrist, fighting for the knife.

We watched in horror as the two men grappled,

falling to the floor in a writhing twist of limbs while Esme pressed her back against the helicopter, cowering.

They were going to kill each other if we didn't stop them. But how? The police could be ages away yet. I'd not even heard any sirens. But at least they would be armed.

Guns.

I remembered Barraclough's handgun in the kitchen. It might be the only hope.

'Wait here,' I said to Cam as I turned and ran back to the house.

Jimmy was standing by the door with his phone clasped in his hand, but I pushed him aside and lunged for the handgun he'd put back on the worktop. It was much heavier than I'd imagined and felt alien in the palm of my hand. I knew nothing about guns, but I guessed all I had to do was point it and squeeze the trigger.

A scream shocked me into action. I sprinted back into the garden. Frank was now sitting on the grass under the tail of the helicopter, clutching his shoulder. His hand was stained scarlet, his shirt covered in blood.

'What happened?'

Cam was rooted to the spot. 'Barraclough stabbed him,' he said, like he couldn't believe what he was seeing.

Barraclough loomed over Frank, looking murderous.

'Drop the knife!' I yelled, walking slowly towards them with the gun in both hands, my body trembling.

Barraclough squinted at me as I picked my way across the lawn.

'I said, drop the knife.'

'What are you doing?' Barraclough asked, swaying like the tall mast of a sailing ship on a fast tide. His eyes were black and puffy, and his skin pale. Clumps of crusted blood matted his hair and covered one side of his face.

'The police are on their way,' I said. 'Step away from Frank.'

'I am the police,' Barraclough slurred as I drew closer, my hands sweating.

'No, you're not. I won't tell you again. Put the knife down, nice and slowly.'

Barraclough grinned as he glanced at the blood-streaked knife, a nasty-looking weapon with a sharp edge and vicious serrations along one side. 'You won't shoot me,' he said. 'You don't have the balls.'

He turned towards us. I felt Cam's heavy breath on my neck.

'Sky,' he said with a trace of panic in his voice. 'He's coming.'

'Stop where you are!' I yelled.

But he didn't. He took a deliberate step closer. I closed one eye. Looked down the barrel of the gun. Pulled the trigger. It jolted me backwards, a loud crack splintering in my ear. A puff of earth kicked up a few metres in front of Barraclough's feet, exactly where I'd aimed. He stopped. Looked up at me, surprised.

'I won't miss next time,' I said.

Now he was taking me seriously. He dropped the knife. It embedded itself in the grass.

Behind him, Esme rushed to Frank's side, peeling his hand from his shoulder to inspect the wound. He grimaced in pain. As my insides cramped again, my kidneys screaming, my legs weak, I felt no sympathy for him. He'd plotted with Esme to frame me, happy to let me rot in jail for a crime I didn't commit so they could be free.

But I didn't wish him dead. That would have been too easy. I wanted them both punished for what they'd done. I wanted my day in court, to look them in the eye and for them to understand I was worth more than that. I had my entire life ahead of me.

'Frank, get in the helicopter.' Esme tried to pull him up, but he cried out in agony, unable to move. 'We've got to go!'

'He's not going anywhere,' I said, stepping closer, shifting my aim past Barraclough, towards Esme's chest. I didn't want to shoot her, but I'd do it if I had to.

'Sky, that's enough. Put the gun down before someone gets hurt.' I wasn't expecting to hear Jimmy's voice right behind me.

'Not until the police get here,' I said.

'And if they see you with a gun, you're going to get yourself shot,' he said.

'He's right,' Cam chipped in. 'Drop the gun.'

What was wrong with the pair of them? Couldn't they see the danger? Either Barraclough was going to kill Frank and Esme or they were going to escape. I had to stop them. 'I won't hurt them,' I said.

'Sky, give it to me!' Jimmy ordered. He was up alongside me now, crowding me, putting me under pressure.

I tried to push him away with one hand but instead of backing off, he reached for the gun, wrapping his hand around it, trying to wrench it out of my grip. I barged into his chest with my shoulder. He grunted but didn't give up. This was crazy. Why was I fighting with Jimmy?

'Get off,' I screamed in his ear as the sound of the first distant siren drifted across the garden. Thank God, the police were nearly here. An ambulance too, I hoped. The pain in my abdomen was getting worse. It was almost crippling.

Jimmy came at me again. A thunderbolt ripped through my gut. My body convulsed. Jimmy's hands wrestled for control of the gun. A single shot rang out.

I looked up in horror. Esme was clutching her stomach, a look of disbelief on her face, eyes wide and jaw loose. Her legs folded, and she collapsed, scarlet rivulets of blood creeping out between her fingers.

'Esme! No!' Frank frantically tried to stem the bleeding with one hand.

I couldn't move, paralysed with shock. What had I done? As much as I hated her, I didn't want Esme dead. One death on my conscience was enough.

Jimmy relaxed his grip on the gun. But I no longer wanted it. I dropped it like it was a hot coal onto the grass. Barraclough rushed forwards as I backed away and snatched it up with a grin of delight.

'Stupid girl,' he sneered. 'You should have kept out of this.' He aimed the gun at my chest and ordered the three of us towards the helicopter where he made us all lie down on our stomachs next to the pilot, our hands on the backs of our heads.

A short distance away, Frank was kneeling over Esme begging her not to die. Jimmy shot me a look of apology.

'What are you going to do with us?' Cam asked.

Barraclough tilted his head as if the thought hadn't occurred to him. Was he thinking about killing us? Behind him, Frank pulled himself onto his feet, his face screwed up in pain and his shirt and hands almost entirely stained scarlet with blood. He inched forwards, silently. Plucked Barraclough's knife from the ground. Raised it up. Gritted his teeth. And plunged it into Barraclough's back, between his shoulder blades.

Barraclough screamed. A mixture of agony and anger. He grunted and gurgled. Twisted to reach the knife. Tried to pull it from his back. Not quite able to locate it.

I turned my head away, unable to watch. It was all too horrific. Of all the things I'd forgotten when I'd blacked out after partying too hard, this was the one thing I wished I'd never seen, that I could instantly forget. But I had a feeling it was an image that was going to haunt me for a long time. Another gunshot made me jump. I squeezed my eyes tightly shut, whimpering with fear and the swell of another pang of agony in my gut. I thought I was going to be sick.

When I finally summoned the courage to open my eyes, Barraclough was lying face down in the grass, unmoving, with the hunting knife buried in his back, his head twisted towards me, his glassy eyes staring blankly. I clamped a hand over my mouth to stifle a scream as I saw Frank a few feet away, on his back, his arms open wide and a gaping hole in his chest where he'd been shot.

Cam stirred beside me and helped me to my feet. 'Are you okay?' he asked.

I nodded, even though I felt far from fine. Jimmy and the pilot were slowly getting up, both looking as shocked as each other.

Esme moaned. I rushed to her side and took her hand. Her skin was cold and clammy. Wet, sticky blood soaked the fabric of her dress and pooled on her stomach. As much as I hated how she'd treated me, how she'd try to kill me, I really didn't want her to die.

'I'm so cold,' she said.

'An ambulance is on its way. You're going to be okay,' I said.

Jimmy and Cam were checking on Barraclough and Frank. The slow shake of their heads confirmed both men were dead.

'I wish I'd never met you,' I told her. 'Or found your stupid diary.'

Even as she lay dying, she found the strength to

smirk. It infuriated me. But what had I expected from her? Remorse?

'It could have been anyone,' she said, coughing. Spittle formed at the corners of her mouth. 'Don't take it so personally.'

Cam joined me and pressed his hands to Esme's stomach, trying to stop the bleeding, but it looked a thankless task. She'd already lost so much.

'You made it personal,' I said. 'You thought you could trade my life to save yours. What kind of sick bitch does that?'

Another thick needle of pain in my side nearly made me vomit, like my kidneys and liver were slowly shutting down.

'I hope you rot in hell,' I said, catching my breath.

That made her smile. Her face was turning blue, and her eyes narrowed to slits. Her breathing had become slow and shallow. She was drifting away.

I heard several sirens now, much closer. 'Don't die on me,' I yelled at her. 'You're going to pay for what you did.'

'It's too late,' she gasped. She coughed again, her voice weak. 'Look in the helicopter,' she whispered. I lowered my ear to her mouth to hear. 'A black, zip-up bag. Take it. Don't let the police find it. I want you to have it.'

I shushed her quiet. 'Save your strength,' I said.

'Use it. Start a new life. Get off this island.'

Her eyelids fluttered, and I squeezed her hand. 'Esme!'

'Give them my diary. It's in my handbag. It'll explain everything.'

Her grip on my hand loosened. She was going. 'Esme, stay with me. Help is nearly here. Don't you dare die on me!'

But her head fell to one side and she let out one last gasp of breath.

Cam removed his hands from her stomach. 'She's gone,' he said.

'No.' I shook my head, not wanting to believe it. She couldn't die, not without paying for what she'd done. There was no justice in her death. 'Esme, come on, wake up.'

'Sky, she's gone,' Cam repeated. 'There's nothing more we can do.'

CHAPTER FORTY-NINE

A t the hospital, they said I was lucky. Not that I felt fortune had favoured me after the events that had unfolded that morning. The doctors confirmed the paracetamol I'd ingested shouldn't leave any lasting damage to my liver and kidneys. They kept me in hospital for a few days, hooked up to a drip while they carried out all sorts of tests on the function of my inner organs. At least I had my own room and a police guard, even though Esme, Frank and Barraclough were all dead, and it gave me plenty of time to dwell on everything that had happened.

It was difficult, looking back, to make sense of everything and soon a gloomy veil of depression descended over my mind. It was as if I'd woken from a bad dream, all the details a little blurry around the edges, and several times I caught myself wondering if I'd imagined it all.

I had to speak to two detectives from my hospital

bed. They closed the door to my room and pulled up chairs before bombarding me with questions. I tried to be as honest as I could and told them everything I remembered. After all, I had nothing to hide. Well, almost nothing.

'We've found several handwritten diaries,' one of the detectives said. 'They document everything over the last few months, including Duncan and Pamela's attempts to vanish and their move to Kent after appropriating a deposit of money that was paid into Mr Whittaker's business account.'

It was weird hearing Frank and Esme called by their real names, like they were different people. The detective explained that they believed Frank had become caught up with a criminal gang of Romanian money lenders who'd recruited him after tricking him into accepting an overpayment on what he thought was a legitimate loan. When subsequent sums appeared in his bank with increasingly bigger sweeteners, Frank had soon ended up over his head.

'The problem is, once you're in and you've taken the money, it's hard to get out again,' the detective said. 'It appears that's why Duncan stole the last instalment and tried to disappear.

'The diaries we found seem to corroborate your version of events,' the detective continued. 'The Whittakers planned on faking their own deaths when their new identities were discovered and intended to persuade you to confess to Duncan's murder. However, we have a few questions remaining about how they died.'

I explained to them several times how Jimmy had tried to take the gun from me after Barraclough had stabbed Frank and that in the struggle I had accidentally shot Esme, but they didn't seem satisfied with my account.

'You both had good reason to want Pamela Whittaker dead, didn't you?' the second detective, a man with a suspicious look in his eye, said. 'She and Duncan had not only tried to frame you for murder, but when that went wrong, they fed you an overdose of paracetamol. Meanwhile, they'd blackmailed Mr Steele into assisting them by suggesting they'd planted child pornography on his laptop.' He looked up from his notepad and licked his lips. 'Not that anything untoward was found on his hard drive.'

'It's not like that,' I said. They were twisting what happened, making it sound like we'd plotted together to kill Esme. 'I never wanted Esme to die. I only wanted to stop them leaving.'

They also asked lots of questions about Cam and our relationship. I could only hope they weren't giving him a hard time. He'd only become involved because of me.

'Am I under arrest?' I asked.

The first detective frowned. 'Of course not.'

'It's just that you're making it sound like I'm guilty of something.'

'Are you?'

'Only of trying to help someone I thought was in trouble,' I said.

'Why didn't you alert the police when you first suspected Duncan of domestic abuse?' the second detective asked.

I shrugged. 'I didn't have any proof. And as it turns out, I was wrong. Esme, I mean Pamela, maintained all along that he'd never laid a finger on her. If anything, it was the other way around.'

'Most people would have reported a suspicion like that.'

'But I thought it would make things worse for her. I figured it would be better if I could persuade her to leave him and get her to a women's refuge,' I said.

They kept going, asking the same questions over and over, trying to find holes in my story, for more than two hours, before they finally left me, drained and exhausted. 'What happens next?' I asked.

'We'll be continuing our investigations until we're satisfied we have the entire truth,' the first detective said.

'I've told you the truth,' I said.

'In which case you have nothing to worry about.'

CHAPTER FIFTY

The tattered remnants of a strip of blue and white police tape tied to the gates fluttered in the breeze as we approached Shurland Hall in Cam's father's car, but there was no other sign of any police presence or TV news crews at the house. After two weeks, it looked like the story had blown over and the hordes of journalists who'd descended on the island to report on the triple deaths in the grounds of the mansion had moved on to other, more important things.

Cam pulled up outside the front entrance, the tyres crunching on the gravel. He killed the engine, and we sat staring up at the house for a moment, lost in our own thoughts. It was weird being back. Disturbing.

We'd both been given the all clear from the police who'd accepted our stories and told us they were planning to take no further action against me or Cam. Nor were they pursuing any prosecution against Jimmy

Steele, who'd temporarily moved out of the house to stay with his sister in Oxfordshire while the press interest died down. So we knew we had the place to ourselves.

'Are you okay?' I let Cam take my hand. He gave it a gentle, reassuring squeeze.

I nodded. Although being back stirred up some powerful emotions, I was determined they wouldn't get the better of me.

'Do you want me to come with you?'

'Absolutely,' I said, not wanting to be left alone for a second while we were in the grounds.

It was a beautiful clear day without a cloud in the sky and the warmth of the early spring sun carried the promise of hot summer days to come. I led the way through a gate in the hedge, following a narrow path around the side of the house and out onto the expansive lawn at the back that overlooked fields of grazing animals and solitary oak trees bursting with the new season's growth. I half expected to see the helicopter still standing where it had landed, but there was no sign it had ever been there.

'That's it, over there,' Cam said, pointing to a sprawling camellia bush heavy with fragrant pink blooms.

We crossed the lawn in silent anticipation, unsure whether the police had discovered the black holdall Cam had pulled out of the luggage hold in the aircraft shortly after Esme had died. They'd never mentioned it when they interviewed us, but my heart was galloping as we approached the bushes.

Cam pulled apart some of the lower branches and dived in, reappearing a moment later with the bag in one hand.

'It's here,' he cried.

I could have wept with joy. 'I was sure the police would find it,' I said, unzipping the bag. It was filled with velvet jewellery boxes of all shapes, sizes and colours.

I picked out a random box and flipped it open, just to be sure. Inside was a beautiful silver statement necklace studded with diamonds. The rest of the boxes contained earrings, bracelets, tiaras, necklaces and rings all set with rubies, diamonds and pearls. A real-life treasure trove of riches. I'd never seen such an incredible collection of jewellery before in my life. Esme died before explaining, but I guessed it was from Frank's business when he'd stopped trading and they'd left in a hurry. A nest egg for their future lives.

I wasn't sure if I was going to take it at first. I didn't want any reminder of them. But Cam had talked me round. He said that if Frank and Esme didn't have any family and the police found it, they'd simply auction it off. Esme's dying wish was for me to take the jewellery and use it to rebuild my life. I figured it would be fitting compensation for everything she'd put me through.

'You've decided to keep it then?' Cam asked.

'I think so. It's my ticket out of here.'

'You're definitely leaving?'

I zipped up the bag and moved close to Cam, resting my hands on his hips, our noses inches apart. 'I want to follow my dreams,' I said.

'Right.' Cam looked disappointed, gazing over my shoulder, refusing to meet my eye.

'I thought I'd sell some of it and use the money to go to college and finish my education. Who knows, I might even study to become an architect after all.'

'You should. It's a good idea.'

'You don't sound so sure,' I said.

'I'm going to miss you, that's all.'

I reached up and cupped his face with my hands and kissed him softly on the lips. 'Come with me,' I whispered. 'We could start a new life together.'

'You know I can't do that.'

'Why not? Don't you want to be with me?'

'Of course. I want that more than anything.'

'So what's stopping you? Let's leave this island behind and start over. It'll be an adventure. We can do whatever we want.' I tried to kiss him again, but he pulled away, rejecting me once more. It didn't sting any less than the first time.

'What about the shop?' he said.

'Your parents can look after it, right?'

'It's not that simple. You know that. Dad needs to look after Mum, and I can't leave them, not when she's so ill. I don't even know how long she has left.'

I shrunk away from him, feeling foolish. I was asking him to choose between me and his family. It wasn't fair. 'I'm sorry,' I said. 'I wasn't thinking. You're right. You should stay.'

'I can come and visit you when you're settled,' Cam said, his eyes lighting up.

'I'd like that.'

'You understand, don't you?' he said.

'Of course.' I patted his chest, smoothing out the fabric of his t-shirt. 'You're lucky you still have your family. You definitely should put them first.'

I threw the holdall over my shoulder and we walked back to the car hand-in-hand. I tossed the bag onto the back seat with a small rucksack of clothes I'd packed.

'What now?' Cam asked.

'Can you take me to the bus stop?'

I'd spent much of the previous two weeks moping about on my own in the caravan, shutting myself off from the world while I replayed everything that had happened over and over in my mind. I'd been determined to save Esme, to not have her death on my conscience. And yet it was me who'd shot her in the stomach and killed her.

Cam and I spent a lot of time on the phone chatting about everything, going over every little detail, while I convinced myself I could have handled things differently.

'You're not responsible for Esme's death,' Cam said. 'Even the police don't blame you for that. You wanted to help her and in return she tried to kill you.'

'But I shot her!' I said.

'It was an accident. And even if it wasn't, who could blame you? It wasn't your fault they'd got themselves mixed up laundering money for a crime gang.'

'If I'd let her go, she'd still be alive.'

'You don't know that for sure,' Cam said. 'That gang would have tracked them down no matter where they'd gone. Who knows what they would have done to them.'

'First my mum and now Esme.'

'Stop beating yourself up, Sky. You're a good person. You're kind and caring. Loyal. Funny. Determined. And I love all those things about you, but you need to stop blaming yourself for things that are out of your control.'

I allowed the trace of a smile to creep across my lips. It had been a long time since anyone had said anything so nice to me. 'I don't think I am a good person.'

'You can't carry around this burden of guilt with you for the rest of your life. It'll destroy you, and for what?'

And he was right. It was time to face my demons and stop letting them rule my head.

On the day the police confirmed they'd closed their investigation into me and Cam, he'd turned up at the caravan with a bottle of champagne to celebrate.

But the pop of the cork echoing off the thin walls reminded me of the gunshots at Shurland Hall. I squeezed my eyes shut and shoved the memories away. Champagne fizzed out of the bottle in an exploding foam, and Cam caught most of it in two glasses.

He offered me one, but I refused, holding up my hand. 'Sorry, I'm giving up alcohol for a bit,' I said with an apologetic shrug.

'Detoxing?'

'Something like that.'

'Fair enough.' He put his glass to his lips and then thought better of it. 'Actually, you're right. A break from the booze is probably sensible.' He poured his glass and the rest of the bottle down the sink. 'There, temptation gone.'

'That was probably expensive.'

'It doesn't matter. I'm proud of you for saying no.'

We waited for what seemed like an eternity, taking it in turns to peer down the road, anticipating the arrival at any minute of the bus to the mainland and the beginning of the rest of my life. We had so much to say to each other but stood in awkward silence.

Finally, a single decker coach trundled into view and pulled up in a hiss of air brakes.

'This is it then,' Cam said, handing me the holdall as I stepped on board.

'I'll call,' I said. 'I promise.'

'Where will you go?'

'I'm not sure yet.'

'Be careful with that bag.'

I leaned down and pecked him on the cheek. He hugged me tightly. 'It's not too late to change your mind,' I said.

'I'll miss you, Sky Warehorn.'

'I'll miss you too, Cameron Searle.'

The doors rolled closed, and the bus moved off. I stumbled to the back seats and stared out of the window at Cam, a forlorn figure on the side of the road. But there was no time for sentimentality. Or weakness. I needed to do this, to escape the island and learn how to be myself. My new self. The idea was exciting and terrifying, but as the bus chugged along, heading towards the arching bridge off the island, I knew in my heart I was doing the right thing. I just needed to make a phone call.

'Amber, it's Sky.'

'Oh my God, Sky, how are you?' She sounded giddy with excitement.

'I'm good. And you?'

'I was going to, you know, call after I heard what happened, but I wasn't sure… ' Amber said.

'It's okay. I probably wouldn't have answered, anyway. It's been a hard couple of weeks.'

'I'm sorry about Esme and Frank. It's shocking, isn't it?'

'You don't know the half of it.'

'But you're okay?'

'I'm leaving the island. I'm starting over,' I said.

'Amazing. Where are you going?' Amber asked.

'It's funny you should ask that. Is that offer to stay with you for a bit still open?'

'Oh my God, of course it is. I'll have to speak to

Mum and Dad, of course, but I'm sure they'll be totally fine with it.'

'Great. I'm on the bus.'

Amber reeled off her address and gave me detailed instructions on how to find the house. 'How long will you stay?'

'I don't know. A couple of nights maybe if that's cool with your parents.'

'Totally. We can hit the town and I can show you around.'

'I'd rather have some quiet nights in catching up. I'm not sure I can face going out.'

'Yeah, sure, whatever you want.'

'I'll see you in a few of hours then. Make sure you've got the kettle on.'

I hung up and slumped in the seat with the holdall firmly gripped between my knees, my eyes fixed on the road again. Would I ever come back to the island or see Cam again? I wasn't sure.

I'd meant it when I'd said I was going to miss him, but it was time to live life for the here and now and to stop dwelling on the past. No regrets. No remorse.

I took a deep breath and let it out slowly. I'd been given a second chance by the strangest of circumstances, and this time I was determined to make the most of it.

ACKNOWLEDGMENTS

She Knows was born from an idea that occurred to me while riding my bike. I'd spotted something in the gutter at the side of the road and started to imagine, what if it had been a diary? Someone's deepest, darkest secrets they never intended anyone else to read.

Would you be tempted to read it?

I think most of us would. It's a human frailty wrapped up in our desire for knowledge, to solve mysteries and to understand how other people live their lives.

And probably we'd all feel guilty after reading it because we know diaries are supposed to be personal and private.

The characters of Sky, Hanlon, Esme and Frank all came later as I began piecing a plot together around this central idea.

The ending is in fact the second ending I plotted. Originally, I had Esme being tortured to death by

Hanlon, strung up in the shower and suffering a death of a thousand cuts.

On reflection, it seemed a bit too brutal and not a fitting end for any antagonist.

The setting, the Isle of Sheppey, is only a few miles from where I wrote the book, as the crow flies.

I'd wanted an island location where it was conceivable a couple like Frank and Esme might have fled to disappear and I knew Leysdown reasonably well.

It only occurred to me afterwards that the novel was written entirely during the coronavirus lockdown period and the island is a great analogy for that period.

It's somewhere that can feel remote, distant and detached. And that's a feeling, I'm sure, anyone who lived through any of the pandemic lockdowns can totally empathise with.

Greatest thanks as always to my small but dedicated team, but particularly my wife and fellow psychological thriller author, Amanda (you'll know her as AJ McDine); Rebecca Miller, my editor, for her wonderful eye for detail and for pushing to be a better writer and the team at Books Covered for another incredible cover image.

Finally, if you enjoyed, *She Knows*, I'd be grateful if you could leave a review on Amazon. It will help me to find new readers and allow me to keep writing. Thank you.

Adrian

His Wife's Sister

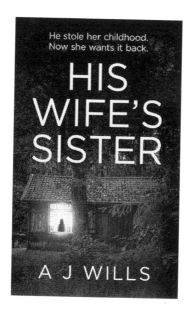

He stole her childhood. Now she wants it back.

Mara was eleven years old when she went missing.

Nineteen years later she's been found, claiming she was kept chained up in an underground cell for all that time.

But her brother-in-law, Damian doesn't trust her. There's something about her story that doesn't seem right.

He fears his young children might even be in danger when his wife insists Mara moves in with them to recover.

The only way he can save his family is to prove what really happened to her all those years ago.

But the truth is hard to find when it's been buried so deep. . .

Between the Lies

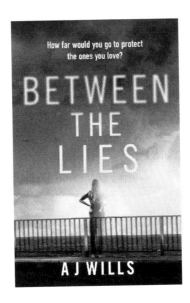

He thought he was living the perfect life – until he discovered he was living with a perfect stranger.

Jez believed he'd finally found happiness when he met the alluring Alice Grey.

She's elegant, stylish and beautiful, the kind of woman he never imagined would look at him twice.

But his life's shattered when Alice goes missing with her young daughter– and the police accuse him their murders.

The only way to prove his innocence is to find them alive.

But that's not so easy when Alice is running from a dark family secret and doesn't want to be found.

At least without any evidence he's killed them, it'll be hard for the police to charge him.

Unless they discover the body Alice asked him to hide…